Books by H

Single Titles

Little Rainbows
Scenes from Adelaide Road

1

LITTLE RAINBOWS

HELENA STONE

Dedication

For Dermot, who stayed with me when even I wanted to
leave me behind. You are my heart and soul.

Prologue

"What do you need, sub?"

The young woman's panting reverberated through the room. The fine sheen of sweat covering her body reflected the lights shining down from the ceiling, making her glow and sparkle. Wearing nothing except her high heels, her feet held apart with a spreader-bar and her upper body tied to the spanking bench, the beautiful blonde was a picture of vulnerability. Arousal wafted from her, strong and enticing — and it left him cold. He had no desire to touch. Hell, he didn't even want to be here.

"Do you think you've earned your orgasm, my dear?"

So far the only response he'd been able to get from her were moans. And they both knew he'd do nothing to release her need unless she asked him — no, begged him for it.

You can't blame the girl for being incoherent, he thought. The clamps on her nipples were as tight as he could make them, exerting the kind of pain she craved. Her arse and upper thighs were a glorious shade of red, courtesy of his hands and the black leather flogger. He knew all it would take to make her come was the lightest of touches to her clit. But he wouldn't touch her again until she begged him for it. He knew it and she knew it. It was a crucial part of their play. He had mastered the game over the years and played it very well, even if the enjoyment he used to derive from it was gone.

"Please, Sir, please."

He leaned forward and whispered in her ear. "You know that isn't enough. You have to tell me what you want. You won't get it unless you name it. Tell me what you need."

5

The young woman groaned and shook her head, the tips of her long blonde hair stroking his face. He grabbed a handful of the soft locks and pulled her head backwards.

"Tell me!"

"Please, Sir, I need to come. Please make me come, Sir."

"Good girl. That wasn't so hard now, was it?"

He moved his hand between her legs and found exactly what he'd expected, a soaking wet pussy. For a moment the memories of the pleasure he used to derive from these shows guided his actions. He indulged himself and teased her, stroking his fingers through her wetness, between her folds, managing to miss her clit on every pass. He changed direction and pinched her hard little bud between his thumb and index finger before stroking it with purpose.

He'd been right. It only took a few seconds before her body tensed and started to shake. Her groans turned to screams as her orgasm took hold of her body and mind. He prolonged her release with his finger's continued pressure on her clit. When she at last started to come down from her high, he freed her from the bench and helped her up. He caught her when her legs, still kept apart by the bar, gave way. With a look to his left, he summoned one of the many dungeon assistants. The young man released the sub's legs and picked her up, carrying her to a couch where he wrapped her in a soft blanket and enveloped her in a tight embrace.

Satisfied his aftercare instructions were being followed to the letter, Jason left the stage and made his way to the exit. He accepted compliments and greetings on the way but didn't stop to talk to anyone. The show was over and he needed to get away from the scene. He stalked through the resort he'd opened less than a year ago with high hopes and expectations, not seeing anything or anyone. He was blind to the guests making their way to private rooms, impatient to alleviate the sexual tension he'd ignited in them with his show. He pretended he didn't see the worried expression on his best friend's face as he exited the BDSM area and he ignored the vanilla guests taking advantage of the facilities in the more innocent part of his club. Waiting for the elevator would take too long and give others an opportunity to approach him, so he took the stairs two at a time, impatient to be alone and in his own environment.

He slammed the door to his apartment. *What the fuck's wrong with me?* This wasn't, had never been, just a job. This was his life. He'd been born to play this role, to be this man. He'd finally reached the stage where his life resembled everything he'd dreamed about and the feeling was gone. Why had it been months since he'd felt the need to bed one of his subs? Why was the portrayal of his dominance, their willing submission to his will, not enough for him anymore? Why had these exhibitions started to feel like a chore rather than a welcome side benefit to his chosen profession? He had to find out—and soon. In just over a month's time the elite of the Irish BDSM community would be meeting here, in his club, for its first anniversary. His reluctance was growing so fast he feared it wouldn't be long before he'd find himself incapable of putting up a believable performance.

He groaned out loud while he poured himself a large whiskey. His anger made him restless and he ignored the comfortable large couch and chairs. The walls of his spacious and bright apartment seemed to be closing in on him. A need for fresh air brought him to the glass wall opening onto a building-wide balcony. The clear night sky combined with the distant sound of waves hitting the shore went some way toward settling his edginess.

He forced himself to be honest. It wasn't just about being believable. He felt as if he'd lost himself. He'd always known he was dominant from his first, clumsy, sexual experience. Opening his club in Ireland, the country he'd grown up in and had always seen as home, had allowed him to turn his desires into an income while giving other people the opportunity to discover everything sex had to offer in a safe environment. Sure, he could still earn a comfortable living and offer that service without ever rediscovering his inner Dom. He just didn't know who he was without that need. His sense of self had disappeared as his dominant side receded and he didn't know what to do about finding it again or how to go about discovering who he was without it.

The star-filled sky, the moon and the sea watched but didn't provide answers as he struggled with his inner demons.

Chapter One

There it was, her opportunity to kick-start her life again. And, as restarts went, it made quite an impression. The hotel or club—she wasn't quite sure how to label the building—looked rather grand at the end of the long drive. The Atlantic Ocean, throwing up a spray in the distance, only enhanced the picture. Even on this bright summer's day she could see small rainbows in the watery mist the waves were producing. It would be easy to confuse this place with any of the up-market tourist traps the west coast of Ireland was peppered with. This could be any other posh resort catering to Americans trying to find their roots and golfers looking for an opportunity to try the links courses littered along the coastline. The heavy gate blocking the entrance told a different story. She knew too much about this place, its purpose and what happened behind those gates to confuse it for anything except what it was, a dream from the past and—if everything went according to plan—the start of the rest of her life.

She'd been looking at the building, the grounds, the gate and the little buzzer on the intercom box for a few minutes. If anybody on the inside happened to be keeping an eye on the entrance through those security cameras, they would have decided she was either scared or crazy by now—and they'd be right. She was apprehensive. Her hands were clasped together, her fingers worrying her wedding ring. After eighteen months of virtually living like a hermit, coming here felt like diving in headfirst. Still, if she'd had any doubts about leaving Dublin, that surprise visitor two weeks ago and his shocking proposal had taken care of those.

The bastard. She refused to even think his name. It still bothered her he'd had the nerve to show up at her door like that. Where would he have gotten the idea she'd be open to his suggestions? It had been clear that he'd expected her to embrace his offer — or should she call it an order — with open arms. His delusions of grandeur must have gotten the better of him, or he'd confused her with someone she clearly wasn't. She didn't get it. Even before her self-inflicted confinement, she'd made a point of staying away from him. Why would he think she'd changed her mind about him just because she was on her own? She didn't know but lingering on that memory right now didn't serve any purpose. She didn't want him in her thoughts, especially not now. It would only make her more nervous than she already was.

She'd thought this place would be the perfect setting for her return to the BDSM world she'd been ignoring for well over a year. Now that the moment was close, now that she had to take this last step out of her confinement, the first step into her future, she couldn't help second-guessing herself. Was she really ready to move forward? Could she do it on her own? She'd never been a part of this lifestyle without her husband and his loving support.

With a sigh she lifted her hand and pressed the little button. She'd come this far. She hadn't driven the five hours from Dublin only to turn away at the last hurdle. If she gave up now, it would be the end of the business they'd built together. If she chickened out of this, there would be no way of ever going back on her own terms. Going forward scared the shit out of her but going back frightened her even more. She could do this. She'd promised she would take this step. Breaking her word was not an option, no matter how scared she was.

"Can I help you?"

The voice from the intercom brought her out of her reverie. "Hi, I'm Heather Staunton, I…"

"Mrs. Staunton, welcome to The Blowhole. You're expected. Please drive up to the parking area and make your way to reception in the lobby."

The voice disappeared at the same moment the black steel gates started to noiselessly open. Heather put her bright yellow Beetle into first gear and with a deep sigh, started the too short drive up to the parking area. She wondered about the name as she drove. The Blowhole. It could be a reference to everything going on behind the resort's walls. Or, maybe the owner enjoyed provoking and shocking people. Anyone unaware of the true nature of this place would probably assume a connection to the numerous chimneys on the roof. Knowing all too well what awaited her once she stepped out of her car, she doubted chimneys had anything to do with the choice.

Heather's curiosity about the name receded as she parked her car and stared at the imposing building in front of her. It was magnificent. Built in gray stone, the resort had the higgledy-piggledy appearance of a manor built over the centuries, with bits added on as circumstances required. Of course she knew this wasn't an old building — she'd done her research — but she liked that it had been erected with materials and in a style that made it appear old and worn. High and low rooflines alternating in an apparently random fashion gave the manor an uneven and fascinating exterior, to which the protruding and receding sections only added. It made her curious about the interior and excited about exploring all its nooks and crannies. She wouldn't be surprised to find secret passageways, dark cellars, roaring fires — although it wasn't quite the season or the weather for those right now — and adventure.

She got a glimpse of the grounds behind the manor and studied the extended garden with at least one other building. Off in the distance, she could still see the Atlantic Ocean. She took another moment to delight in the tiny rainbows in the sky above the sea. The sight took her breath away and made her feel better about the whole enterprise.

She decided to take it as an encouraging sign. She chose to believe that Mother Nature herself had put her stamp of approval on Heather's decision to come here.

She wished she could stay out here and enjoy nature's beauty, but, she wasn't here for the view, breathtaking as it might be. She'd come here to do a job, as well as to restart her life. Daydreaming about little rainbows wouldn't achieve either. Heather's worries resurfaced as soon she thought about the days ahead of her. In a few minutes she would come face to face with a man she knew little to nothing about in order to help him organize the BDSM party of the decade. Someone who called himself Master Jay and had been conspicuous in his absence from the negotiations so far. She'd only dealt with his manager, Karl Mulready. A few minutes from now that would change. Heather and the elusive Master were about to meet.

Almost reluctantly, Heather made her way to the entrance. Close up, the hotel resembled a jigsaw with all its corners, the various doors and height differences. The doors of the one-story extension in front of her were wide open, inviting her to enter.

Once again she questioned her sanity. She'd kept herself away from anything and everyone connected to the kinkier side of Ireland for almost two years. Why did she think she still knew everything and everybody in that world well enough to offer any real assistance? It had been two years since she'd last planned a BDSM party, so why did this Jay—she couldn't refer to a man she'd never met as Master—think she'd still be able to do the job?

For a moment she closed her eyes. Unless she kept on moving forwards, she would never answer those questions.

Heaven or hell? Heather had no idea what she would find on the other side of the threshold. Her fear took her by surprise. She'd known starting again would be daunting but hadn't expected to be this scared.

Another big sigh took her up the few steps, through the doors and into a wide and spacious reception area. The high ceilings and the sun streaming through the open doors and various windows made the lobby bright and welcoming. Through a long hallway she saw a glass wall. For a moment she stopped and stared at the view of the Atlantic those windows provided. There was only one word for what she saw, *stunning*. Even on a quiet day like today, the ocean looked wild and dangerous. She had no doubt the view would be even more spectacular in bad weather.

"Amazing, isn't it?"

The deep voice brought Heather back to earth with a shock. Turning toward the sound, she had to tilt her head back to look into the face of the giant who'd addressed her. Well over six feet tall, he was built like a house. With his relaxed facial expression, his short blond hair and friendly eyes, he reminded her of Sting—be it a much larger version—an artist she'd been attracted to for as long as she could remember.

"It's fabulous." She knew the smile on her face didn't begin to reach her eyes, but since she'd never felt less sure of herself in her life, there wasn't much she could do about it.

"You're Jay?"

The giant smiled and his features transformed from rather stern into warm and welcoming. "No, I'm Karl Mulready. The Master is in his office." The smile faded from his face again to be replaced by something she couldn't name. "I'll take you to him in a minute."

"That would be great, thank you. I left my car in front of the building, I hope that's okay?"

Heather wanted to kick herself. She shouldn't be feeling and sounding this insecure. She was supposed to be an experienced party-organizer. Even if it had been some time since she last planned an event, she shouldn't be feeling as if this was her first ever project. When a little voice in the back of her head tried to suggest party planning wasn't the only thing she'd ignored for almost two years, she slammed a mental door in its face.

13

The man, Karl, walked around the desk and approached her. "If you give me your keys I'll make sure your luggage is brought to your room and have the car parked in the staff area."

Either the manager didn't pick up on her insecurities or he'd successfully mastered the art of disguising his thoughts. If Heather had to make a guess, she'd pick the second option but that didn't lessen her relief. She was grateful he didn't make her feel any more stupid than she already did. Handing over her keys, she watched as Karl passed them on to a younger man who smiled at her before walking out of the door.

"If you'd follow me?"

Karl strode off down the corridor, glancing over his shoulder to make sure she was behind him. Her surroundings turned into a blur as Heather rushed to keep up with the manager, grateful she didn't have the time to worry about her upcoming meeting with the man Karl had called *the Master*. A few minutes from now she'd know who she'd be dealing with and would hopefully be able to scratch one item off her long list of worries. She'd do this one step at a time. If she could stop herself from obsessing about the big picture and her personal issues, she might just make it through the next few days. Maybe...

* * * *

He wanted to scream. No amount of staring at the pile of papers on his desk or the schedules on his screen made it any clearer how he could possibly turn this weekend into anything but an unmitigated disaster. What had seemed a great idea four months ago had turned into a nightmare of apocalyptic proportions. He only had just over two weeks left before everybody who was anybody in the Irish BDSM scene would descend on his *Blowhole*, expecting to be — as he'd so poetically put it in the invitations — blown away by the facilities he had to offer.

Of course, four months ago he'd still been himself. He'd been happy in this setting he'd created and secure in the knowledge he'd found his place in the world at last. Now he didn't know who or what he was and felt like an imposter. He almost laughed. An imposter who happened to own and run the show. He'd introduced himself as *Master Jay* on the invitations, a title that could only be interpreted one way. A title he was less comfortable wearing with each passing day.

He got up and walked to the window, taking in the view in front of him. The sight usually filled him with calm and pride. The gardens were impressive, a riot of colors lit up by the sunshine. The Atlantic provided a glorious backdrop. Under most circumstances, the beauty surrounding him was enough to set his mind at ease. Today the perfection outside only served to feed his inner turmoil.

Besides, it was too late for second thoughts. The invitations had been sent and accepted. All but one or two of his rooms had been booked for the anniversary weekend. Nothing short of the place burning down would stop this party from taking place.

The idea of having to spend a weekend with practicing Dominants while having lost his urge to dominate filled him with horror. He knew they would immediately recognize something wasn't right. The people he'd invited had no way of knowing he was indeed an experienced and well-respected Dom—in America. He knew his last scene, a month ago, had raised eyebrows. He'd been fielding concerned questions from his friends for weeks. His guests would take one look at him and see a man incapable of living up to his self-proclaimed image. A wannabe. A failure.

A low buzzing sound brought him back to the here and now. That would be Karl, warning him his visitor had arrived. He was about to come face-to-face with another one of his many questionable decisions. Leaving the initial planning to Karl had been an escape mechanism, making it possible for him to pretend he didn't have a party and possible public relations disaster in his near future. But now that she'd arrived, he had to deal with somebody he knew next to nothing about. And to make the situation even more prone to disaster, Karl had seen fit to hire someone who'd been out of the loop for the better part of two years.

He turned to his desk, moved the mouse and watched as the website sprang to life. He'd better have a quick look at this woman Karl had hired before she walked into his office. The website looked professional enough and a quick glance at the testimonials showed nothing except lavish praise. But all the information was nearly two years old. Still, the time for second thoughts had long since passed. With the party taking place in a fortnight, and this company apparently being the only one specializing in events like the one he'd be hosting, he had no other options. He'd left it much too late to get somebody from America. He only had himself to blame. If he hadn't abdicated all responsibility for the preparations to Karl, he wouldn't be in this position.

He'd just have a quick glance at the picture gallery and…

A firm knock on the door interrupted his thoughts. *Party time*. With a frown, Jason got up and turned to stare out of the window again while he listened to the door opening behind him.

Chapter Two

"Master Jay."

Heather heard the surprise in Karl's voice but wasn't quite sure what had elicited it.

"Your guest, Heather Staunton, has arrived."

"Thank you, Karl."

The voice was gruff and faintly familiar.

Heather took advantage of the fact that the man on the other side of the bright and spacious office had his back to her and studied her surroundings. She liked this room with its uncluttered feel. The furniture was big, made of dark wood and very masculine. The window on the other side of the room gave her another spectacular view of the Atlantic. She didn't think she'd ever get tired of that picture. A slight change in the light provided Heather with a vague reflection of the man who had to be *Master Jay*. Something inside her stuttered. She knew this man. But no, it couldn't be. Surely she had to be imagining things. There was no way on earth Master Jay could be the same person as the man she'd known as...

"Mrs. Staunton." The man turned and stopped talking. "Heather?"

"Jason?"

She would have laughed at both of them speaking at exactly the same time if she hadn't been so shocked about finding herself face-to-face with somebody she hadn't expected to ever meet again.

How long had it been? It had to be at least twenty years since she'd last seen this man she'd known as Jason Hudson. Twenty years since that summer in Wexford when they hadn't quite managed to get together. A chill ran down Heather's spine. What did this mean? Would this make her project harder or easier? Would she have preferred to deal with a complete stranger? Then again, wasn't he a stranger anyway? A few weeks over one summer twenty years ago didn't mean she knew who this man was — or how to work with him.

"Jason. It's okay to call you Jason, isn't it? Should I say Jay? Or even" — she couldn't stop herself from smiling — "Master Jay?"

It was a relief to see him return her smile as he took her hands and squeezed them lightly. The frown that had formed on his face when he first recognized her had been worrying.

"Jason is fine, Heather. It is my name, even if I rarely use it these days. And I'm not your Master."

The smile disappeared again.

"In fact..."

Heather watched, trying to make sense of the unfinished sentence and the deepening frown. It reassured her Jason was as surprised by this meeting as she was. On the other hand, she'd enough reservations about this project without having to take on the possible complications resulting from their previous acquaintance as well. She needed him to be sure of what they were doing because she knew she wasn't. One of them had to be in charge or they'd never get this party organized, never mind turned into a success.

She recognized the moment he gave himself a mental shake and took control.

"How did we not know we were dealing with each other?" Heather couldn't keep the confusion out of her voice. "I know I've been talking to Karl until now, but how did you not know you were hiring me?"

"I..." A frown crossed his face again. "I've left all the preliminary work up to Karl. What's the point in having a manager if you don't allow him to manage?" His smile seemed forced. Jason's gaze dropped to the screen on

18

his desk and his frown returned. "If I'd taken the time to study your website before now... But somehow I never got around to it."

When Jason gestured with his hand, Heather sat down in one of the luxurious leather chairs in the corner and watched as he instructed Karl, who'd been patiently observing their confusion, to send someone along with coffee.

Jason seated himself in the chair opposite hers and Heather studied him. "There are no photos of you on your website, Jason. Why not?"

The question appeared to surprise him and he took his time answering.

"The website has been set up to advertise The Blowhole, not me. In fact, I'm not on the menu, so to speak."

The frown, a facial expression Heather didn't remember from the past, returned again.

"The website only has pictures of those members of staff who are available to the visitors. I try to avoid raising unrealistic expectations. If I show pictures of people whose job description doesn't extend to playing with the guests, it may lead to disappointment. I try not to elicit feelings like that in my visitors."

Nodding her head, Heather looked around the office again. His answer made perfect sense and yet, she'd never come across a club owner who wasn't available to his clients at least some of the time. There had to be something else going on to make him so publicity shy. Now wasn't the moment to ask deeper questions though.

"What about you? Why is all the information on your site at least two years old, Heather?"

She couldn't quite suppress her frustration. She didn't want to get into all of this right now. "As I explained to your manager"—it might have been embarrassment flashing across his face—*serves him right*—"that's when Darren got too ill to continue."

She saw the confusion in his eyes and sighed before explaining.

"Darren was my husband and business partner." *As well as so much more*. The thought hurt. She refused to indulge in those memories right now. "He died eighteen months ago."

"I'm sorry." His voice was soft. "For your loss and for having to explain that to me now. I should have known."

Damn right. The thought flew through her head and nearly out of her mouth. Instead she forced herself to smile.

"Tell me about your anniversary party." She didn't want to talk about the past right now — or ever. She had to keep Darren out of her mind as much as possible if she wanted to do this job.

Rubbish. She would never be able to keep Darren out of her head. She could try to keep him out of her conversations though. If she managed that, she might just make it through the coming weeks without turning into a drama queen... maybe.

It surprised Heather to see Jason look as relieved as she felt when the conversation turned to matters of business. He didn't appear to be any more eager to talk about personal issues than she was.

"It's like Karl pointed out in his emails."

Jason smiled at the beautiful young woman, placing coffee cups, a cafetière and a plate with treats on the table.

"It's been nearly a year since I opened The Blowhole and for all those months I've been entertaining visitors from overseas. I lived in America for close to twenty years and have extensive contacts in the BDSM world there. Having old friends and acquaintances as my first visitors made the starting up process a lot easier than it might have been."

Heather nodded as she listened to Jason. Visitors from abroad, even if they weren't friends, would be so much safer than guests who were part of the Irish BDSM community. For starters, those Americans wouldn't see him as potential competition. She relaxed into her comfortable chair and sipped from the excellent coffee as he explained how he'd been able to create a relaxed environment in which to find his feet and train his staff to his personal standards.

"Of course, I can't continue this dependence on customers from overseas. Not to mention that if I'd wanted to cater to Americans, I could have stayed there." Jason looked at her, lost in thought for a moment. "I don't think there is a place just like mine here in Ireland. I also believe there is a market for what I have to offer. So it is time to take the next big step and allow the 'locals' to discover The Blowhole. But—" Jason smiled. "That's enough for now. You've had a long drive to get here and must be tired. Let me show you to your apartment and we'll get together again in a few hours."

As if his words had triggered the sensation, Heather felt tiredness descend on her. She could do with a shower, maybe a nap and definitely some time to gather her thoughts. She wasn't at all sure how she felt about this coincidence. Some time alone might clarify things for her—or not.

"That would be wonderful. Thank you."

She watched him as he walked to the desk and picked up the phone. Jason hadn't changed a lot in the past twenty years. He was older, of course. His face was less round, and more sculpted. His chin was stronger and there were fine lines next to his eyes, indicating both the passing of years and an inclination to smile a lot. His lips still had the tendency to turn up at the corners, although she had no doubt he'd make a domineering presence without that smile on his face.

When he held out his hand to help her up, Heather took the opportunity to look into his eyes. They were as brown and beautiful as she remembered. Well, not so much remembered but recalled again, now she found herself face-to-face with this blast from her past. She couldn't say she'd thought about him a lot since she last saw him, but the memories rushing back made it clear she hadn't forgotten him either. She'd loved his short but unruly black hair when she'd first met him, and was glad he hadn't felt the need to change his style over the years. Tiny spots of gray streaked the black now, but it still had the tousled look suggesting little concern about styling and lots of running his hands through his hair.

Staring at Jason the way she was should have embarrassed Heather. Since he studied her with equal intensity, she didn't feel too self-conscious about it. To her surprise, the fact that he held on to her hand longer than was strictly necessary didn't worry her either. With both of them on their feet she noticed that, of course, he was still as tall as he'd always been. But then, she was still as short.

Heather considered pulling her hand free when Jason started to lead her from his office but decided against it. To her surprise she didn't mind the contact, and pulling away now would only draw attention to the fact that he appeared to be reluctant to let go of her hand in the first place.

"I hope you don't mind you won't be staying in one of the guest rooms while you're here, Heather."

"I guess it depends on where you've decided to put me." Heather couldn't stop the laughter in her voice as she faced him while the elevator took them up.

"I don't think you'll have any objections."

Jason returned her smile as they exited on a hallway with two doors facing each other. When he opened the door on the right, Heather's feet stopped in their tracks.

"This will be your home away from home while you're here."

She looked around in wonder—a whole apartment to herself. She'd hoped her room wouldn't be too small and claustrophobic. Not in her wildest dreams had she imagined she'd have this much space. She took a moment to study her surroundings as Jason showed her what appeared to be living quarters. The sitting area was spacious and the blue leather chairs and sofa looked as comfortable as the chair in his office had been. The large desk at the window, overlooking the ocean, would make an ideal spot for writing or day-dreaming. There was a small but fully equipped kitchen off to the right.

"You are, of course, free to use the restaurant and room

service whenever you want." Jason's voice broke through Heather's thoughts in a way that made her wonder if he could read her mind.

"If you need anything else, just let me or housekeeping know."

Lost for words, Heather could only nod her head as Jason led her farther into the apartment then opened the door to the bedroom. It was luxury personified. A whole wall length worth of wardrobes was far more than she could possibly need for the clothes she had brought. But the four-poster bed had to be the star attraction. Big enough to sleep at least three people comfortably, she couldn't help feeling it was wasted on her. As were those bars and hooks she saw, strategically placed on the posts and headboards and footboards. This was a bedroom for someone who wanted to play. She wasn't that someone. She might be taking her first tentative steps back into this world. She wasn't sure if she'd ever be ready to play again. Playing without Darren... She couldn't imagine it.

Once again, Jason's voice brought her out of her thoughts and into the present.

"I'll leave you to get settled then. Take a few hours to freshen up and rest. I'll meet you downstairs for dinner at eight, if that's okay."

Heather smiled. "I would like that. Thank you for everything." Heather waved her hand at the luxury surrounding her. "I'll see you later."

* * * *

Jason knew the smart thing would be to go back to his office and spend some more time staring at the plans and schedules but found he couldn't be bothered. He crossed the short hallway and opened the door to his own apartment. Unlike Heather's rooms, his place took up more than half of the floor and was more palatial than big. He walked straight through his living room to the sliding doors on the far side. Sitting down on one of the loungers on his balcony, he allowed himself to release the big sigh that had been trapped in his chest ever since he'd recognized Heather. He still felt as if someone had dumped a ton of bricks on his head. Not in his wildest dreams had he thought he'd ever meet her again.

Heather. A smile appeared on his face as he remembered the sweet and innocent girl she'd been twenty years ago. The woman who'd just walked into his club couldn't be mistaken for anything but the grown-up version of that girl, although he'd be hard pressed to call her innocent now. She still had those honey-colored curls tumbling around her head in wild abandon. Her big, almond-shaped eyes had stared into his, filled with a combination of wonder, depth and sadness. Jason shook his head, he had to be imagining things. He didn't know—had never known—her well enough to recognize those feelings.

She'd certainly grown into her body since he'd last seen her. And she definitely knew how to fill a pair of jeans. Just one look at her arse in those trousers…well, the stirring had been a surprise after all those months without the sensation.

Restless, he got up and stalked up and down the balcony.

He had to stop these thoughts. He was supposed to work with Heather, not fantasize about her. He was a grown man, an experienced Dom, not some drooling teenager getting off on mentally undressing her. Still, what were the chances of meeting her again like this? Surely, such coincidences didn't happen in real life? His past had just walked into his present and was scheduled to work with him this fortnight. Two weeks during which he could get to know her again, provided he could convince her to stay. As it stood, the plan was for her to be here for a few days and then return before the event started. If he played his hand right though…

No.

He raised his head to the sun, hoping the warmth would sooth his fevered thoughts. What was wrong with him? Just because he hadn't seen the woman in twenty years didn't

24

mean he had to lose his mind over her. He might once have said that if he'd ever... He wasn't going to pursue that line of thought either. *For fuck's sake*, she'd lost her husband and partner, who had probably been her Dom as well, not too long ago. Even if she didn't look like the typical grieving widow, he had no doubt he'd seen pain in her eyes. He had far more pressing problems to deal with right now than a sudden infatuation with a memory. Like how he'd get through that weekend without exposing himself as the fraud he'd turned into. Or how he'd ever find his way back to what had been such an important part of his life for so long.

Even if Heather hadn't been recently widowed, seducing her would have been a bad idea. There were a few exceptions, but in general, fucking somebody you had to work with only led to unnecessary complications. He had a party to organize, a business to sustain. He needed to keep his eyes on the ball and off his balls, and Heather's arse, and her beautiful green eyes. He had to stop his mind from creating these images unless he wanted to set himself up for a one-way journey into endless amounts of pain.

Chapter Three

When the alarm on her phone went off, Heather woke up from a sleep much deeper than she'd expected to enjoy. She'd needed that. She hadn't realized how tired the combination of the drive from Dublin and the shock of meeting Jason again had made her.

It *had* been a shock and she still wasn't sure how she felt about *Master Jay* being Jason. It had been great meeting him again. Of course it had. But it would have been a lot easier if the circumstances had been different. If she didn't have to work with him. If Darren had been with her.

She got out of bed and walked to the bathroom for a quick shower. Darren...she had no idea if she could do this without him. He'd made her promise she wouldn't let their business die. He'd even made her promise that one day she'd... No, she wouldn't allow her thoughts to go there. Continuing their work was one thing, giving herself to someone else?

The unfairness of the whole situation hit her like a slap. Darren would have loved this place. The Blowhole and everything it offered, this apartment, that bed... All of it could have been custom-made for her and Darren. Yet here she was, alone, without the only man she'd ever loved, the only man she'd given herself to body and soul, the only man she could imagine ever submitting to.

The tears streaming down her face were easy enough to ignore. Under the shower they were just more wetness, indistinguishable from the water falling on her head. This was not the way to start her new project. If she couldn't look at a bed built for bondage, she had no hope of dealing with everything else she would be encountering over the next few weeks. Heather turned her head into the spray and groaned. Maybe she should just leave—take her luggage back down to the lobby, apologize to Jason and go back home. Put the whole thing down to experience and give herself more time.

As tempting as the thought was, she could hear Darren's voice in the back of her mind. *"Pull yourself together, Heather. You're being silly and you know it. Of course you can do this. Remember your promise. Face those fears and defeat them. Do it for us. Do it for me. But most of all, do it for you."*

She could hear him so clearly. She knew he would want her to stay. He'd tell her to go and familiarize herself with The Blowhole and work out the best possible plan for a spectacular party. He'd expect her to make the anniversary a success then share the details with the world. Knowing Darren—and she knew him so well—he'd even tell her to open herself up to the idea that it might be…

But no. He would have been wrong. She might be able to organize this party, to observe people while they enjoyed everything that would be on offer, but she was nowhere near ready to throw herself back into the game. Not now… maybe not ever. Although… Much as she didn't like the thought, she couldn't deny she'd been getting restless lately. Isolating herself wasn't working anymore. Recently she'd found herself yearning for something she'd rather not name. Her unexpected visitor might have been an unwelcome intrusion, but he had also made her realize her desires and needs weren't as dead as she'd thought they were.

She had some time left before she had to get ready for dinner with Jason. Determined to stop her mind from bombarding her with more doubts, Heather opened her laptop and had another look at The Blowhole's website. She'd been studying the information for weeks now, but it didn't hurt to be as prepared as she could be.

Welcome to 'The Blowhole', *Ireland's largest, all inclusive adult playground.*

The words *adult playground* made her smile.

Welcome to a world where people are allowed to be who they are and enjoy whatever their hearts desire without judgment. Whether your tastes are innocent or adventurous, ranging from luxurious vanilla to full-fledged BDSM, 'The Blowhole' will provide you with the environment and equipment to fulfill your every fantasy.

Yes, the idea impressed her. She had visited many sex clubs, swingers meetings and BDSM gatherings with Darren. They had organized quite a few of those events. Yet she had never come across a place catering to such a wide variety of customers until now. In theory, the idea sounded inspired. Whether or not it worked in practice remained to be seen and depended on how comfortably all the various tastes could live together. Of course that wouldn't be an issue as far as the party she'd be organizing was concerned. The event would be exclusively BDSM. In the meantime, it would be interesting to see how Jason had dealt with the risk of alienating vanilla-minded people as a result of the kinkier excesses.

The familiarity of research did the trick. Heather could feel herself relax into the information. When she couldn't postpone getting ready for dinner any longer, she was almost calm again.

Almost calm. She couldn't quite put her finger on the source of the apprehension she felt when she thought about having dinner with Jason. *It would be nothing more than a business meeting,* she thought as she pulled a dress from the wardrobe.

She knew how to conduct herself, what questions to ask, what queries to expect and even most of the answers she'd give to those. She might not have done any of this on her own before but that didn't mean she wasn't capable. Of course, she would probably have been completely sure of the way forward if she'd been dealing with anyone other than Jason. She ignored the thought, refusing to linger on what it might mean, just as she wasn't going to spend too much time thinking about the past.

She glanced at herself in the mirror and decided she would do. She looked nice — not too sexy and not too modest either. With a bit of luck people — Jason — would see a dedicated professional. That's what she was. She was here to do a job and do it well. Nothing else should matter... *Should* being the operative word.

* * * *

Jason found himself in the lobby, waiting for Heather, a few minutes before the appointed time. He still couldn't get over her showing up here. What was more, he couldn't get his head around his reaction to seeing her again. For twenty years he'd barely spared the girl — no, woman — a thought. And now, ever since she'd walked into his office, he couldn't get her out of his mind. Pictures of that long-ago summer in Wexford surfaced in his mind. The four of them, two couples and six weeks of love, lust and drama. It had been one of the best summers of his life and he'd allowed the memories to slip away. He wondered if maybe it would have been the best summer of his life if he'd spent it with Heather instead of Moira. But Heather back then had been so young, so innocent and too sweet to take advantage of. Moira, on the other hand, had been more than eager to embrace everything he threw at her and to introduce him to concepts he'd never known existed.

The lift doors opened and Jason's heart skipped a beat, only to settle again when four guests stepped into the lobby.

He looked from the stairs to the elevator again but still saw no sign of the woman who had taken up permanent residence in his mind. He couldn't get over the irony of the situation. Back then he hadn't been able to bring himself to be intimate with Heather. Now his imagination was running riot. He would have to find a way to bring himself back to his senses. He had hoped a few hours away from her presence, hours of studying her website and all her suggestions for the party, would help him get used to the idea of having her stay here. They should have cleared his head off any images of him seducing her out of her mourning. Unfortunately his thoughts weren't cooperating.

Staring at the elevator he became aware of a presence behind him. Turning around, he found her standing on the stairs. This was a Heather he hadn't seen before. Her hair had been tamed and fell sleekly down her face, coming to rest on her slim shoulders. Without the curls, her face looked longer, less round, more grown-up. Okay, it took her straight from sweet and attractive to sexy and hot.

He still had no control over his thoughts. The red dress she wore showed every inch of her body off to its best advantage, making her look at least as lush as she was in his memories. Those gorgeous, full breasts were allowed to show just enough cleavage to excite. She exuded sexiness without being provocative, although the picture she presented did trigger a few sinful thoughts in Jason's mind. The dress hugged her curves. The little red number ending just above her knees allowed him to appreciate her shapely legs, elongated by the heels she wore.

As Jason took his time walking toward her, he couldn't stop the smile from spreading across his face. She was beautiful and unless she'd changed a lot over the years, she would be delightful company. Even if he had to restrain his urge to touch her, to bring her to his bed, to play his games with her and, God help him, take her to his dungeon, he could have a good time with her while she was here.

With Heather standing on the second step of the staircase, their eyes were at the same height and Jason took advantage of the opportunity to look straight into her beautiful green irises. His groin tightened when she lowered her gaze for a moment, only to flash it back up and stare right back at him. There it was. Such a small sign. A slight indication that the submissive inside this woman hadn't died with the man she'd called Sir. He saw the slight blush coloring her cheeks and realized she was as aware of the signal she'd just transmitted as he was. Jason forced that piece of information to the back of his mind as he reached out and took both her small hands into his.

"Heather, you're a sight for sore eyes." Unable to help himself, he bent forward and placed a soft kiss on her cheek. Her perfume was light and flowery. The aroma mirrored the way she looked — beautiful, self-assured and subtle.

"And you're still as imposing as you always were." Heather's teasing smile didn't stop him from treasuring the little shudder he'd felt going through her when his lips had met her cheek.

He needed to deflect his thoughts, keep this meeting light. "Imposing? My dear, you have no idea. If you think I'm imposing now..." He allowed the sentence to die. She'd never see that side of him. It no longer existed, regardless of his reactions to her. Still he couldn't help wondering if her reaction to him could possibly resemble the thoughts she elicited in his mind.

He stopped himself from pursuing the question. What was wrong with him anyway? She was here to do a job, to help him make a success of this party he'd decided to throw. The doubts he had about this professional partnership were disappearing fast. He wanted their cooperation to be a success — and not just for the sake of his club. He wanted to get to know her again. Scaring her off with hasty advances would make that impossible.

"Do you have everything you need in your apartment?" He started toward the restaurant, holding on to one of Heather's hands as he went. He noticed when her hand tensed and relaxed again, as if she'd been thinking about pulling back before deciding against it. He would love to be able to read the thoughts running through her head right now but knew better than to ask. As long as he pretended that holding her hand was nothing other than natural and friendly, she might leave it there. He didn't know why it seemed so important to him, but holding her hand made him feel good. He loved that tiny bit of skin-to-skin contact — all the skin-to-skin he was likely to experience with her. He wasn't going to spoil it by opening his big mouth.

"I do, Jason. Thank you so much for those amazing rooms. I still can't believe I have a whole apartment to myself." Heather's smile was genuine and relaxed, even if her words sounded rather formal. He wondered whether she found it as difficult as he did to keep things strictly professional. He knew it was unlikely, but couldn't stop himself from hoping that maybe, somewhere deep inside, Heather felt some of the same attraction.

"Over there is the bar, which is open more or less twenty-four-seven."

"You allow your clients access to unlimited amounts of alcohol? Isn't that a recipe for disaster?"

He could see the confusion in Heather's eyes and understood what lay at the root of it. Alcohol and kink could be a dangerous, in some cases lethal, combination and most clubs had strict rules with regard to drinking.

"It has not been an easy decision and I haven't made up my mind about the party yet." He saw the question in her eyes and continued.

"You see, we don't only cater to lifestylers here. There is no real reason to deny vanilla couples, just because alcohol and BDSM don't mix." He sighed, thinking back to the endless to-ing and fro-ing he'd done about the decision. "Security keeps an eye on everybody entering the BDSM area and will demand a breathalyzer test if anybody appears to be even slightly intoxicated. So far we've managed to avoid any trouble. If that ever changes, the bar policy will be revisited." Jason pointed to his right. "That there is the games' room."

The way she looked up at him left Jason in no doubt about her assumptions and he laughed.

"Different games, Heather. The kink part of my club starts farther down this corridor. In there all you're going to find are a pool table and table football, as well as a collection of board games."

He watched her nod her understanding before adding, "Of course, even those everyday games have been known to transform into something more risqué."

As soon as he said the words, his treacherous mind flashed on Heather in a short dress with a deep V-neck, playing pool. He imagined her bending and stretching to hit the ball while her skirt rode up her legs, and her breasts... He felt his cock stirring in his trousers. He didn't get it. For months now, playing with beautiful, willing and naked women hadn't been able to excite him. Yet here he was, picturing Heather in a provocative pose and all his systems were firing.

"Do you play pool, Heather?" The way she blushed made him think she might be able to read his mind.

"I have been known to shoot a few balls, yes." Heather's blush deepened and her eyes grew distant for a moment. God, what he wouldn't give for just a glimpse of the thoughts going through her head.

Chapter Four

Heather hated the blush creeping up her cheeks. Again. She had to stop this ridiculous behavior. Why did being around Jason make her so insecure? Everything about him set her nerves on edge. The way he looked at her, the light kiss he had given her, his hand holding hers. All of it made her feel things she hadn't felt in a long time. Images jumped into her mind of pool tables and everything you could do with them and on them, when you weren't trying to pot balls.

She listened to Jason telling her more about the various rooms they walked by while her mind went back to the moment when he'd looked into her eyes. She hadn't been able to stop herself. She'd lowered her gaze instinctively as soon as his met hers. She wanted to pretend it had meant nothing, that anybody would have done the same thing, but she'd be lying. She'd lowered her eyes because everything in her system had demanded it. A small part of her had yearned to fall to her knees and stay there until he told her to get up again.

When Jason released her hand and placed his on the small of her back while steering her into the restaurant, it barely registered. The room was dimly lit, dark enough to make it hard to clearly see the other diners, and the atmosphere was intimate.

The table Jason led her to was set in a rather private corner. Heather didn't know how she felt about that. Until this afternoon it had all been simple. Her only intention, when she'd accepted this job, had been to resurrect her business. This party was supposed to be the perfect opportunity to let her customers know her retreat into obscurity had ended. She had not expected to feel anything resembling lust, never mind the need to submit. She wasn't ready to deal with these feelings or the sultry atmosphere around her. She needed this to be a pure and simple business meeting far removed from the confusing emotions assaulting her. She'd been so sure she would never feel attracted to another man again and resented her feelings for betraying her. And yet...

A sharp dart of anger shot through Heather. *Damn Jason.* If only he'd been someone else. Working with a stranger would have been so much easier. Now she had to deal with this attractive, dominant and kind man while memories of their first meeting, twenty years ago, were snaking their way back into her mind, taking on an importance they'd never had in the past.

"I've ordered for both of us. I hope you don't mind."

Jason's voice brought her out of her thoughts and back to the present.

"We're having small portions of most dishes I would like to serve during the weekend. Let me know what you think."

She jumped on the opportunity to get away from confusing personal thoughts and concentrate on work.

"I love that idea, Jason. In fact, I'm looking forward to hearing about your plans for the party."

She knew she sounded both relieved and over eager, but she couldn't help it. Anything had to be better than the thoughts and feelings running through her head, trying to destabilize her.

"I'm going to need a lot more details before I can make useful recommendations, beyond the ones I discussed with Karl."

She looked up into Jason's dark eyes and forced herself not to look away. This was business. And she'd better remember it before she either made a fool of herself or left an impression she'd no intention of living up to.

"I thought we might leave those discussions for tomorrow,

Heather." His smile suggested he knew exactly where her thoughts had taken her. "I want to get to know you again, find out what you have been up to for the past twenty years."

She couldn't hold his gaze any longer. Her eyes would betray too many of the feelings rushing through her, so she looked down and admired the small bowl of cucumber soup a waiter had placed in front of her. Taking a taste, she was delighted with the combination of cold and creamy in her mouth and grateful for the few seconds of respite it bought her.

"This is delicious, Jason."

Heather was all too aware of Jason's gaze on her as she enjoyed her soup. She knew he wanted a response to his suggestion. *Feck it.* She'd have to be honest and hope he'd understand. Forcing herself to look into his eyes again, Heather took a deep breath. "I'm not sure I can do that, Jason." Seeing he was about to interrupt her, she continued, "I'm trying to move forward, revisiting my past will only hold me back."

"But" — Jason hesitated for a moment — "aren't your memories happy ones?"

Shit. She so didn't want to get into this right now. "Yes. Yes they are, but it hurts they're *only* memories. It shouldn't be my past. I should be doing this with Darren, not on my own." She hated the tears trying to make their way to her eyes, betraying themselves in her voice. "I'm not sure I can do this if I don't keep the past behind me, where it belongs." She felt the one tear rolling down her cheek despite her best efforts to hold it back. "Please don't make me do this."

"I'm sorry."

Jason brushing the tear from her cheek fueled her confused feelings even further.

"I won't ask you again if it's too painful. Sure, we can talk about anything you want."

It was pathetic how relieved and grateful she felt. "I'd love to hear all about your life though, Jason. How did you end up owning The Blowhole? I know it's not fair to ask when I'm not willing to share" — she smiled — "but I am very curious."

She couldn't suppress the sigh of relief when Jason sat back in his chair and nodded his head.

"I guess that's only fair. You need information about me, and what I want to achieve if you're going to help me. And I suppose I do know more about the work you do, thanks to your company website, than you could ever have found out about me."

Heather sat back and took a long sip from her glass of wine while Jason started.

"After Wexford — you do remember Wexford, don't you, Heather?"

As if by magic, his words brought her back to that glorious summer when she'd only been eighteen years old. It had been her first holiday without her parents, without any adults to restrict her freedom. The summer before she'd started college, the summer before she'd met... No, she wasn't going there.

Once she'd switched her thoughts off again, she found she enjoyed listening to Jason as he revisited those weeks in Wexford. The long sunny days on the beach, the lazy afternoons and those midnight walks all had conspired to make it six weeks of pure pleasure. The more he talked, the more vivid her memories of those days became.

She and her friend Moira had only just settled into their cottage when they'd run into Jason and Rick, who were staying next door.

Heather nodded her thanks as a waiter placed a small seafood platter in the middle of the table and smiled when she remembered how they'd paired off almost immediately.

"There was one moment, Heather, when I thought you were the one for me."

She thought she heard regret in Jason's voice and despite her reservations, Heather opened her mouth.

"Then why did you pick Moira?"

Jason's smile held a quality she couldn't identify.

"Remember what we were like back then, Heather. You were so innocent and Moira was… Hell, Moira was Moira. She was up for anything and didn't have an innocent bone in her body. I hadn't yet figured out what I wanted and needed at the time, but I knew it wasn't innocence."

The naughty smile on Jason's face did funny things to Heather's insides.

"The things I wanted to do to you, everything I ended up doing to, and with, Moira, all the experiences she brought me. Back then I couldn't imagine you in those scenarios." The smile turned wistful. "Maybe if I'd known then what I know now, I would have made a different choice. But can you honestly say you were ready that summer for everything you discovered later on in life?"

Heather felt herself relax further. These were good memories to focus on and she allowed herself to go back there. Jason was right. She had been innocent. It hadn't lasted much longer, but during those weeks, she'd still thought all she needed was someone to love, someone who would treat her as if she was fragile. Those were the days when cuddling brought all the excitement she needed. Fucking, or lovemaking as she had thought of it at the time, had been something to save for the future and the someone special she'd hoped to meet one day. Back then she'd wanted attention and validation far more than intimacy, and Rick had fitted those needs perfectly.

She barely noticed as the dish of Eastern treats was placed in front of her by the unobtrusive waiter.

"You were right, of course, Jason. I wasn't ready." Heather couldn't stop herself from grinning. "Although I think the vibes you and Moira sent out did have a lot to do with my later curiosity." She allowed her mind to flow freely for a moment. "I think I needed Darren to fully awaken those needs in me."

Shock robbed Heather of her words. She couldn't believe she'd said that. She'd been so determined to keep Darren out of her dealings with Jason. Wexford was supposed to be a safe subject between them. Bless Jason for ignoring her last statement, as if he knew how much she'd surprised herself when she'd said those words.

"Heather, you and Rick looked good together back then. I thought you two were well matched."

She thought she might be imagining it, but for a moment Jason seemed troubled.

"I remember you as being happy. Weren't you? Was I fooling myself? Trying to make myself feel better about picking the easier option?"

Her heart made a little jump inside her chest, taking Heather by surprise. As she delved into a salmon-filled pastry wrap, she wondered why the fact that Jason had felt the same attraction she had experienced, made her happy. It was safer to not explore that line of thought right now though.

Smiling at the handsome man across the table, she shook her head.

"No. You were right. Rick and I were well matched. I don't think either of us was ever in love. But the attraction was there."

She paused. How honest did she want to be? If she wasn't prepared to talk about Darren, should she not at least have the courage to admit to everything she'd felt and thought before she had met him?

"Don't get me wrong, Jason. I didn't spend those six weeks pining for you. But I would catch you looking at me and in those moments I always had these 'what if' scenarios running through my head."

They'd also shared an afternoon on the beach. She wasn't going to mention that though. Not unless he did.

Without thinking her next words through, Heather continued. "When I found out later that you'd said..."

She couldn't finish that sentence. If Jason had never said those words, saying them out loud now would be too embarrassing. Even if it were true, she didn't want him to think it was still important to her now. Because it wasn't—it couldn't be.

"That I said what?" The tone in his voice left her in no doubt Jason knew exactly what she hadn't said. His teasing smile only added to her embarrassment.

"Never mind. Forget I said anything. I must be misremembering things."

Jason just continued to smile. "That I'd said that if I were to ever marry, it would be to a girl like you."

Strange how it wasn't difficult to admit to those words. Jason had meant them at the time. And he'd never married. Whether it was because he'd never met another woman like Heather was a question he didn't want to answer right now—not even to himself. He'd never known those words had made it back to Heather, but he was glad they had. He could never have said them to her face back then, had been too much of a coward. Saying them now was easy though. He was glad she'd known how he felt about her. It was good to confirm now that she had been special to him, even if his actions had indicated otherwise.

"You remember that?"

He couldn't disguise the wonder he felt. She still remembered those words, after all these years.

A warm smile lit up Heather's face.

"Of course I remember. It's one of the nicest things anyone's ever said about me. It's hard to imagine a bigger compliment than being the sort of person somebody hopes to marry." The smile deepened. "Finding out you'd said those words did wonders for my self-esteem."

Jason was glad the conversation was interrupted by the arrival of their desserts. The fresh strawberry mousse looked tempting, and watching Heather dive in with obvious pleasure gave him an excuse for the happy feelings rushing through him.

He hadn't imagined it. Heather had been as interested in him when they were in Wexford as he'd been in her. While he regretted ignoring the attraction, he still felt it had been the right—the only—decision. He'd been so inexperienced then. All enthusiasm with nothing to back it up. Moira had been able to deal with that. She'd known what it was he needed, because she'd needed it too.

Against his better judgment he asked. "Are you saying Moira and I made you curious enough to find out more when you met Darren?"

Stupid.

The shutters came down. The warm smile evaporated as if it had never been. Pain and anger were clearly visible in her eyes. She'd told him she didn't want to talk about her husband. He understood why and had still opened his big mouth.

"Heather, I'm sorry." He picked up her hand and stroked his thumb over the soft flesh. "I had no right to ask that question and I don't expect an answer."

The weak smile she shared went a small way to alleviating the guilt he felt.

"Don't apologize, Jason."

He watched with admiration as she shook her head and visibly forced the tears and the pain back.

"Most, if not all, of the guests coming to your weekend know me only as part of Heather and Darren."

He watched her as she stared off into the distance, as if the real implication behind her words only now became clear to her.

"If I'm going to be here then, and that *is* the plan, I'd better be prepared to talk about him. And about losing him."

Jason could have sworn he saw the exact moment she made up her mind to find the strength somewhere.

"I'll have to get used to talking about him."

A weight he hadn't known he'd been carrying lifted from his chest when she smiled rather ruefully.

"Do you mind if I use you as a guinea pig? If I get used to talking about Darren with you, it might make dealing with all those people who knew us as a couple, easier."

"Not at all, I'd be honored."

He looked at her, trying to figure out what her real feelings were. She might be pretending to make him feel better. It worried him that he couldn't tell for sure.

"Yes, Karl?"

Jason looked up at his manager who had succeeded in approaching their table without being noticed, despite his size.

"You asked me to warn you when Hector was ready to proceed, Jason. He'll be starting in about fifteen minutes."

"Thank you, Karl. I'm not sure if... Never mind. You go back to what you were doing." He saw the curiosity in Heather's face and knew he had to explain. "I know I said we'd postpone the party planning until tomorrow, but I did want to show you one thing tonight, because I'm not sure we'll have another opportunity." He rushed on before Heather could ask questions. "Hector is my best Dom. He and his sub Amber are about to start a demonstration. They'll be doing one or two during the weekend as well and I thought you should see what I have in mind." He nearly didn't say the next few words but forced them out anyway. "Now I'm not so sure though."

This time he had no problem reading her facial expression as she thought about his words. Excitement, probably at the thought of a demonstration, almost immediately followed by fear as she realized watching it would bring her closer to her past then she'd been in over a year. He could only hope he'd managed to disguise his relief as he watched her take a deep breath and make up her mind.

"I appreciate your concern, Jason. But I think I should bite this particular bullet now. If it turns out to be more than I can take, I'd rather find out tonight than during the festivities."

So brave.

She amazed him and herself as well by the looks of her. Since he was still holding her hand, he used it to help her up.

"If it gets too much, just let me know and we'll go, okay?"

The gratitude in her eyes as she nodded her head almost broke his heart. He had to live up to the trust she'd just placed in him. He had to protect her from getting hurt, even if it did mean denying the feelings growing stronger inside him. He'd find a way. He wouldn't let her down.

He held a tight grip on her hand as he led her out of the restaurant and down the corridor to all those other play areas.

"You know this isn't *just* a BDSM club."

Of course he did get a lot of customers — the majority if he had to take a guess — from those who lived the lifestyle. He wasn't aware of other clubs operating as a resort, not in Ireland. But quite a few of his customers were the sexually curious, those who wanted to find out what exactly was possible and available in a safe environment. He'd seen his fair share of bored couples arriving in the hope that a few days on the west coast of Ireland would reignite the fire in their relationship. He liked to think that most, if not all of the time, he delivered exactly what those people were expecting.

He led them through double doors into a wide, dimly lit hallway. "This first part of what we call the Recreational Area is reserved for our less adventurous visitors." Pointing to the doors on either side of them he continued.

"Those rooms are all available to our guests to use as and when they please. They do contain some toys but nothing suggesting either bondage or pain."

He shrugged. "Guests can request any other toy or implement they want from the staff, of course."

He watched Heather as she took a good look around her, observing the few couples making their way to the free rooms, most of them so engrossed in each other they were barely aware of anybody besides themselves.

"Guests can, and most often do, close these doors if they want privacy, but none of the doors lock and all rooms are monitored by cameras." He watched Heather switch into her professional persona. He'd been right to end the personal talk. She was far more at ease, now she could concentrate on her work rather than her memories.

"Through there" — Jason pointed at another set of double doors — "things get more adventurous. All the guests are allowed to enter, but they do so in the full knowledge they may see things that will make them uncomfortable. Just as they know they can't object to anything they may encounter there."

Again it hit Jason that his guests' comforts weren't the only ones he had to worry about right now.

"Are you certain this is what you want to do Heather?"

He looked at her, relieved to see her giving his words the attention they deserved.

"Yes, I am. I need to know for sure."

He heard a strange combination of courage and fear in her voice.

"Having doubt lingering in my mind will only make things worse and blow this out of all proportions." Uncertainty flashed in her eyes before disappearing again. "If I can't do this, you deserve to find out now, while there's still time to find somebody else to help you."

He almost laughed out loud. There were no other BDSM party planners in Ireland. He needed an insider, someone familiar with the Irish scene, to steer him right. If Heather couldn't do this, he'd be on his own.

Because he knew what she meant, he stifled the laughter and appreciated what she'd said. She had to be worrying she would end up wasting his time and money and had no way of knowing he wanted her to stay, even if she didn't contribute anything to his party. He'd no intention of telling her that either.

"Promise me you'll let me know if it gets too much, Heather." He knew he was about to take a risk and used the words anyway. "Consider it a safe word scenario. You reach your limit, we go."

He saw her hesitation at the mention of a safe word and

cherished the smile that crept across her face as she looked up at him.

"I will, Jason, I promise. My safe word is black."

Chapter Five

Safe word.

It had been a while since she'd had to think about using one of those. In fact, she couldn't remember the last time she'd used one. Darren had known her so well and had been so tuned into her body language, that she'd rarely come close to even considering hers. It did emphasize the risk she was about to take. This decision might well be what would make or break her. She wasn't sure where she'd found the courage to tell Jason she wanted, needed, to do this now. Of course every word she'd said was true. If she wasn't up to this job, both of them were better off if she found out sooner rather than later. Still, to voluntarily walk into a confrontation with everything that had brought her such delight in the past, everything she feared she might never enjoy again, scared her. She wasn't quite sure if she'd label herself brave or insane. On the other hand, she couldn't deny that lately she'd become aware of a longing she'd been reluctant to investigate.

She listened to Jason as he told her he would show her all the rooms they were passing tomorrow morning.

"They're mostly occupied now, and while these rooms have cameras too, we try not to interrupt sessions unless it can't be avoided."

The smell of sweat, leather and almost tangible lust in the area invaded her senses. The sounds of floggers hitting flesh, moans of pleasure and shrieks of pain, all of them brought back memories. Everything she saw, heard and smelled filled her with a great sense of loss, as well as an unexpected rush of arousal.

A crowd of waiting people filled the large area Jason steered her toward. She could feel the anticipation in the air and couldn't escape the excitement buzzing through the room. A path cleared in front of them and Heather followed Jason to a spot, just outside the exhibition area, allowing her a clear view. Her first instinct was to turn around, look away, close her eyes, do anything in her power not to see the scene in front of her. She couldn't.

It had been so long, she could barely remember the sensations displays like this aroused in her. She knew it would hurt later, but right now she needed to experience those feelings. She'd dealt with the pain for almost two years. She could deal with it for a while longer.

Her breath caught as she watched a man dressed only in dark denim pants lead a naked and blindfolded woman to a bench. Heather studied it more closely. This didn't look like a standard spanking bench. A big dildo was fixed near one end.

The man brought the woman to the purpose-built piece of furniture and made her place one foot on a small step before helping her to straddle it. With her other foot positioned on the step on the far side, the woman's crotch hovered over the phallus. Of course, deprived of her eyesight, she didn't know that—yet. When the man took the woman's hands and pulled them forwards to the other end of the bench where two pieces of ribbon were waiting to tie them, her body lowered just enough. Heather recognized the moment the woman became aware of the dildo between her legs. Her face tensed then relaxed into a lazy smile.

Amazement filled Heather when she felt her own face mirror the girl's satisfied expression. The full and instant reaction of her body to the scene shocked her. Her nipples tightened and heat and wetness gathered between her own legs. She wanted to shake her head, deny the feelings. But she remained still, suddenly aware of Jason behind her, his hands on her hips. For a second she felt the urge to just lean back and find some of that physical contact she'd missed for so long. She couldn't. It was Jason behind her, not Darren. She wanted it to be Darren. She needed to feel him behind her, pressing his hardening cock into her arse, whispering suggestions in her ear. She could hear his voice in her head, telling her all the things he'd be doing to her later, once they were alone. She felt his hands squeeze her hips.

They weren't Darren's hands. Disappointment shot through her body and she tensed. The hands squeezed again and some of the tension disappeared. No, those weren't Darren's hands, it wasn't her husband and Dom standing behind her, but she couldn't deny those hands were grounding her, making it possible for her to watch the scene in front of her instead of running away as fast as she could.

She relaxed further and gave her full attention to the beautiful couple in front of her. The woman's hands had been tied to the bench now, and the man walked toward her legs. A soft but resounding slap on her arse had the woman slip down onto the waiting dildo, her excited groan almost lost in the gasps coming from the audience. Heather watched as the man talked to the woman, his voice too low to carry to the watching crowd. Whatever he was saying, the woman must have been reacting according to his expectations. He had a satisfied grin on his face as he rubbed his partner's arse with languid strokes. Heather watched as if hypnotized as the woman started to squirm, only to stop as soon as the man murmured something else. He took something from his pocket, looked at it and pressed with his thumb. Instantly a low buzzing sound filled the room and the woman started squirming again. The man's hand went back to her arse to keep her still and in place, victim to the vibrations the dildo sent into her core.

"You're not to come."

For the first time, the man spoke in a voice loud enough to carry to the audience. Heather could feel the crowd around her tensing in sympathy with the woman's plight. Her own body stiffened, her vagina contracted. Heather's breathing quickened and she could feel herself getting hotter. Somewhere in the back of her mind, she knew Jason had to be aware of all these reactions as well. His hands were still on her hips, his thumbs stroking her, his presence only adding to the need running through her system.

Again she forced her attention away from her own body and back to the scene now nearing its end. The woman appeared to be reaching her limit, moaning loudly and pleading with the man who continued to keep her arse still with his hand. After a few more minutes of what Heather knew was exquisite torture for the woman, the man gave her shapely arse another light slap then walked around the bench to face her. As the woman took advantage of her freedom and bucked herself to a long and violent orgasm, the man bent forward and took her mouth for a long and deep kiss.

Too much. It was too much. She couldn't do this. The heat, the love, the way the man so obviously cared for his sub. Memories rushed through Heather's head, lights flashed in front of her eyes. She had to get away, she couldn't breathe. Turning around, she blindly stared up at the man behind her, the man she didn't quite recognize. "Black... Black. Please...black."

* * * *

Shit, she safe-worded.

Instantly he turned her toward the exit. Putting his arm around her shoulder and pushing her head into his chest, he steered them through the clearly excited crowd. He felt the tears as they landed on his shirt. How had he missed the signs? There had to have been signs. He should have seen this coming, should have been able to recognize it and get her out before it got too much. He'd failed...again. He had no right to call himself a Dom. Twenty years of experience and he'd failed to see a meltdown coming. He wanted to kick himself, needed to scream, shout, punch somebody, be punched by someone.

Jason took a deep breath. He had to look after Heather, make her his priority and stop his selfish thoughts. Shaking and barely supporting herself, Heather sounded close to hyperventilating. Staving off his panic, he looked around and sighed with relief when he saw an empty room. He closed the door behind him and guided the frantic woman to a comfortable couch in the corner. He sat down and settled Heather on his lap, cradling her in his arms.

"It's okay. You were so brave. Shhh now, you're fine. You're safe. I've got you."

His stomach churned and his heartbeat grew faster at the sight of Heather's despair. Her crying got louder, making it almost impossible to hear her words.

"So sorry. I'm so sorry. Jason, I can't. I was wrong. Too soon."

He couldn't remember the last time he'd felt this helpless.

Reduced to allowing her to cry her tears, listening to the words she had to say and holding her close, a sensation of impotence engulfed him. His mind scrambled, trying to identify the moment when it had all gone wrong. The crucial moment he'd managed to miss.

He'd thought she was fine. He'd loved having his hands on Heather. He would have left his hands on her hips forever if he could. Her curves had felt every bit as good as they looked and it had taken all his restraint not to stroke her too much, to stop his hands from squeezing her lightly, just to see what sort of a reaction that would get. He'd felt it when she tensed as the scene started and had been ready to let her go when she'd surprised him by relaxing again. He'd been aware of what had been happening to her body and had allowed himself to think that bringing her to this display had been a good idea. There had even been a moment when he'd thought she was about to lean back, rest her body against his. Maybe he'd been wrong or maybe she'd stopped herself. Either way it was probably best that she hadn't. At least she hadn't discovered how excited having her close had made him.

Shit.

He'd been able to disguise his hard-on earlier but knew there was no hiding it now. Despite her obvious pain, her panic, her tears, his cock throbbed against her legs. She'd realize it as soon as she calmed down. And what sort of an impression would that make? He'd appear a pervert, getting off on her despair. He had no possible way of preventing that from happening. He couldn't let go of her now. He had to hold her until she rediscovered her equilibrium. He'd created this mess and now he'd better deal with it. If it all ended with Heather thinking of him as an insensitive bastard, it was no more than he deserved. If he couldn't stop himself from lusting for her while she felt this bad, he wasn't worth her good opinion, or anybody else's.

Heather's crying sounded less hysterical, her breathing less harsh. She still hid her face in his shirt though and continued to murmur sentences he only caught flashes of.

"Stupid... Too soon... Can't... Too much."

He'd been so sure bringing her to see this couple would be good for her. Hector and his sub were so obviously in love with each other. The dynamic between them was so beautiful. His domination and her submission were vivid, the power exchange between them complete and instantly recognizable. They were everything Jason had always hoped to find one day. Everything he now knew he would never have because he just wasn't perceptive enough.

His mind went back to the end of the scene. Until the very last he'd been convinced Heather had if not enjoyed then at least relaxed into the display. He'd been aware of her body reacting to the scene in front of her. He'd been able to sense it when she got excited. He'd convinced himself he could smell her arousal. He'd been about to congratulate himself for bringing her there when Hector had kissed his sub and...

The kiss.

He would have slapped his head if he hadn't needed both

hands to hold Heather. Of course it had been the kiss. How had he not seen it coming? Heather had been fine as long as the scene had been about bodies, arousal and satisfaction. The display of love had undone her. Of course it had. She'd clearly been devoted to her husband. Only a blind person could fail to see how much she still missed him. He should have gotten her out of there before that kiss. Hector always ended his scenes with a display of his love for Amber. Damn it. He could and should have known.

"Jason?" Heather's whisper broke through his fevered thoughts. "You're holding me too tight."

Bollix.

To add insult to injury, he couldn't even hold her through her breakdown without hurting her. "Heather, I'm sorry. I should have known, should have gotten you out of there before it got too much for you."

He relaxed his hold on her and took a deep breath. Looking into her eyes was almost too much. They were red and tears were still glistening, trying to break free again. And yet she looked at him...not angry. He'd expected anger. *Fuck*, he deserved her anger. Instead he saw trust. He didn't get it. Why wasn't she upset with him? She should be shouting at him, trying to break free, running away.

He nearly broke when she brought her hand up to his cheek and stroked it.

"No, Jason. Don't go blaming yourself." She swallowed visibly, her emotions still very close to the surface. "You told me to safe-word if it got too much for me." She shook her head. "It's not your fault I waited too long."

"Yes." He all but shouted the word at her. "Yes, it bloody well is. I know how fragile you are, I've seen enough of Hector's exhibitions to know how they end. I should have been smart enough to foresee how it would affect you." His voice nearly broke. "And I didn't. I failed to think ahead and I failed to get you out in time, to keep you safe. Don't you see, Heather? I should have recognized the signs and I didn't."

The glimmer of a smile appearing on Heather's face made no sense, and neither did the humor in her voice.

"You men, you're all the same. Thinking you know it all, convinced you can read any woman's mind." Heather's face grew serious. "I want you to listen to me, Jason. You don't know me. You have no idea what I can and can't take and you're not responsible for my feelings." Anger flashed across her face. "Nobody is responsible for my feelings except me. Not now, not in the past and not in the future. It is my job to keep me safe. That's what safe words are for. The only person to blame when I fail to use mine is me." The anger disappeared again. "Don't you see? Taking that responsibility away from me makes me helpless. Don't make me feel as if I can't look after myself, please."

Jason's mind struggled to keep up. He'd never thought about it in those terms. Of course he knew it all, in theory. He was well aware the real power in a D/s relationship rested with the sub. He knew the Dom could only push as hard as the sub would allow. He'd never needed to fall back on it though. He'd always put the responsibility upon himself. He'd prided himself on knowing when his subs were reaching their limits before they did, always tried to get them as far as he could without them having to use their safe word. Did that mean he'd not trusted his playmates to look after themselves? Was it just one big power trip for him?

He realized he'd been stroking her hair and bent his head to plant a soft kiss on her head.

"Heather, I just don't know." He looked at the beautiful face and marveled she was still in his lap, leaning into his hand. "I can't help it. I do feel responsible. I've allowed you to get hurt, and there are no circumstances under which that's acceptable.

She frowned and shook her head. "You're still not getting it. I decided I was ready to come here, to take on this job. I could have said no when you suggested watching this scene. I felt the tension rising inside, knew what it meant and forgot to use my safe word." She swallowed, hard. "Maybe I got it all wrong. Maybe it's too soon for me to get back into this world. Hell, right now I think I may never be ready to get involved again. And that's not the end of the world. I'm a party planner. I could plan other parties, weddings. It doesn't have to be about BDSM."

Her voice sounded strong and determined, while her face crumbled.

"You may have bet on the wrong horse. I'm sorry about that. You need someone who knows what's she's doing, capable of dealing with her working environment. I'll pack my stuff and go. You have enough time to come up with a different solution for your party."

Her mouth tried to smile while her eyes teared up again. The sight all but broke his heart.

"You've got such a wonderful place here you probably don't need a planner at all, and even if you do, that person isn't me."

Panic gripped Jason. He didn't want to let her go. He'd only just found her again. He wanted her to stay. Not for the party. Right now he couldn't care less about how that went. He wanted her to stay so he could get to know her better. Because he felt this connection to her he'd never felt with anybody else. Because he had this suspicion she might be the only woman who could stop him from falling apart. And he couldn't tell her any of those things.

"Let's not make any hasty decisions, Heather." Grateful he just about managed to keep the panic out of his voice, he plowed on. "This has been an emotional rollercoaster for both of us. We'll sleep on it and talk in the morning." He managed what he thought had to be a weak smile. "It's too late for you to start driving back to Dublin now anyway."

He planted another kiss on her hair and gratefully accepted his reward when she snuggled closer.

"We'll have breakfast together tomorrow and see how we feel then. We'll come up with a solution. I'm sure of it."

Holding his breath, he waited for her reply. He couldn't

see her face which still pressed into his shirt and had no idea what she might be thinking. Words were rolling through his head in a continuous loop of selfish prayer. *"Please stay. Please stay. Please say you'll stay."*

When Heather looked up at him he recognized the doubt in her eyes. Her deep sigh sent fear rushing through him.

"Okay, Jason. Breakfast tomorrow. We'll talk and then I'll decide. I just don't see how…"

"Not now, Heather." He couldn't allow her to finish that thought. "Tomorrow. We'll settle it tomorrow."

Neither of them spoke as they made their way to Heather's apartment. The silence didn't break until they were standing in front of her door and Jason lifted Heather's face to look into her eyes.

"If you need me, for whatever reason, I'm just across there." He pointed at the door facing hers before looking down at her face again. So beautiful and so fragile. The need to comfort her, to show her he really cared overwhelmed Jason. He couldn't have stopped himself for any reason and placed a soft, lingering kiss on her lips.

She couldn't be kissing him back. Surely that had to be his imagination.

Chapter Six

She'd kissed him?

Heather leaned against the door she'd just closed behind her. She'd accepted his lips and kissed him back? What was wrong with her? As if she didn't have enough confusing thoughts running through her head, she just had to go and return his kiss? She felt her breathing getting faster, her heartbeat increasing. She had to calm down, organize her thoughts, try to figure out what had just happened and find a way of dealing with it.

Walking across the room, she stripped out of her clothes then put on her pajamas. She'd write about the whole sorry affair. Writing always allowed her to sort out her thoughts, make sense of the jumble of emotions running riot in her mind.

She waited for her laptop to boot up before clicking on the folder named 'Darren'. She'd started this file the day after he'd died. Every time she needed to work something out or get her emotions under control, she'd written a letter to her husband. In the past it had always helped her put things in perspective. She could only hope it would have the same result tonight. Of course this would be the first time she'd have to write about being aroused or admit to kissing a man, but she couldn't think of another way to calm herself down.

Darren, my love
This will be among the hardest letters I've written to you since you left me on my own. I need you so much right now. I'm confused and scared. I don't know what I'm doing here. I

have no idea why I thought I could do this. Would you be very disappointed if I gave up and just went home tomorrow?

Wait, don't answer that. I know what you would say. You would expect me to soldier on. You'd be proud of me for having come here despite my fears and would have applauded my decision to go and watch that scene.

Have you got any idea how hard that was? That couple? They could have been us. It was the same dynamic, the same level of love. And it was so hot, Darren. There were moments when I wished I was her. I wanted that big dildo vibrating inside me, a hand holding me down, denying me the release I needed. I craved that kiss at the height of an orgasm.

Jason thinks I panicked because I couldn't deal with watching the scene. I didn't have the courage to confess to him it was envy more than panic that made me lose it. I have a hard time even admitting it to myself, or you. But it was. I was jealous. I suddenly couldn't deal with the thought of being alone anymore. In that moment I wanted someone to hold me, kiss me, love me. And I want that someone to be you. Of course I do. But it can never be you again. So does it make me bad that I cherished those moments in Jason's lap, that I couldn't stop myself from returning his kiss, small as it was?

I'd like to think you'd want me to move on. I imagine you telling me to continue living. But would you? And is now the right time? Is eighteen months long enough to mourn a loved one — too long, not long enough? And even if I kick-start my life and allow my emotions free reign again, does that also mean I should be open to the idea of submitting to someone other than you? I'm not sure I can do that. Jason isn't you. He's nothing like you. What if I end up comparing you two? He wouldn't have a chance against the eighteen years we had together. And I like him. I don't want to hurt somebody I'm fond of, somebody I want to keep as a friend. But I'm so hot. I need someone close to me again. I thought I might be able to live the rest of my life alone. I truly believed my memories and some toys would be enough. They're not. I'm yearning for skin-to-skin. I want to submit so badly it hurts.

If I leave tomorrow, will the need go away again? I managed to get used to being without you after spending many happy years together. Surely I'd forget Jason within a matter of days.

And yet, I'm not sure I want to forget him. I think he wants me too. That makes it harder. What if I'm wrong? What if I give in to this urge only to discover it's not what I want at all? Would I hurt Jason if that happened? Do I have the right to take a risk for both of us?

There are times I wished I didn't know you so well. I know exactly what you would tell me to do if you were here. And I hate you for being right. Of course I should be honest with Jason, give him the opportunity to deny he's attracted to me, a chance to decide for himself if he wants to see what would happen if we did move forward. I KNOW IT'S ALL ABOUT COMMUNICATION, DARREN. There's no need to remind me. All right, maybe there is. I'm just not sure I'm brave enough to initiate that conversation. I may not be strong enough to deal with the rejection that might follow. I don't think I'm ready to deal with the emotions going forward would unleash.

Darren, for the first time ever, writing to you has not provided me with the answers I need. I'm still no clearer on what I want or need to do. And I guess that means Jason was right. I need to sleep on this day and see how I feel in the morning. How did I end up with two men in my life who think they know it all?

Frustrated, Heather closed her laptop. Writing it all down should have helped her. She'd expected to have a clear plan of action after committing her thoughts and feelings to her laptop. It had always served her well, but not today. This day of all days her sure-fire solution had failed. And, to make matters worse, she'd admitted to feelings she'd been trying hard to ignore and, when that had failed, deny.

Barely aware of her movements, Heather walked to her suitcase and opened it. She stared at the big pink vibrator she hadn't unpacked earlier. She was so hot. She could still hear the woman's moans in her ears—the images of her riding that dildo, the ecstasy when she came, the love in her Master's eyes as he'd kissed her while she climaxed. Heather couldn't shake any of them anymore than she could ignore the feelings sitting in Jason's lap, feeling his lips on hers, had awakened.

This was a need she *could* deal with though. It wouldn't be the same as having a body close to hers, it couldn't take care of her need for skin-to-skin contact, but it might just take the edge off her desire.

As she shrugged off her pajamas and threw herself down on the bed, she didn't need to check her pussy. She knew she was wet, open and ready. She moved the vibrator between her folds, not turning it on yet, just getting it lubricated with her juices until it was slick. And still she didn't enter the head into her yearning vagina. She pushed the button and shivered as the vibrations traveled through her folds, bucked a little every time she allowed the vibrator to tease her clit.

Her mind started wandering. The hands holding the vibrator were no longer hers. She could hear Darren talking to her, teasing her as her need grew. Darren's laughter rang in her ears as he asked her what she needed. His voice telling her not to come once he started fucking her with the vibrator, making sure the little rabbit ears hit her clit just that way every single time, was familiar and welcome. She heard herself begging Darren for permission to come when her need grew too strong. His voice in her ears was loud and clear as he said those words she'd heard so often in the past. The words she treasured and would never hear again.

"Give it to me, coinín. Show me what you've got." With one hand lodged between her teeth and tears once again streaming down her cheeks, Heather screamed his name in complete silence, unable to repress the thought that this orgasm had also been a form of goodbye.

Sleep came swiftly after her release. Her mind and body were both exhausted and more than ready to flee to the safety of oblivion. Exhaustion, however, didn't result in a peaceful night. Images of the couple in the playroom haunted Heather and whenever they faded, Darren would be there. Darren as he played with her, Darren in full Dom mode, Darren at his sickest, Darren in his coffin, Darren fading, morphing until… Jason looking down at her with his dark eyes. Jason kissing her lips.

When her alarm went off, she was more than ready to leave the dreams behind and face the day, even if it meant deciding whether or not she could stay here and explore all the new emotions assaulting her.

* * * *

Jason thought he might be losing his mind. He didn't think he'd manage to sleep. He couldn't get his mind to shut up, couldn't stop cursing himself. It didn't matter that Heather thought he wasn't to blame for the night's fiasco, he knew better. It was his duty, his job to know what he was doing, to keep his subs and his clients safe. And he had failed.

He'd walked straight from the door to his bedroom. One look at his bed told him he was in the wrong place and he walked out again. He could hear the whiskey bottle whispering his name but knew one glass could easily turn into a full bottle and he needed to be clear-headed tomorrow morning. He went to the kitchen and turned on the kettle. A cup of tea, the Irish answer to every problem, would have to do.

He should never have mentioned the exhibition to her, should have refused to take her to see it. Why hadn't he picked up on her distress earlier? If he'd walked her out of there the first time she'd tensed up, none of the rest would have happened.

Now Heather thought she wasn't up to working with him. She thought she had to leave when all she'd been was brave, and kind and all too generous. It didn't matter what she said. He knew it had been his responsibility to keep her safe, and he had failed.

When the kettle boiled, he poured the steaming water into a mug, added a teabag and some sugar and waited for the liquid to the turn the right shade of red. Sitting down at the kitchen bar, he allowed the fragrant steam to blow into his face while his thoughts continued to spin through his head.

At least he now knew why his body had stopped reacting when he played with subs and why he had lost all interest in dominating. His body knew what his mind had been slow to cop on to. He couldn't be trusted to do his job. Whatever it was he used to have that allowed him to read women, to anticipate their wants, needs, desires and boundaries, had been lost somewhere along the way. He'd have to figure out how to run this place without participating in the scenes. It wouldn't be easy and there would be questions, but it had to be possible. If he didn't — he shuddered at the thought — he might well end up causing real harm before too long. He'd never allow a so-called Dom as insecure as he was right now, to play with one of his subs. The conclusion was easy. He didn't have the right to break his own rules.

The decision brought him a sense of relief. He'd no idea what his life would look like without the BDSM dynamic, couldn't quite imagine not being in total control. But he could learn. Surely he'd be able to adjust. He might even find a way of enjoying vanilla sex and 'plain' relationships.

Of course it had never worked for him in the past. But that had been before he'd lost his drive as well as his instincts. Without those he was no different from any other vanilla male. Forgetting about the high he used to get out of being in control had to be easier than living with the risk of doing serious harm. His choice had been made. It wasn't easy, but it was for the best. It would be one thing less to worry about, and God only knew how badly he needed fewer things to worry about.

He nearly burnt his tongue when he took the first sip of tea. It felt appropriate. He deserved the pain. Still restless, he got up and walked into the living area and sat down on the couch only to get up again and pace around the room.

Heather. He couldn't stop thinking about the woman. Ever since she'd walked into his office, his mind had been buzzing with images of her. Even now, just thinking about her, remembering those eyes as they'd looked into his before she'd lowered her gaze, his cock stirred in his pants. He couldn't believe it. He hadn't felt anything close to lust in months only to have the sensation return to him the moment he decided he had to give up on domination.

He wanted Heather badly, so much more than he'd wanted her twenty years ago. He'd no idea where the thought came from, but if there was a woman he could be vanilla with, it was her. And there was one of his problems. She wasn't vanilla any more than he had been. Even if he could convince her to stay, even if he managed to seduce her, he probably wouldn't be enough for her, not the way he was now.

Walking around his apartment without spilling his drink proved hard but he managed. The lack of clutter and unnecessary furniture helped. He stopped for a moment and looked around, trying to imagine what his rooms would look like to Heather. Masculine, without a doubt, but would she like that?

He was getting ahead of himself. Right now he shouldn't be worrying about getting her into his bed. He needed to make her stay. He had to convince her he required her help with this party, that she was the only one who could provide the necessary assistance. And it would be true. There were party planners a plenty. But only Heather specialized in BDSM events. She'd know most, if not all, of the guests he'd invited. Only Heather would be able to give him information about these people. There would be so many Doms walking around The Blowhole that weekend, he needed to know who he could trust, who he had to be careful around, which among them had delicate egos and whether any of them were likely to try and take over proceedings.

Would it be enough if he just asked her not to leave? If he

told her she didn't need to watch another demonstration, wouldn't have to be involved in the activities during the weekend beyond supervising. If he were to be honest and told her how much he required her help, could she be persuaded to stay? He wasn't beyond begging. He'd even admit to the attraction he felt for her if he thought it would help his cause.

His smile was wry as he sat down again and drank the finally cool-enough tea. If he mentioned how much he wanted her, she'd run without waiting for him to finish his sentence. And he wouldn't blame her. He'd never let anybody down as badly as he'd failed her this evening. He'd been so caught up in the way his hands felt on her body, the soft curves of her hips, the way her breath had quickened as the scene unfolded, he'd completely forgotten to pay attention to any warning signs. Surely there had been warning signs?

He glared at his phone as it rang, before answering. "What?"

"Whoa, Jason, easy man."

Hearing Hector's voice send shockwaves through Jason. The Dom had never called him before. Why would he when they lived on the same grounds? Something had to be wrong. Jason nearly groaned. Not something else to add to his list of disasters.

"What's wrong, Hector? Why are you calling me?"

"Just checking you and that gorgeous young lady are all right. I saw you leave. The beauty appeared distressed."

And didn't things just get better and better. Not only had he fucked up, no, he had to do it in such a way it was obvious to everybody else as well.

"No, I'm not. She's not. Jaysus, Hector, I completely fucked up and I'm not sure how to fix it."

He considered it. For a moment he was tempted to just let it all out. If there was anybody he could confess to, it was Hector. He trusted the Dom with his life. But he was also the man's employer. He couldn't just drop his garbage on him.

"Bottom line, Jason."

"Bottom line? She doesn't think she can stay. I need her for this party and she's planning on leaving in the morning."

He should have known he'd never get away with only half the story.

"I'm sure there's more to it than that, Jason. If that was the only issue, you'd find your way around it. I won't ask though. I'll tell you this—not that you don't already know it, but clearly you need to hear it again—be honest with the lady. She deserves it. Honesty works wonders and is the basis for any relationship, work or otherwise."

Jason sighed. Of course Hector was right, and it wasn't his fault he didn't know things were a lot more complicated.

"I know, Hector, and I will. She's still here and we're talking tomorrow over breakfast. I'd love to have the conversation in private, but don't want to scare her any more than I already did, so I'll be taking her to the restaurant."

He thought for a moment, grateful Hector stayed silent and waited for him to finish. "I'll find a way to convince her to stay. If it means putting her up in another hotel to keep her on the job, so be it. Thanks for calling."

He wasn't ready to admit it, but this voice of reason had arrived at just the right time.

"Let me know if there's anything I can do, Jason. And go to bed. Sleep. Nobody thinks clearly or operates well when exhausted."

Jason nodded before realizing the man couldn't see him.

"I will, Hector. Thanks again."

Hector was right, of course. He did need to sleep. He needed to relieve some of the tension first. A shower, some lotion, those images of Heather flashing before his eyes and his hand would take the edge off. He would find a way of convincing her to stay. The alternative was unthinkable.

Chapter Seven

She was ready when she heard the knock on her door. Well, she was awake, showered and dressed. She still hadn't made up her mind about leaving or staying. It would be so much easier to just leave. There'd be no tension, no revisiting of memories she'd rather avoid and no tempting Doms to confuse her dreams. Of course there would also be no more business and she would have to live with the knowledge she'd broken her promise to Darren.

What she really wanted was to hide here, in her rooms. Look out of the window, enjoy the view of the ocean, lose herself in the colors of those little rainbows appearing and disappearing in the spray. Another knock on her door ended the daydream.

"Heather, are you there?"

She squared her shoulders, took a deep breath and stepped forward to face the inevitable.

She opened the door and looked up into Jason's tired features.

"Jason, you look exhausted." She shook her head at her own stupidity. "I'm sorry, Jason. Good morning."

His tired eyes seemed to be filled with something resembling fear.

"Morning, Heather, how are you?"

The disappointment surging through her when he didn't follow his greeting with a kiss took her by surprise. She didn't think about it, just got on her toes and planted a light kiss on his cheek.

"I think I'm okay, thank you. You do look tired though." A thought ran through her head and she had to voice it. "God,

I hope that isn't the result of my meltdown last night."

Jason just shook his head and took her hand. "Let's not have this conversation here, Heather. We'll go down and talk over breakfast. We have a lot to discuss."

She felt safe when his big hand swallowed hers. The sensation still confused her, as did her disappointment at the missing kiss, but she couldn't deny either. Yesterday his kisses had startled her and now, less than twenty-four hours later she found herself expecting them. Her mind was all over the place. How was she supposed to decide what to do if her thoughts and emotions changed from one moment to the next?

The journey down in the elevator felt a lot longer than it could possibly be. She couldn't stop herself from staring at Jason, who looked back at her in silence. Something in his face had changed. Yesterday he'd been delighted to see her again, happy to have her here and eager to work with her. Now she couldn't escape the feeling that just the sight of her hurt him in some way. She guessed she'd scared him off with all her drama last night. Who wanted to hire a party planner who couldn't control her emotions? The last thing he needed while throwing a party that would make or break his business was somebody who couldn't hold it together.

At least it meant she could stop agonizing. Cleary he'd decided she was not what he needed. They'd have breakfast, he'd break the news to her in as kind a way as possible and she'd be on her way.

Sadness engulfed Heather. Staying was obviously no longer an option and the thought hurt far more than she'd expected.

The restaurant had been transformed overnight. It might as well have been a different room. The light, bright and airy space in front of her barely resembled the dim environment they'd dined in. A huge breakfast buffet had been set up against one of the walls and on the opposite side, two large double doors opened to what appeared to be a patio area.

Jason's hand on the small of her back felt good as he steered her toward the food. The layout was beautiful, the choices endless and both were wasted on her since she had no appetite whatsoever. Jason appeared to be feeling much the same. As she followed him along the long table, she noticed he was as disinclined to put food on his plate as she was. He ended up with a child-sized portion of the full Irish breakfast, which was better than she managed. A spoonful of scrambled egg and one slice of toast could hardly be called a hearty start to the day. Still, she'd be surprised if she managed to eat at all.

"Coffee for me, please. Heather, what would you like to drink?"

The question brought her back to her surroundings. Lost in her thoughts, she hadn't even seen the waitress approach.

"Coffee would be great, Jason. Thank you." She smiled at the young woman taking their order before following Jason as he led her through the double doors to a table on the far side of the patio.

The beautiful surroundings took her breath away. There was color everywhere. The garden was in full bloom and grew right up to the patio. Pathways twisted their way through the flowers in what appeared to be a random fashion. In the distance she could see water, a pond or small lake, surrounded by grass and deck chairs. For the first time since waking up, she smiled.

"It's good to see you smiling, Heather. What's so funny?"

Maybe it was safer to start off like this, on an easy subject. God knew the Irish were champions when it came to talking about the weather.

"I can't help wondering how often you have the opportunity to put those chairs out." She couldn't stop herself from smiling again. "The West Coast of Ireland is not known for its beautiful weather."

It was such a relief to hear Jason laugh, to see his face relax, even if it was only for a few moments.

"No, it isn't. In fact those chairs are brand new. When the

weather stayed warm and sunny for three consecutive days and the forecasts announced continuing high pressure, I decided I'd better provide some outdoor seating."

The grin appearing on his face lifted Heather's heart.

"Nudity allowed of course, although not required."

She grinned back and sat down. She still didn't have much of an appetite and started with her coffee. She couldn't put this off for much longer. "Jason, listen…"

"Heather, I…"

She forced a smile. This was much harder than she'd expected. The realization she didn't want to leave this place or this man at all took her by surprise. But it was for the best. He'd obviously made up his mind. If she had to leave she'd rather it was her decision.

"Just let me finish please."

His nod was reluctant.

"I'm so sorry about last night. If I'd known how badly I would react I would never have gone to watch the demonstration with you." She could see he was about to interrupt again and put her hand on his to stop him. "Don't deny it, Jason, my reaction freaked you out."

"Yes, but…"

"No buts, Jason. My behavior last night was over the top and out of proportion. I'm not new to this world. I didn't agree to go there with you all blue-eyed innocence. I knew what to expect." She took a deep breath. Getting all worked up about this wouldn't help, after all, the hard part was still to come. "I completely understand you no longer want to work with me. I couldn't have been more unprofessional if I'd tried." She gave it her best but couldn't quite keep the disappointment out of her voice. "Consider our contract terminated. I'll pack and leave after breakfast."

Eating would be easier than looking at Jason, so Heather picked up her fork and stabbed at the unappetizing pile of eggs on her plate. When he still hadn't said a word after she'd worked her way through three forkfuls she dared to look up at the man across the table. Whatever she'd expected, it wasn't the open-mouthed wonder on Jason's face as he looked at her.

"Jason?"

"Excuse me? Master Jay, Mrs. Staunton, may I have a word?"

Heather looked up into the face of the beautiful young woman she'd watched the previous night. The redhead had been gorgeous in the dim lights, all flushed with desire. If possible, she looked even more fabulous in daylight. The sun lit up her hair, turning it into a wild flame. Heather glanced at the thin silver collar around the woman's neck. Darren had never felt the need to collar her. She glanced at her left hand and the golden band on her ring finger. Of course there was more than one way of claiming your partner.

A frown appeared on Jason's face. "Good morning, Amber. Everything okay?" His eyes shifted to hers. "I'm sorry. Heather, this is Amber Somerville. Amber, you know who Mrs. Staunton is."

"Heather, please call me Heather."

With nerves and regret already coursing through her system, Jason's stiff formality only added to her apprehension.

"Pleased to meet you Mrs... Heather."

The girl's smile managed to be both open and shy.

"Everything is fine, Master Jay. My Master sent me down to invite the two of you for dinner tonight."

A small stab of pain hit Heather. No matter how much this couple had reminded her of Darren and herself, or maybe because they did, she would have loved to get to know them better.

"That's so kind of you, Amber. I'm so sorry it won't be possible. I'll be leav—"

"We'd be delighted to join you two tonight, Amber. Thank you, and don't forget to thank Hector as well."

As the young sub walked away, Jason shifted his attention

back to Heather and registered the shock on her face.

"Jason, I just told you I'll be leaving. I thought you'd be relieved. Isn't that what you wanted?"

"No, Heather, it's not."

"Don't lie to me. Don't be polite. I saw your face this morning. I know I ruined it last night, I…"

"Heather, listen to me."

He almost didn't recognize his own voice. It had been a while since he'd used that tone with anyone. Heather's gaze dropped instantly. Her simple but immediate reaction to his change of tone stirred feelings in Jason he didn't want to examine too closely.

"My face and mood this morning had nothing to do with me wanting you to leave. Quite the opposite, in fact."

He watched Heather for a reaction while she refused to look up from her plate with the unfinished, now cold, eggs. He reached out and gently lifted her chin.

"I want you to stay. I need you for this party. But it's more than that." He stopped himself. Now wasn't the time to have that particular conversation, if ever. "I was worried you'd want to leave. I was sure I'd scared you away and wasn't sure how to fix it."

Fear gripped him. What if he was wrong? Maybe she really wanted to go and had only used his face or reaction as an excuse. "I don't want you to go unless it's what you want. I can't ask you to stay if it's only going to cause you pain. But please don't leave because you think that's what I want." He hadn't really been aware he'd been stroking her cheek. When she leaned her face into his touch, some of the tension he'd been holding evaporated.

"You sure you're not just saying that because you're feeling sorry for me? I don't want or need your sympathy."

He could see the conflict on her face. She wanted to give in, enjoy his touch, accept his offer but couldn't allow herself to trust his motives. It didn't matter. He'd convince her. She wanted to stay. His failure hadn't scared her away. He'd get his second chance to get it right.

"You'll always have my sympathy, Heather." He watched her eyes as they heated up, glaring at him. "That's not the reason I want you to stay though. I would like you to stay because you're good at what you do and I need your help. I want to get to know you again. I like spending time with you."

Decisions, decisions. How far did he want to take this honesty?

"You've returned something to me I thought I'd lost forever. I want you to stay, even if you don't want to be involved in the party."

When her hand reached up to touch his, he held his breath. Would she remove it, reject his touch? His sigh was audible when her fingers stroked his and a small smile relaxed her anxious face.

"If you're sure."

This time she didn't avoid his eyes and apparently found the confirmation she needed there.

"I'd love to stay and help you with your weekend." Her small smile turned into a huge grin. "It's going to be the best BDSM party Ireland has ever seen by the time we're finished with it."

He wanted to shout, punch the air, and couldn't believe the prickling sensation in his eyes. Heather would be staying. He'd no idea how things would develop from here, but if she stayed, there would be opportunities to find out. He needed to know. He needed her here. He needed her too much.

Jason took a deep breath and thought for a moment. Last night and this morning had been emotional and difficult for both of them. Heather needed time to think about something else besides her job and all the other obstacles she might be running into. And he, he just wanted to spend some uncomplicated time with the woman he found himself more attracted to by the minute.

Her face was soft under his touch and the way she leaned into it warmed his heart. "Listen, I know we can't postpone work indefinitely, but let's ignore it for now. There's a magical place nearby I would love to show you. We'll get down to business in the afternoon."

"Works for me, Jason."

The last signs of tension left her body. It was good to see her face completely free of stress. There was no sign of worry, fear or strain. She should always look relaxed. A frown didn't suit her. He would do whatever it took to keep her looking like this.

"I don't know about you" — he smiled, feeling relaxed for the first time since waking up — "but I need another go at the buffet first though. I'm suddenly starving."

Chapter Eight

He watched her come down the stairs and wondered if she had something against elevators or just enjoyed the exercise. She'd paid attention to his words. Jeans, a T-shirt and what appeared to be a waterproof coat over her arm.

God, she'd been made to wear jeans. Strike that, she looked edible in everything she wore, but these tight jeans were something special — not to mention the instant effect they had on him and his groin. The sensation reassured him as much as it worried him. Every time his body reacted to her, it filled him with gratitude. A part of him he'd thought had died turned out to be alive and happy to make its presence known. He couldn't, shouldn't, act on it though. Much as his mind and body were screaming at him to make a move, Heather had some way to go before she would be ready for everything his reaction to her implied.

"Good girl."

Jaysus, where had that come from? He bent toward her and gave her the kiss he'd denied both of them earlier, while relishing her reaction to his words. A small smile, a quick drop of her gaze, followed by a light return of his kiss. The perfect response, if only he hadn't sworn he wouldn't indulge that part of himself again. He couldn't be trusted to get it right and Heather was too fragile to take chances with.

Jason forced himself to abandon that line of thought as he settled Heather in his Range Rover before getting in himself and driving toward the gates.

"Have you ever seen a blowhole, Heather?"

"Something called a blowhole actually exists?" Heather

grinned. "I thought the name was a reference to either the amount of chimneys on your roof or some form of kink I haven't yet encountered."

Jason couldn't help returning her grin. A relaxed Heather was delightful company. "Yes, blowholes are a real and rather magnificent natural phenomena. You'll love it."

"I'm curious now, tell me more."

"It's not easy to explain. You'll understand better when you see it." He thought for a moment. "A blowhole is a deep opening in the ground a short distance away from the shore. There's an underground connection between the sea and the hole where water gathers. Every so often the water erupts. It is a powerful sight when a huge column of water shoots straight up into the air, only to disappear again."

"And that's the reason for the waterproofs. I get it now. It sounded like a strange suggestion on a glorious day like this."

"Oh yes, you'll get wet. And as much as I would love to see…" What was wrong with him? He couldn't say things like that, shouldn't even been thinking them.

"As much as you would love to see what, Jason?"

Was she teasing him? Did she know what he'd wanted to say? He hesitated.

"See me in a wet shirt? I bet you would."

Heather's sudden playfulness took him by surprise. "Well, what can I say? I'm only human. And you are rather beautiful." Had he gone too far?

Her grin reappeared. "Interesting idea. We'll see."

He pulled the car over and parked, relieved to see that despite the beautiful day, they would have the place to themselves for now. He wrapped his arm around Heather after he'd helped her out of the car. They turned toward the sea and as if on cue, a huge column of water shot up into the air. He heard Heather's gasp and wasn't surprised. From where they were standing, it looked as if the water had come through solid ground.

The water disappeared as suddenly as it had shown itself.

"Jason, that was...wow. You're right. There are no words to do the sight justice."

Power surged like heat through Jason's veins at the delight and wonder in Heather's eyes, making his heart pump faster and causing warmth to spread throughout his body.

"Come. It's even better when you're close. Better put on your coat though if you want to stay dry. There'll be another one soon."

Coats on, he put his arm back around her and pulled her closer. Touching her felt too good to let an opportunity slip. And she wasn't trying to get away. In fact, she leaned in to him. If he could get her to put her own arm around him... *Small steps,* he reminded himself, *small steps. Don't scare her off again. You've already got more than you thought you would. Don't bloody ruin it.*

As he led her toward the hole, he explained the set up to her. "This passage" — he pointed at the two sloping stone walls on either side of them—"is part of a monument that was erected here about ten years ago." He stared ahead at the gate they were approaching. "The fencing is from the same time. Before then, the only thing here was the hole itself. After one too many tragedies, well... Let's just say it is now a lot harder to fall into the hole, either by accident or on purpose."

Heather looked shocked.

"You mean people actually... No, don't tell me. I don't think I want to know."

"You're right, I shouldn't have said that. Sorry, my big mouth ran away with me." *His stupid big mouth.* Would he ever learn when to shut the fuck up? "Here is the blowhole. Have a look, and tell me it isn't amazing."

Heather's breath caught as she looked down into the hole. She'd expected to see water, flowing in and out. What she saw, at least ten meters below didn't resemble the sea at all.

"That's water? It doesn't look like water at all. It's more

like, I don't know, liquid metal? Mercury?"

It was beautiful, amazing. She had never seen anything close to the miraculous sight in front of her. Heather used her phone to take a few pictures, in the hope they would do the beauty justice.

"I've no idea why it looks like that, Heather. I'm sure there's an explanation for it, I haven't a clue what it might be."

A shudder went through her. "See how the water down there appears to be solid? That's how I feel sometimes. I appear strong to anyone who doesn't know me. But it only takes a tiny bit of pressure to make me dissolve, only a small push to cause an explosion."

As if it had heard her words, the sea took that moment to send another spray of water into the air. She relaxed into Jason's arms as he pulled her back tight against his body.

"I'll be here, Heather, if you let me. Whenever you dissolve, the moment you explode. I'll be the friend ready to support you, to stop you from sinking."

As the water drenched them, Heather drank in his words.

"I'll catch the pieces and put them back together when you blow apart. I promise I won't let you down again."

She hadn't known it, but she needed to hear those words. For the first time in eighteen months, she didn't feel alone.

"Thank you. I need a friend. I'm grateful it's you."

She wasn't sure what the combination of joy and disappointment on his face meant but was too caught up in her own thoughts to give it much attention.

"Surely you have friends, Heather. Don't tell me there's nobody in your life."

"Of course I have friends."

She leaned back against his solid chest and thought. Maybe now would be a good time to open up and share some of the past eighteen months.

"I sort of pushed people away after Darren died. All my friends had been his as well. I found being alone much easier than spending time with mutual friends."

It had been the perfect solution in the short term. By the time she'd realized how alone it left her, she'd felt so ashamed of pushing those people away, of ignoring their offers of support, that she couldn't bring herself to contact them again.

"I only now realize a lot of those people I've ignored for so long will probably be here for your weekend." She turned around in his arms and looked up into his face. "Is that going to complicate things for you?"

His eyes were warm and completely focused on her face. She wanted to let herself fall into those eyes, forget about the world for just a few minutes.

"Not for me. Won't it be difficult for you though?"

Another thing she hadn't thought through. "No. I think it will be fine. Most of them will be happy to see me out and about again. The one or two who resent me after my confinement..." She laughed. "What a word, confinement. Anyway, if some of them are upset with me, they weren't the friends I took them for. And" — she wanted to make it sound teasing but could hear the pleading note in her voice — "didn't you say you'd be there to catch me when I fall?"

She couldn't detect any teasing in Jason's voice when he answered. His face was warm and solid, his voice reassuring.

"And I meant it. I'll hold you together, no matter what happens."

"Thank you." She got on her toes and kissed his cheek. "You've no idea how much that means to me."

And neither did I.

The thought took her by surprise. She hadn't known how much she needed a friend, someone she could trust. She'd also been unaware how much she craved this physical contact, someone to hold her. The urge she'd felt, just a moment ago, to kiss his mouth instead of his cheek, to open her lips while kissing him, confused her. Only twenty-four hours ago she'd been certain she would never be able to move beyond Darren. And now, if she was honest, all she wanted was Jason. If she could, she'd have Darren back in a flash. But Darren was gone, for good. And Jason... He made her feel again. He'd reminded her she had a life to live. Just being near him made her feel things she hadn't felt in a long time. When his voice changed, the lower, demanding tone made her body want to do things she'd never done for anyone except Darren.

"Jason, I need a moment to think. Do you mind if I walk on my own for a while?"

"Are you okay? Having second thoughts about staying?"

She hated she'd made him worry again, as the look on his face clearly showed. "I'm fine and I do want to stay. I just need to sort some things out in my head. It won't take long. I promise." Maybe if she tried to joke about it. "It's hard thinking straight while your arms are wrapped around me."

His smile was weak as he released her, but at least it had been there.

"Take all the time you need, beautiful. I'll wait here."

Heather slowly walked away from the monument and Jason, thoughts flying through her head. When she saw a large, flat rock close to the end of the cliff, she sat down and stared out over the ocean. Looking at the waves, rolling in with force, despite the almost wind-free summer's day, she allowed her mind to go where it wanted, hoping it would lead to the answers she needed.

Darren her lover, Dom and husband had been her life, her everything for so long. Jason, the man she'd secretly lusted for twenty years ago, who had now somehow managed to resurrect her body from the grave she'd sent it to when Darren died, could be someone in her life. She knew what her body wanted. She could feel it yearning for contact, touches, heat, intimacy. If she gave in to the need, would her heart be able to cope, would her head?

"Tell me what to do, Darren. You always knew what was best for me. I need your advice now."

Grateful Jason couldn't possibly have heard her words over the sound of the waves, she turned and looked back at the blowhole where he stood, patiently waiting for her. Another column of water shot up from the hole and for a moment Jason was surrounded by hundreds of tiny rainbows, illuminating him as if he was a pot of gold, waiting to be found.

Thank you, Darren.

Relieved and with a smile on her face, Heather walked back to the man who'd done what she'd imagined impossible. He'd brought her back to life.

Chapter Nine

Jason watched as she walked back to him. It wasn't easy to be sure, but he thought he saw a smile on her face. He'd been worried. He could admit it to himself. Even as she'd told him she didn't have second thoughts, he'd been sure her next words would tell him she wanted to leave after all. He didn't want her to go, needed her to stay. It was as if he'd found his lifebuoy, was clinging on for dear life while it was trying to pull away from him.

"Are you okay?" He took her hand and looked into her eyes, searching for but not finding any sign of fear or insecurity. Instead he saw relief, as if a weight had been lifted off her shoulders.

"Better than okay, Jason. Thank you for bringing me here. This place is magical. It helped me put a new perspective on a few things I've been worrying about."

She got on her toes and looked from his mouth to his cheek and back again before kissing him on the lips.

Need shot through him and he wrapped his arms around her as he pushed his mouth against hers, only to pull back again. *Damn.* Could the timing be any worse? He had Heather where he wanted her, in his arms, lips touching, and of course now several cars pulled up by the side of the road. As he lifted his head, he saw families with hordes of children moving to where they were standing.

"Let's go. There's another, hopefully quieter, place I want to show you."

It satisfied him on a deep level to see Heather look as disappointed as he felt. The thought that this interruption might be a sign — that maybe they weren't meant to be together—shot through his head before he ruthlessly pushed it down again. He would not allow himself to create problems where none existed. It wasn't as if they didn't have enough issues to overcome between the two of them.

The lighthouse was only a few miles away, on one of the most western points of Ireland. As he'd hoped, they were on their own. Not many people ventured this far. Taking a blanket from the boot of his car, and with his arm once again around her, he walked Heather as close to the edge of the cliff as he dared.

"Let's sit here and enjoy the view."

Jason spread the blanket on the grass. His heart skipped a beat when Heather sat down close beside him. Nothing could convince him she hadn't meant for their legs to touch.

"This place is amazing."

A smile as bright as the sun shining down on them lit up Heather's face. The setting was perfect. A calm and warm day, blue skies and hardly any wind, and yet the ocean appeared wild. They were alone, the peace and quiet only interrupted by the sound of the waves crashing against the rocks. Just him, Heather and the sea, again.

"Remember the last time it was just us and the sea, Heather?"

"In Wexford? Yes, I do. That was different though."

His mind traveled back. He couldn't remember why, but Heather and he had been alone that day. The walk on the beach had been delightful, as had lying down in the sand for a rest. They'd had no intention of falling asleep, but the combination of warm sunshine and soft sand had been too much for both of them. When they'd woken up, they'd found themselves on a sandbank of sorts, surrounded by water. Not in any danger of ending up in the sea, thankfully, but with no way back to the rest of the beach without getting soaked. They'd sat there together for hours, looking at the sea, talking and, eventually, kissing.

"That kiss." Heather paused. "Those hours with you in the middle of the sea… It was the only time during that summer I thought I might have made a mistake when I decided not to pursue you." She smiled. "I didn't believe I could give Moira competition when it came to you, but that afternoon I thought maybe I should have tried."

"I know. I felt the same." And he could still kick himself that he'd been too much of a coward to just drop Moira and hang on to Heather. "It felt right when I kissed you. Felt right in a way it never did with Moira."

Jason looked at Heather and saw in her eyes the same hunger he knew had to be shining out of his.

He moved closer, giving her plenty of time to stop him or pull away. She didn't. Just as slowly she moved closer to him. Her teeth nibbled on her bottom lip, her gaze jumped from his mouth to his eyes and back again, but she didn't try to prevent what was about to happen.

Mouth against mouth. Soft lips moving over his, finding every corner of his mouth. A small sigh and her lips were caressing his again. Her hand touched his cheek, stroking as her lips continued their investigation.

"Jason." His name was a breath against his lips, her slightly open mouth an invitation. No hurry, no rush, no force. Just lips stroking lips, tongues finding each other, touching, teasing, playing.

Without removing his mouth from Heather's, Jason pushed her until she was flat on her back. Leaning over her, he pulled away and drank in her beautiful features— her face relaxed, her eyes open and smiling at him, her lips parted. He traced his fingers over her skin, her lips, her ears. So soft. She pushed her face into his hand, searching for his touch, asking him for more. He needed to taste her again. His mouth on hers, her tongue against his. His hand in her hair, on her face. Her hand on his neck. This was perfect, it was too much and it wasn't nearly enough. He wanted more.

"Jason?"

He heard the confusion in her voice when he abruptly pulled back. "Shhh, beautiful. It's all good. I want you more than I should."

"Yes." She panted rather than spoke the word.

"But not here, not right now. I don't want to rush this. We're not making the same mistake twice." He hesitated. "When I do get you naked, I don't want to have to look over my shoulder."

"But Jason..."

"No, we're going to do this right. I'm going to get you alone, in my bed and take my time to discover every inch of your skin. I want to know what makes you giggle, when you squirm, where your sensitive parts are. All of it, all of you. And" — he couldn't help but take enjoyment from his cruelty — "before we get to play, we need to work."

He saw the slight frown on her face, and continued, "This party isn't going to organize itself. We don't have much time."

The thought nearly ruined his happiness. She'd only been asked to come for a few days to get the preliminary planning out of the way. If he'd known who she was, he would have invited her to stay the two weeks between now and the party. As it was, she'd leave in two days and he'd no idea how to ask her to stay on without sounding pushy and demanding.

"I hate it when you're right." Heather pushed herself up, turned, and grinned at him.

"Take me back to your estate, Sir. Let's get the work out of the way so we can concentrate on other things."

Sir.

The word went straight to his cock. At least she'd been getting up when she said it and had missed his instant physical reaction to her words. This woman made him feel things he'd not expected to feel again, feelings he wasn't sure he was comfortable with anymore.

The realization hit him hard. She had no idea, but Heather had the power to make or break him. The thought scared the shit out of him. If he'd met her six months ago, if he'd been able to hang on to his needs for longer, if... He hated the word. Part of him wanted, needed to get her under his spell and make her submit to him. A bigger part was sure he'd get it wrong, harm her. He didn't want to see her hurt ever again. If that meant putting his dominating self to rest permanently it would be a price well worth paying. He'd find a way to make it work. One way or another he'd learn to be satisfied without the play. He would, somehow.

* * * *

Heather couldn't keep track of her thoughts and feelings. Walking back to the car and during the drive back, all she could think about was Jason's mouth on hers, his tongue, his hand. She wanted those body parts of his all over her body. She wanted his body parts in her hands, his skin against hers. Her body was excited, her skin felt alive, her nipples hard. She felt the wetness in her panties increase as the car bounced over the pothole-riddled road.

She was glad Jason seemed as lost in his thoughts as she was in hers. Her mind went back to that one afternoon in Wexford. It had been about a week before the end of their holidays. She'd been delighted to spend the day with Jason. He and Moira had been so caught up in each other, or at least in each other's bodies, that she and Rick rarely saw them. Looking back, she realized it had been strange she'd missed contact with Jason, who she barely knew, more than time with Moira, who was supposed to be her friend.

She hadn't expected anything from their one day together except a chance to get to know him better. Not in her wildest dreams had she imagined kissing him. She'd been convinced Moira and he were made for each other. Any guilt she might have felt for kissing her best friend's boyfriend had been tempered by the knowledge Moira had no interest in Jason beyond a holiday fling. Those kisses, with the calm sea flowing around them, had been magical and a wake-up call. Even while kissing Jason, she'd known she'd only been pretending with Rick. All she'd felt with

Rick was comfort. It had been fun and sweet. Jason had brought her excitement, had woken up her body when she hadn't known it was asleep. He'd made her yearn for things she couldn't have named if her life depended on it. Things she hadn't discovered until months after she'd met Darren.

She waited for the stab of pain she always experienced when she thought about her husband, and found she only wanted to smile. Maybe this really was okay. Her body had no doubts. She only regretted they'd not been able to take their exploration of each other further.

She sighed as The Blowhole appeared in front of her. A few hours of serious party planning before they'd be able to... She nearly groaned out loud. Dinner with Hector and Amber... How had she managed to forget? She looked forward to meeting them, to finding out if they were as similar to her and Darren as she imagined. Spending time alone with Jason was much higher on her list of priorities though. Patience had never been one of her virtues, and she needed a lot of it today.

Chapter Ten

There.

With one final brush, she finished her mascara. This was the best she could do. She couldn't remember the last time she'd put this much time and effort into her appearance but had to admit it felt good. *And didn't look too bad either.*

She thought she'd managed to strike the right balance. Sexy but not too over the top. The little black dress couldn't be called original, but it fitted her well and was just short enough to tease without looking slutty. She loved how it supported and emphasized her breasts without the need for a bra. It had been a while since she'd worn heels this high and hoped she wouldn't have to walk too far, but it was worth it. Her legs looked longer and her posture was better.

Disgusted, she turned away from the mirror. When had she become this vain? The last time she'd worked this hard in the hope of impressing a man had been the first time Darren had taken her on a proper date. In fact, she'd been even worse then. She'd also been almost twenty years younger, of course.

Surprisingly, admitting she wanted to impress Jason didn't worry her. She wasn't afraid he'd change his mind, not really, but she didn't want to leave anything to chance either.

She shook her head, marveling at her sudden and rather extreme conversion. Less than forty-eight hours ago she'd been sure she'd never revisit sex, only to find herself doing everything in her power to ensure it wouldn't elude her now. It was as if someone had pressed a switch in her head.

She thought back to all the work they'd done after they'd returned from their outing. It had been nonstop. Jason had organized lunch and coffee in his office and they'd gone over his plans, his expectations and the guest list. Yes, the guest list. She'd expected most if not all of the names and had been surprised and relieved to find one name missing. She'd been sure he would top the list and wasn't sure what his absence meant. Still, it was one potential headache less.

There had been one or two other things left to address, but those were details and could be ironed out closer to the date. For now, the catering had been organized and the preliminary timetable established. Being a party planner for the BDSM community meant you rarely needed to come up with a theme for the event. Still, they'd managed to divide the weekend up into several sessions with a different focus. Overall it had been a productive afternoon and it was good to know that all the basics had been covered.

She sighed. Except that with the work done, there was no reason to stay. The schedule had made perfect sense when they'd agreed on it. She was supposed to return the Monday before the weekend kicked off to finalize all the details. In theory therefore, she was good to go home. There was no official reason to stay here any longer.

Two days ago, when she'd driven up from Dublin, the only thing stopping her from turning around and driving straight back had been the knowledge it would only be for a few days. Now, with nothing preventing her from returning to Dublin, she wanted to stay longer.

A knock on her door stopped her from pursuing that thought further. That would be Jason collecting her for their dinner with Hector and Amber. Her earlier excitement about meeting them fought with worries she couldn't suppress. They seemed nice but reminded her a lot of herself and Darren and she wasn't sure how much she wanted that reminder now that she was about to give in to her lust for Jason. One last glance at her image in the mirror and she opened the door, only to forget how to breathe.

Jason looked overpoweringly male. The man standing in front of her personified dominance. She'd had her doubts about how dominant he actually was over the past few days—it was one of her worries about this party. Any reservations she might have had were gone. All her long dormant instincts kicked in. One look at this face and she lowered her gaze, felt her nipples tightening and her pussy contract. She wanted to fall to her knees and stay there, worship him—and only just managed to stop herself.

His hand underneath her chin had her looking into his dark eyes again. Shivers ran down her spine as his gaze skimmed over her body and back to her face.

"Beautiful."

One word, in the tone of voice she recognized on an instinctive level, sent thrills through her.

"Jason, you look… Wow."

She found herself completely tongue-tied, and the smirk on his face did nothing to alleviate her tension.

His kiss did help. When he pushed his tongue past her lips and pulled her flush against his body, she felt herself relax. Oh, God, she wanted this. She yearned for contact. The moan escaping her mouth still took her by surprise.

"So beautiful and so eager."

Jason's smile set all her nerves off again.

"Ready to have dinner with friends?"

"No. Yes, of course I'm ready." His smirk told her he knew exactly what he was doing to her. She'd better get her shit together before they reached wherever Hector and Amber lived. She was liable to make a complete fool of herself otherwise. And Jason wasn't helping. In fact, he appeared to be taking great pleasure from her discomfort.

The elevator felt too small for the two of them. Jason's personality filled the space and Heather backed away. He didn't give her an inch. Every step back was copied by a step forward until her arse hit the wall, their feet toe to toe and his face so close his breath touched her hair.

"I want you."

Jason's hand was in her hair, pulling her head back and up, his mouth on hers again. It was only a few floors, but by the time the doors dinged their arrival, Heather's breathing sounded more like panting. Grinning, Jason took her hand and led her down the corridor, through a back door and into the garden.

In the early evening light, the colors were less vibrant than they'd been during the day, but the smell of recently cut grass combined with the wide variety of flowers almost overwhelmed her senses.

"Most of the permanent staff have apartments over there." Jason pointed toward a large, two-story barn conversion partially hidden behind a line of trees. "Hector and Amber live over to the far side, close to the pond you saw this morning."

The water in the pond was still and shone like a mirror. The deck chairs had been folded and piled away. Through a gap in a high hedge, Heather spotted the cutest cottage she'd ever seen. She stopped walking and took her time, drinking in the sight. The house wasn't big, just about the right size for a couple. It appeared to be built from loose stones of various sizes. Plants in full bloom climbing up the walls gave the whole picture a fairytale feel.

"This is idyllic, Jason."

"Isn't it?"

The voice coming from her right, apparently out of nowhere, gave her a shock.

"We're privileged to be allowed to live here."

"Nonsense, Hector. I'm privileged to have the two of you working for me. This was the least I could do. The house was here anyway." Jason seemed embarrassed by the other Dom's praise.

"Heather, you haven't met Hector yet. Hector Kelly, meet Heather Staunton."

The Dom's scrutiny made her want to squirm. "How are you, Heather? May I call you Heather?"

She knew her smile was feeble, but it was the best she

89

could do. "Of course, S... I'm sorry, how would you like me to address you?"

"Call me Hector. I'm Sir to only one person in this world. We have to put up with guests who don't know any better addressing me as Sir, but everybody else calls me Hector."

This time her smile was strong and heartfelt. Knowing he wasn't an egomaniac Dom made the evening less intimidating than it had been a moment ago. It also confirmed her first impressions of him had been right. She'd never been a fan of addressing men she didn't know, and would never submit to, as 'Sir' and neither had Darren, but there were quite a few Doms who demanded it. She couldn't help feeling it was because they weren't too sure about themselves. Not that she'd ever say such a thing out loud, but the suspicion was there.

"Please, walk with me. We've set up for dinner in the back garden. The evening is too beautiful to waste inside."

The walk around the little house was magical. The garden appeared to be wild, although Heather had no doubt a lot of planning had gone into making it look like a quirk of nature. This sort of garden, with all its corners and bushes in unexpected places, invited games like hide and seek, and the perfect climbing tree she saw near the far wall made her wish she'd put on trousers rather than a dress.

"You've got yourself a piece of heaven here."

Heather was rewarded with the Dom's huge smile. "We certainly think so. Jason may make light of it, but for us, having this house is what has made The Blowhole our home. Amber, love" — Hector turned to face the cottage — "our guests have arrived."

Heather laughed out loud when she saw the beautiful girl walk into the garden. If they'd planned it, they couldn't have worked it out like this. Amber's outfit was an almost exact copy of hers although the girl wore all white for Heather's all black.

"Must be a case of great minds." Amber smiled.

"Or great taste." The pride in Jason's voice was mirrored

in his eyes when Heather glanced up at him.

"What would you two like to drink?" Hector opened an outside fridge.

After beer and glasses of wine had been dispensed, they sat down and Heather took her time taking in the Dom and his sub. She recognized it in the small things. The way he touched Amber constantly. The adoration in Amber's eyes whenever she looked at Hector. Only needing half a word before finishing the other's sentence. The love between these two was so clear Heather could feel it in the air. This was a happy home occupied by two people who were made to be together.

Just for a moment, the sadness was back. A little sting in her heart.

"Heather, what's wrong?"

Two voices asking the same question simultaneously made her smile and the pain faded away. She should have known she wouldn't get away with stray feelings around two experienced Doms.

"I'm fine. It's just that I recognize so much of what I had with Darren in you two." She nodded at Hector and Amber. "It was the same, only much stronger last night." She swallowed. "About last night. I apologize if I disrupted your scene. If I'd known I was going to react like that…"

"No need to apologize. You didn't disrupt anything." Hector hesitated. "While I hated seeing you in pain, it is always gratifying when our displays touch people."

She thought about it and nodded. She wouldn't have reacted last night if it hadn't been for the obvious connection between the two players. Heather wasn't sure why the knowledge made her feel better but it did, and she felt herself relax. "I'll stop worrying about it then." She shook her head. "Still, I'm glad you're taking it so well. I've seen some Doms lose the plot over the slightest disruption while they work."

"You know there are reasons for that, Heather. Distracting a Dom at the wrong time can have disastrous consequences for the sub." Jason's voice was stern.

"She didn't interrupt the scene, Jason. Let's not create problems where there are none."

The more time she spent with Hector, the more she liked the Dom with the voice of reason.

Hector continued. "Besides, you're both right. There are good reasons for frowning on interruptions, just as there are Doms out there who completely overreact when it does happen. Let's leave it there. Jason, why don't you give me a hand with the barbeque? We'll leave the ladies to their drinks."

* * * *

"Wanna talk about it?"

Jason tore his gaze away from Heather and looked at his friend. He wasn't surprised Hector didn't waste any time before getting on his case. "Not really." He stared at the glowing coal as Hector put steak and chicken on the rack.

"What happened with Heather last night?"

"Not my story, Hector. Not for me to share."

He hated keeping his friend at arm's length, but he just wasn't ready to talk about all the doubts and confusing emotions running through him. If he started talking about Heather, he'd eventually end up having to admit to his own feelings.

"Fair enough."

Hector studied him and for a moment Jason knew exactly what it had to be like to be submissive. He almost wanted to open up to this man.

"You going to tell me what's up with you then? You haven't been yourself for weeks now."

Jason sighed. "It's complicated."

Boy was it ever complicated. It had been straightforward until Heather had walked back into his life. He'd been ready to admit defeat. But now...he didn't know what he wanted or needed anymore. All he knew was that he craved Heather, that she made him feel things he'd thought he would never experience again. He had no idea how to deal with all the conflicting feelings.

"And not something I want to talk about now." *Or ever.* He couldn't see himself ever admitting to having lost his drive.

"You know you need to talk, Jason. Don't be a fool. Don't shut yourself off."

Hector's voice sounded both stern and encouraging. Sometimes Jason felt like hitting the man. Why did he have to be so damned reasonable and almost always right?

"I know. Damn it, I do know. Just not now."

Jason glanced away, focusing his attention on Heather and Amber, who were talking and smiling. Both women looked beautiful and relaxed. This was how Heather should be all the time, happy in her skin and at ease with the world. He couldn't quite believe this was the same woman as the nervous creature who had walked into his office only yesterday.

Hector's voice brought his attention back to the Dom next to him.

"I'll let it go for now. But, Jason?"

Something in Hector's voice warned him he might not like the man's next words.

"I've known you for over a year now and I've never seen you look at anyone the way you're looking at Heather. Whatever is going on, don't be stupid. Don't ruin it out of some idiotic sense of pride. And find me when you're ready to talk."

Jason nearly growled. The bastard didn't even say 'if'. *'When you're ready to talk'*, as if it was a foregone conclusion. Keeping his thoughts to himself, Jason just nodded.

"I think that meat is ready to be eaten. Let's join the girls."

Maybe he was a coward, he just didn't know anymore. He couldn't talk about things he hadn't worked out for himself yet. He'd get there. And when he did, he would talk — or not.

"Heather."

The dominant tone in Hector's voice took Jason by surprise. Heather had obviously picked up on it as well. Her reaction was as instant as it was automatic. Her eyes were down, her shoulders back and a small smile touched her lips. Then she was out of the zone again. Just like that.

"Yes, Hector?"

"Tell me about last night. What happened? I hate that we upset you."

Jason held his breath. Would she open up and talk about her feelings with the three of them? They were virtual strangers. She'd no real reason to trust them with her emotions. He watched her intently as she looked from Hector to Amber and finally rested her gaze on him, clearly coming to a conclusion.

"You didn't upset me, Hector, although the scene did unsettle me. You woke me up."

Surprise, relief, shock flashed across her face, betraying her every emotion. He saw the big breath it took for her to continue and relished her smile when she found the courage.

"You two reminded me of Darren and me. It was the first visual reminder since he died. It shook me." She shrugged her shoulders as if it wasn't anything big.

For a moment he thought she'd leave it there.

"It was so beautiful. A reminder of what I used to have and a confirmation of all I've lost."

"I'm so sorry, Heather. If I were to lose Hector—" Amber's voice was a whisper and the sub's eyes were filled with tears as she glanced at her Dom. "I don't know how I'd go on living."

"Neither did I."

Heather's honesty astounded Jason. Maybe she needed to work it all out for herself in the company of people who hadn't known her husband.

"But last night and this morning—after I'd calmed down—I realized something." Suddenly her smile was bright. "I'll always have those memories, and I'll always treasure them. But I can't live my life on old memories."

For the second time he thought she'd reached the end of what she wanted to share.

"And?"

Anger flared in Jason. Who was Hector to ask Heather all these questions and force her to share her pain? Without thinking about it, Jason picked up her hand and stroked his thumb over her soft skin.

"Enough about this. We're supposed to be having a fun and relaxing dinner. *All* of us. Lay off the third degree already."

Heather squeezed his hand. He looked at her. She was fine. She didn't appear to mind. It was as if she was lighter. As if someone had lifted a weight from her shoulders.

"If I'm going to live rather than exist, it is time to start treasuring the memories I have while opening myself up to new ones."

Jason would have been hard pressed to name the emotions running through him. She wanted to make new memories. Surely that meant she didn't regret what had happened earlier. He knew what he wanted. Her, in his arms, in his bed, under him, above him, around him. And so much more. He wanted her on her knees, submitting to him, trusting him to give her everything she needed. If only he could trust himself, things would be perfect.

He felt more than saw Hector staring at him and ignored it, digging into his juicy steak instead. "This is great, just what we needed after an afternoon of party planning." He was well aware he was less than subtle in his change of topic, but *fuck it*. The personal stuff had gone more than far enough. "You and Amber still up for one or two exhibitions during the weekend?"

Chapter Eleven

Heather took comfort from Jason's arm around her shoulder. The garden at night took her breath away. The low lights, evenly spaced along the various meandering paths, gave her surroundings an almost mythical glow. It was as if she'd stepped into another world.

Heather wasn't sure what to make of her sudden transformation. Only yesterday she'd been scared and sad. She didn't know why she suddenly felt her life was once again filled with opportunities, but she embraced the feeling.

She'd occasionally wondered what moving forward would be like. And she'd been sure she would feel as if she were betraying Darren and their shared past. Now the moment had arrived, it amazed her how easily she'd slipped into this new phase of her life. She was excited. She'd even admit to being a little scared. The good kind of scared though. The scared you feel when you're about to take a step into the unknown. The kind of excitement she associated with new opportunities.

It had been a strange but wonderful evening. She would never have believed she could open up to strangers the way she had done. But Jason wasn't really a stranger, and Amber and Hector felt familiar, as if she'd known them for a long time. She was grateful Hector had forced her to put her emotions into words. She hadn't realized it was all about memories, old and new. But it was true. She'd never forget Darren. She'd never regret a single moment she'd spent with him, and there would always be occasions when she'd wish he was with her. But she was ready to create new memories without him, to live again. As he'd known she would be. As always, he'd known her better than she did herself.

"Heather, look at me." Jason lifted her chin, forcing her to meet his gaze. She'd been so lost in her thoughts she hadn't noticed he'd steered them off the path into what appeared to be a pergola. There were flowers everywhere, at her feet, climbing up the posts of the structure around her and blooming over her head. The perfume surrounded her as if it held her in a sweet embrace.

He looked straight into her eyes as he softly touched her face. She couldn't stop herself from leaning into his hand as he stroked her cheek and pushed her hair behind her ear.

"I want you."

His voice was gruff, and where she would have expected to see confidence, she encountered doubt.

"I know. I want you too."

"You don't have to do this, Heather. We are probably going too fast. I don't want you to do anything you're going to regret."

For a moment, doubt filled her. "I don't think I'd regret being with you. I feel ready. But, Jason, you don't have to. I know I'm a mess. The kisses don't mean we have to go on if you don't..."

His mouth was on hers before she could finish the thought. His lips attacked hers, fierce and demanding. She parted her lips without thinking about it, wanting, needing more. He withdrew. Heather felt like screaming.

"You broke down last night and I couldn't stop it. I don't want to hurt you again, Heather. Tell me to stop now if you're not sure."

She knew he wouldn't kiss her again until she'd reassured him, but at least his arms were still around her. Resting her head on his chest, she took a moment to listen to his heartbeat. She had to find a way of explaining her turn-around to him.

"For eighteen months I've kept my grief close. I lived

it. Loss was my whole life. Everything I did, everywhere I went, my pain was with me, holding me tight. Grief became the faithful companion Darren had been when he was alive." She stared into the darkness. "Last night was a wake-up call. You know how sometimes when somebody is hysterical you slap them to snap them out of it?"

She felt the slight nod of his head.

"Last night's meltdown had the same result. Watching that scene took me out of my comfort zone. It showed me everything I've been missing. It made me realize I can't live without intimacy for the rest of my life."

She was tempted to stop there, but didn't want to give Jason reasons to think she was using him to get back into the scene.

"My body has been reacting to you since the moment I recognized you in your office. I didn't want it to then and tried hard to deny it to myself, but my reluctance doesn't make it any less true." She forced herself to lift her head and look at his face. "I want this, Jason, with you. I can't explain it, but somewhere between my meltdown and now, I've made peace with the past."

She listened to herself with wonder, suddenly aware she needed this explanation as much as Jason.

"I'm ready to leave the past where it belongs. I want to start the future. I want...need you to take me there."

His mouth was back, softer this time. His lips exploring, the tip of his tongue teasing. She pushed her own tongue out and stroked back. She felt both their bodies shudder and relished the sensation.

"Not here."

He sounded as breathless as she felt.

"Come."

She wasn't aware of the gardens as he walked her, as fast as her heels allowed, back to the house and through the corridor. People were just vague forms as they rushed to the elevator.

When the door to his apartment closed behind them,

Heather was breathless. Whatever air she still had left her lungs when he turned her, pushed her against the door and attacked her lips with his again. Those lips...stroking, pulling, the soft nibbling of his teeth, his tongue on hers, twirling, teasing, inviting.

Heather closed her eyes and surrendered to the sensations, grateful for the arms holding her up since her legs didn't feel strong enough to support her. She swayed in his arms and couldn't stop the moan escaping her mouth. His tongue pushed in and out of her mouth, reminding her of all the things that tongue could do to other needy parts of her body. Her already over-sensitive vagina pulsed with desire. So long ago...too long ago...so good.

His stroked her all over her back, her bottom, her sides, squeezed her waist and brushed along her breasts. His fingertips flittered over her neck, brushed her cheeks, and stroked her earlobes until they were in her hair, holding her head still while he continued devouring her mouth with his. Heather felt dizzy. All the sensations running through her body made her head spin. She couldn't concentrate, couldn't think, so she returned his long hot kisses and surrendered to the tumult caused by every single nerve ending in her body waking up simultaneously.

"More."

It was a moan. She wanted more. She wanted them to be naked, skin-to-skin. She needed to lick him, smell him, taste him. She needed him on top of her. Inside her. Underneath her.

She pressed her body against Jason's. The sensation of his hard cock pressing into her belly nearly undid her. Her vagina contracted, pulsed with need. She couldn't stop herself from squirming against him, just to feel his reaction to her body. She heard his groan as she circled her tongue around his, as if it wasn't a tongue at all. How had she lived without this contact? How had her body not withered and died? She'd forgotten how much she loved creating this need in a man, how much she craved the need in herself.

He found the zip on the back of her dress. She sighed in tune with the lowering of it and almost groaned when her breasts fell free. They were heavy. She knew her nipples were hard and would be ultra-sensitive. When his thumb rubbed one hard peak, she moaned into his mouth. Need rushed through her as the nipple became so hard it hurt.

"Yes, Jason. Oh yes."

He explored her breasts with his hands as his mouth continued to explore hers. His fingers were teasing her nipples, brushing and pulling them. When he pinched her, she wanted to scream. A flash of desire ran from her breasts straight to her pussy. She needed contact.

A slight movement and her vagina pressed against his thigh. She couldn't stop herself from pressing, squirming, anything to create pressure on her sensitive flesh, to answer the need flaring through her body.

He unzipped the dress all the way and Heather felt it glide down her body before it hit the floor. The stab of despair when he loosened his grip, took a step back and allowed his gaze to roam over her body was immediately followed by the rush of recognition. She lowered her eyes, feeling safe under his scrutiny. This was familiar because this was her true nature.

"God, woman, you're so beautiful."

Jason's voice, more than his words, took her breath away. He sounded awed, as if he'd never seen a semi-naked woman before.

"This is your last chance. Tell me to stop now, if you're not sure."

She shook her head, gratitude warring with impatience. So thoughtful to give her a last out. So cruel to make her wait.

"No, don't stop." The desperation in her voice should have been embarrassing. "Please don't stop."

"Turn around."

He didn't give her a choice and pushed her until she faced the room she'd so far ignored and still failed to take in. She was only aware of his hands touching her back and sliding downwards. His fingers stroked her through her panties.

"Oh, girl. So wet. You're so ready for me."

She could feel the impatience in his hands as he pushed her underwear down. Without thinking, she lifted her feet, one at a time. All her focus was on his hands, now massaging her arse, squeezing, stroking. She wished he'd just raise his hand and...

He didn't. His touch moved up again, around to the front and back to her breasts. His voice was low and growly.

"So beautiful. Jesus, Heather, you're so hot. I've wanted you since you walked into my office. Keeping my hands off you has been torture, but I'm going to make up for it now."

His touch was everywhere, fingers teasing, palms squeezing. She couldn't stop herself from squirming, moved onto her toes so she could push her arse in to his cock, needing the comfort—that physical confirmation of everything he'd said.

"I'm going to enjoy every inch of you. Touch you, lick you, bite you. I want you."

* * * *

Her arse squirming against his cock drove him crazy and he loved it. He stroked her soft skin as he lowered his mouth to her neck. He used his tongue to explore her skin, licking along until he reached her ear and bit into her lobe. When his hands found her breasts again, she pushed into them. Pleasure and relief flooded through him. He could still feel. He did still love and want and enjoy this. He moved his hand down. From her breast, over her belly, toward her folds. When his fingers made contact with the wet heat between her legs, he couldn't stop himself from groaning. All doubt disappeared. She wanted this as much as he did. As if she could read his mind, Heather pushed her wet pussy into his hand, wordlessly begging him for more.

His patience—what little of it he'd had—disappeared. Jason turned her around and lifted her up. Her legs clamped around his middle immediately and she pushed her body into his, pressing herself as close as she could get. He could feel her wetness against his cock through his clothes. He squeezed her arse as he walked, as fast as he safely could, through the living area to his bedroom. He desperately wanted to throw her on his bed, but found the restraint necessary to tenderly lower her to the covers.

His body yearned for her, but he made himself step back and take a long look at the beauty in front of him. She was even more spectacular than he had expected. Her body, so lush and completely open, was made to be touched and worshiped. Her whole being begged him to take her to the heights of ecstasy. The heat and impatience in her huge green eyes were demanding him to take care of her.

"Why are you still dressed?"

Her frown was cute, her voice breathless and her need obvious. He couldn't help himself.

"What's wrong, my dear? Don't like what you see?"

He touched his crotch and stroked himself through his pants. He nearly groaned. He was so hard, he wanted her so badly. He had to be kidding. Teasing Heather, as much as he enjoyed it, only made him need her more.

"Please take them off, Jason. I need you…naked."

He needed to be naked. Focusing on Heather, he opened the buttons on his shirt, relishing her gaze as it followed his fingers, taking in every inch of skin he exposed. It killed him to go slow, but he wanted this to last.

Before the shirt hit the ground, he'd started opening the buttons on his fly. Her breathing grew faster and pure hunger shone out of her eyes.

In one move he pushed his trousers and underpants down. Suddenly in a hurry, he got rid of his shoes, socks, trousers. Straightening himself, he saw Heather's eyes, transfixed on his cock. His balls tightened as she licked her lips before raising her eyes to his.

"Yes. Oh, yes. I want."

He didn't think she knew she'd spoken out loud. Mesmerized, he watched as she raised herself up. Kneeling on the bed, she reached out and touched his cock, one finger stroking him from the tip to the bottom and back again. He hadn't thought he could get any harder, yet the moment he felt her touch, his cock responded. She licked her lips again and moved her face forwards. All he could do was stand there and watch as she puckered her mouth and placed a kiss on the tip of his penis. When her tongue lapped up the pre-cum, his breath hitched.

He looked on as she opened her mouth and took the tip of his cock in, sucking softly. The look in her eyes when she gazed up at him took Jason's breath away. Desire burnt, turning the green darker, almost golden brown. Her eyes didn't leave his as she moved her mouth farther down his cock before pulling back. Her tongue swirled around him, teasing him, finding the stretched ridge of skin, pushing into the tiny hole on top. Something deep inside screamed at him to take her head, push her down, force her to take him deeper. He didn't. He couldn't. The risk was too big. He couldn't be trusted. He knew he'd end up ruining this.

He brought his hand to the back of her head and just rested it there. Even without his help she pushed farther. This was enough. Right now, in this moment, it was all he needed. Every time her head bobbed down, she went deeper until he felt her choke around him, the sensation driving his lust even higher. Her tongue was back, teasing, stroking as she sucked and resumed bobbing. So hot. Her gaze still on his, she groaned, the vibrations driving him crazy. He was going to...

"Stop, enough."

The smile on her face after he pulled back was smug. "What's wrong? Not enjoying it?"

With a growl, he pushed her back until she was splayed out in front of him again in all her heated glory. "Damn you, woman, your mouth is way too clever. I want this to last."

Heather's giggles were like music to his ears.

"And here I was under the impression you are this experienced sexpert."

"I'll give you sexpert."

Kneeling in front of the bed, he stroked his hands up her soft legs. Her muscles trembled under his touch as he skimmed her calves, stroked the back of her knee and moved over her thighs.

"So soft. So beautiful." His hand brushed across her pubic bone and he couldn't stop his smile when she tried to push herself against his hand. "So needy."

She wasn't the only one. He needed this at least as much as she did. He moved his hand a fraction, brushed his finger across her clit and cherished her sharp intake of breath.

"You thought you could get away with teasing me, did you, my dear?" He stroked her folds, spreading her wetness. "Has nobody ever told you that what goes around comes around?" Slowly he pushed the tip of one finger into her and watched as she tried to push her body closer, to feel more, before withdrawing his digit again. "Now we'll see how long you'll last, princess."

He took one moment to look up her body. He felt at home here, between her legs. It was natural to have her stretched out before him, panting. The smell of arousal drifting from her body was so strong he could almost taste it. He would taste it, in just one moment.

Bending forward, he put his mouth on her lower belly and started to lick. He loved how she squirmed when his teeth teased her sensitized skin. He was so close to her heat.

"Please, Jason."

He loved how all of her begged. It was in her voice, her face and her body. Making her wait, teasing her, was even better. He took his time moving his mouth down, licking and sucking and making a point of narrowly missing her clit before moving his attention to her thighs. Her squeals when his teeth clamped down on tiny bits of sensitive flesh went straight to his cock. He smiled against her soft flesh as she squirmed, trying to get her pussy closer to his mouth. Teasing could be very satisfying. He'd always known that, but still it was a relief to discover that right now it was enough. He didn't need to go further.

Her breathing was labored. He watched as her pussy tried to contract around nothing and decided to show some mercy. He couldn't help his groan as his finger slid into her without any resistance. Wet and open and so ready. Moving his mouth from her thigh to her clit, he pushed two fingers into her. The way her body trembled delighted him. She was so close. It would take so little. He pumped his fingers, twisted his hand, pushed again, sucked on her clit and felt like cheering when she arched her body, pushed up against him and screamed.

Suddenly he couldn't wait anymore. He needed to be inside, close, to feel her heat surround him. He kept his fingers inside her, pumping while he blindly reached for the bedside table with his other hand. Her eyes opened when he used his teeth to tear the packaging, a lazy smile spread across her face as she watched him push the protection over his hard cock. As soon as he was covered, she lifted her butt off the bed, offering herself to him.

The need to just push in, to claim all of her in one hard shove nearly overwhelmed him. He would never know where he found the restraint, but he managed to remember her months without and took his time, savoring every inch, as he lost himself in her heat. Keeping his eyes open was just as difficult, but so worth it. He saw the slight shock on her face when she realized how big he actually was and rejoiced when the shock transformed into delight as her body adjusted to his size and took all of him.

Fighting against the need to ride her hard, Jason withdrew all but the head of his cock before pushing back into her. Again and again he withdrew and pushed back, watching as her eyes fluttered shut, hearing her breath catch before coming out in loud moans. Only when she started to move with him, push up to him whenever he re-entered her, did he lift up her arse and drive in harder. He wouldn't last long. His balls were screaming for release.

"Come with me, girl." He recognized the tone in his voice, and saw and felt Heather doing the same. Her body arched when he touched her clit and teased it as he pushed in and out of her with more force.

"Now!" Jason felt her instant reaction. Her muscles pulled at him and with a few uncontrolled pushes, he too flew over the edge, joining Heather as pleasure consumed them both. It was so much better than he'd expected.

Chapter Twelve

"I'm sorry, Heather. But I'll meet you for lunch at about one."

"Don't worry about it, I understand. You do have a business to run after all." Her smile felt stupid on her face, too bright for the conversation they were having, but she couldn't help it. Ever since she'd woken up, she'd felt as if she were floating. It was as if she'd rediscovered herself, as if after months of feeling out of sorts, she fitted her body again. Jason's arms around her, last night while they'd drifted off and the sweet nothings he'd murmured in her ear had allowed her to stay relaxed and satisfied. The thought had crossed her mind she might wake up feeling guilty, but she'd shrugged it off. If she did, she'd deal with it.

This morning she'd woken up to Jason watching her, his fingers combing through her hair with a worried expression on his face. She'd instantly known what he had to be thinking. Searching her mind and her heart, she'd looked for feelings of guilt and had found none. She'd only felt good, very satisfied and like herself.

"I don't like leaving you alone." Jason's voice was gruff and filled with worry.

"I told you. I won't be on my own." She felt as if her face would split if she smiled any brighter. "I'm meeting Amber for a chat and coffee shortly and then I'll have a few things I need to do before we continue our planning this afternoon. It's all good, Jason." She looked straight into his eyes. "I'm all good. Stop worrying about me."

She could see he wanted to smile back at her and didn't like the worry lingering in his eyes. She'd told him she had no regrets. Either he didn't believe her or he regretted what had happened between them last night. She didn't like either idea. Since there was nothing she could do about it while he had people to meet and a business to run, she let it go.

She watched as Jason walked away, taking the time to admire his impressive backside, before turning and entering her apartment. A quick shower and fresh clothes followed by a girly morning with Amber was just what she needed.

It had been too long since she'd simply socialized and enjoyed pleasant company. She looked in the mirror and grinned at herself. She'd been so worried about coming here, about kick-starting her life. And look at her now. Forty-eight hours later it felt as if her world had finally found its rightful place in the universe again. She was back. She'd rediscovered life and looked forward to finding out what might happen next. And she'd have to find a way of sharing those feelings and her excitement with Jason. It was all thanks to him. She wasn't worried. There was no need for him to be concerned about her.

"Oh my, you look amazing." Amber's smile was bright and somewhat mischievous when Heather found her on the patio, waiting in the sunshine. "I'd love to know what you got up to last night."

Heather couldn't hide the silly smirk on her face. "What makes you think I got up to anything besides a lovely dinner in charming company?"

"Only a few things make a girl radiate satisfaction like that. And sexy new shoes are hard to find around here."

Heather just laughed. She liked the idea that her rediscovered lust for life could be read on her face. "Satisfaction is the right word for it, Amber. I won't say it doesn't surprise me, but I feel wonderful this morning."

Amber's hug was a surprise. "I'm so glad. I felt so bad when I saw your reaction two nights ago. And then, last night, after you two left, Hector said he was afraid you might be moving too fast..." She allowed the sentence to fall away. "I know we've only just met, but I like you and I was worried."

A small lump formed in Heather's throat. It had been a long time since somebody had cared this much about her. No, that wasn't fair. It had been a long time since she'd allowed anybody else to care this much about her feelings.

"Thank you, Amber. It's nice of you to care. I'm good. It wasn't as fast as it may have seemed. Jason and I met before, twenty years ago." She thought for a moment. "I'm feeling much better than I would have expected. I just wish I could say the same for Jason."

Shit, she hadn't meant to say that much. She liked Amber, but she'd only just met her. Besides, the girl and her Dom worked for Jason. Her last statement had been too much on so many levels.

"Forget I said that, please, Amber. I shouldn't have."

Amber's understanding smile made her feel a bit better. "It's okay, Heather. I won't repeat it if you don't want me to." The smile vanished. "Hector's worried about Jason too. Has been for some time. And I probably shouldn't be talking to you about that." The redhead sighed. "Let's leave it for now. Hey, do you feel like going to the pond to take advantage of the sun? We could have our coffees there. Couldn't we?" Amber turned to the waitress who'd just arrived at their table.

"I'd love to," Heather said.

As curious as she might be about Hector's reasons for worrying about Jason, Heather was glad the conversation had moved away from personal stuff. She'd no right to go delving into Jason's secrets, if he had any. She pushed the thought away.

"I can't believe all the glorious weather we're having. We better enjoy it while we can." She looked at the clear blue sky and shook her head. "After all, this is Ireland and you know what they say. If you don't like the weather, wait five minutes and it will change."

"Well, if we're lucky, not today." Amber laughed. "Will

you be staying until after the party?"

As if a cloud had moved in front of the sun, Heather's mood shifted. "No. At least, that's not the way we planned it." She frowned. How had that slipped her mind? "I'm due to go back to Dublin tomorrow and return here the Monday before the party." She saw the question on Amber's face and answered it without needing to hear it. "I don't know if yesterday changes the timetable, and I'm not going to ask him."

No, she wasn't going to pester him just because he had given her the best night in a long time. She shrugged, trying to make light of it, for her own sake as much as Amber's. "Besides, I only packed for three days." Suddenly she felt the need to get away from her personal life. "Tell me about you and Hector. You two are so beautiful together. How did you meet him? When?"

Heather had picked the right topic to redirect Amber's attention. The sub's eyes lit up as she launched into her story.

"We met three years ago in a club in Dublin. I was twenty-one at the time and rather innocent. My friends had dragged me to this place I'd never heard of. You probably know it, the DC?"

Heather nodded. She did know the place, the Dark Cellar, and didn't like it—or the man who ran it.

"I couldn't believe my eyes." Those same eyes lit up as Amber continued. "I never knew places like that existed or that people engaged in such acts...and in public." Amber's gaze grew unfocused for a moment. "I was in trouble almost immediately. A masked man dressed in black ordered me to kneel for him. He raised his hand when I didn't. That's when Hector stepped in."

Heather could picture it. She'd visited that club with Darren once or twice and had never liked the feel of it. There were no real rules there. Once you walked in, you were fair game. A woman on her own didn't stand a chance.

"Hector worked there?"

Amber shook her head. "No, he was there with friends too and on his way out when he saved me. He told me I should leave, that me and my innocence didn't belong there." Her smile grew radiant.

"I still don't know where I found the courage, but I told him I was curious and asked him to show me around. The rest is more or less history."

Heather loved Amber's story. It was just what she needed to take her mind of Jason for a little while. "Don't tell me it was love at first sight."

"Oh, but it was. For me at least." Amber grinned. "Hector claims he doesn't believe in that sort of rubbish — his words. But I knew. Then and there I was sure I had found the man I belonged to."

All Heather could do was smile. "I adore a good love story. And you two are so clearly made for each other."

She closed her eyes and lifted her face to the sun and soaked in the warmth. She was happy and didn't feel guilty about it. She'd met a woman who might well turn into a friend and her body still hummed with pleasure. If anyone had asked her, she would have told them life was good.

* * * *

"No. It is not going to happen."

"Jason, be reasonable." Hector glared at his boss. "You know you're going to have to do it. Why are you resisting it so much?"

"There is no need." Jason wanted to hit something. "You and Amber are down for two demonstrations. Roger" — he looked at the man across the table who nodded — "and Leo will be doing one and Margaret is displaying Celia and Evan. That's enough."

Jason fixed his eyes on Hector, hoping against hope his friend would take the hint and leave it alone. He should have known better.

"You're missing the point, Jason, and you're well aware

111

of it." He recognized the confusion in the man's eyes. Of course he didn't understand Jason's reluctance. How could he?

"This is *your* club. You are the *Master Jay* who's invited them all to come here. They will be expecting to see you in action. Not showing them who and what you are is setting yourself up for failure before you've even begun."

Confusion had turned into exasperation.

He couldn't blame Hector. The man had watched as Jason became more and more reluctant to perform in public for no apparent reason. He hadn't explained himself to anyone and had no intention of doing so now.

He nodded. "I'll think about it." He knew he wouldn't be changing his mind, but it might be enough to stop the conversation for now.

He saw Hector open his mouth to continue the argument and turned away.

"Roger, you want to have a practice run with Leo tonight?"

The younger Dom nodded. "Yes, I think I should. We've not been working together for very long and I just want to make sure it works."

Jason nodded, thankful his distraction tactic appeared to have worked and just as grateful his staff cared about getting things right.

"Fabulous. Have a word with Karl about what you need. I'll make sure I'm there for the scene. If it's anything like the last one I saw, we'll be in for a treat." Jason leaned back. "And that's all for today. We'll be meeting every other day until this weekend is behind us." He couldn't wait for the bloody weekend to be over. The only good thing to have come out of it had been meeting Heather again.

Heather... He felt his body relax. Even if she was the only positive to be gained from this mess he'd created for himself, it would have been well worth it.

"I should have a provisional timetable ready for the next meeting." Jason pushed his chair back, unsuccessfully trying to get away before anybody could waylay him.

"Jason, a word."

"Not now, Hector. I'm meeting Heather for lunch in a few minutes."

He didn't like brushing his friend off, but the man was too perceptive. He didn't want to talk about his personal failings with anybody.

He saw the disappointment and confusion on Hector's face and could have kicked himself.

"I'm not sure what is wrong, Jason, but you're going to have to deal with it sooner or later. Sooner sounds like a good idea."

The attempt at a joke was feeble at best, but both men smiled, trying to save the moment from becoming too awkward.

The concession was minor, but it was the only one he could make.

"Hector, I know where to find you if I want or need to talk." For a second Jason considered setting his reservations aside and just confiding in his friend. "Right now I don't." He didn't add the words he heard in his mind *'want to, anyway'* and couldn't help feeling that Hector had picked them up regardless.

Chapter Thirteen

"So, what have we got?"

Heather leaned back in her chair and looked at the gorgeous man on the other side of the desk. They'd had a lovely lunch together.

Jason had seemed tense when they met up and she'd been tempted to ask him about it. One night of mind-blowing sex didn't give her the right to poke into his private thoughts though, so she'd kept her mouth shut. Well, except when they'd been kissing. Her mouth had been open for that, and her tongue busy. She smiled.

"Something funny, Heather?"

She loved how he cocked his head and quirked his eyebrow. "Just a private joke. Nothing important." She forced her mind away from his rather amazing tongue and all the feelings it aroused in her and back on the matter at hand. "Your weekend. We have to try and finish the provisional timetable."

The grin on his face faded and he shook his head.

"Jason, what's wrong?"

"Nothing. Everything." He stared at the wall behind her and frowned. "This weekend is starting to feel like more hard work than it's worth."

She sucked in her breath. If he'd hit her, she wouldn't have been more surprised. Did he mean what she feared? She felt his eyes on her face as she tried desperately not to show all the emotions rushing through her.

"No. Shit." Anger flashed across his face. "Stop your mind, Heather. That's not what I meant."

She was proud her voice didn't waver when she answered.

"What did you mean then?"

He got up from behind his desk and walked around it, toward her. Taking her hand, he looked into her eyes.

"Before lunch, during the meeting I couldn't stop thinking that the only good thing coming out of my brilliant idea was your arrival here."

She could breathe again. "What's so bad about the rest of it, Jason?"

Apparently it was his turn to be stuck for words.

"Everything. The expectations, the work involved, all the various ways in which it could turn into an unrivaled disaster." He grimaced. "The list is endless."

Okay. This she could deal with. This wasn't her first encounter with cold feet. In fact, it was so common it was almost laughable. People decided they wanted to throw a party, got all enthusiastic until they realized the real work involved. By then of course it would be too late. Invitations would have been sent and accepted and canceling would do more damage than a less-than-perfect party ever could. Reassuring them was part of the job description.

"Jason, relax. Tell me what you had in mind and we'll take it from there."

He rattled the list off. "Arrival on Friday, followed by a tour of the premises and a buffet dinner. One exhibition in the evening before people can do what they bloody well please."

Heather listened to Jason with tension growing in her belly. What had him so worried? There'd been no sign of this reluctance during their meeting yesterday. She'd thought they were almost done when they'd finished talking. And now, he appeared to hate the whole idea.

She watched him as he took a deep breath and made the effort to calm himself.

"I thought it might be best to leave the mornings empty and allow people to start the day at their own pace. Saturday afternoon there will be a meeting of all the Doms and Dommes. That should give them the opportunity to check me out." His voice turned harsh again. "Like a bloody monkey in a zoo. I'd just as soon skip that part, but Hector informs me there's no getting around it."

"Hector's right."

Talking business was easier. His behavior worried her.

"The people you've invited will be forming opinions about you, whether you like it or not. Such a meeting gives you the opportunity to have them do so on your terms."

"Still makes me feel like I'll be up for inspection." Despite his words, his mood seemed to be lifting.

"You will be. There's no avoiding it." She took a deep breath. *Might as well get the bad news out now.* "And they'll be looking to find fault." She felt her own anger rising. "And you know this, Jason. Things are the same in America. This is a small and almost incestuous world. Outsiders don't understand our desires and needs, are scared of them and want to find ways to discredit and shame us. It makes insiders suspicious of anything and anyone new."

Suddenly Jason looked tired and every one of his forty-three years. "Yes, I do know. Doesn't mean I have to like it." He shook his head. "And I shouldn't be taking all my doubts and second thoughts out on you. I'm sorry." Jason took a deep breath and continued, "There'll be two demonstrations on Saturday. One in the afternoon and one in the evening, depending on how the *getting to know the Dom session* goes."

He smiled ruefully. She appreciated his attempt to lighten the mood. She desperately wanted to know what had him so down and couldn't help worrying it might be her and the night they'd spent together. She just didn't have the courage to ask.

* * * *

Jason watched as emotions rapidly replaced each other on Heather's face. Surprise was replaced by pain before turning in to fear. Sometimes he was such a prick. He had no right taking his insecurities out on her. She'd been nothing but a delight ever since she arrived and in return he caused her pain because he couldn't get his shit together.

"Weather allowing, I figured we'd have a barbeque outside, near the pond, on Saturday. It may even be possible to have that evening's demonstration outside, provided the temperatures don't change."

He could feel himself relaxing. Listing all the details made it feel less daunting.

"People will start leaving late Sunday afternoon or early evening so the last demonstration will have to take place in the afternoon. Dinner for those who want it and then it will be over."

Just the thought of having the whole affair behind him made him breathe out in relief.

Heather smiled at him and nodded. "That sounds good. What about workshops?"

"Those were offered on the invitations, but the interest was so low I've decided to let the idea go." He shrugged. "Most, if not all, guests have been in the lifestyle for years. Maybe they don't want or need workshops."

He looked at her as she made a few notes on her pad. God, she was so beautiful. So perfect. And if he wasn't careful, he would end up alienating her just because he wasn't sure of himself. He had to avoid transferring his insecurities to her. She'd given him a reason to be optimistic just when he'd been sure he'd never feel good about himself again. She boosted his confidence. She'd wanted him. He wanted more of her.

"So, those demonstrations are delivered by you and..."

"No. I won't be doing one." He saw the shock in her eyes.

"You won't be performing? Why ever not?"

It was on the tip of his tongue. He almost wanted to tell her. Again the need to share his burden nearly overwhelmed him and he still couldn't bring himself to do it. "Because there're others who do it better than me."

He knew he sounded short and gruff again and could see

confusion returning to her eyes. And, *fuck it all*, he didn't know how to avoid worrying her without sharing feelings he didn't want to admit to.

"Hector and Amber will do two. I've got a Domme performing with two subs and one all-male session. That will have to do."

She shook her head while scribbling on her pad. "That's not good enough, Jason. Those Doms will be expecting to see you in action. They'll want to get your measure. Not showing your skills will leave them doubting you. They'll assume you're weak, a wannabe."

And didn't he know it? He just didn't see an easy solution. Performing while he wasn't in the zone would show him up as a fake, just as much as not performing would. It was the worst sort of lose-lose situation and he'd no idea how to fix it. He sighed.

"I know, Heather. Can we just leave it? I'm not going to do it, no matter what impression that's going to leave. No matter what you, or anybody else, say. My mind is made up about this."

"I don't know, Jason."

He saw the uncertainty in her eyes.

"If you're dead set against it, I can't make you. But I don't think it's a good idea. You're creating a problem where there's no need for one." She paused. "With all those egos gathering here, you shouldn't hand them a reason to look down on you. They'll be looking for reasons to do that anyway." She looked into his eyes and swallowed. "And if you're really not open to the idea, I'll stop talking about it now. I'm not promising I won't bring it up again though." She tried to smile but didn't quite succeed. "I like the variety in your exhibitions though. I can't see anybody complaining their particular taste wasn't catered to."

Jason knew his attempt at a smile had to be as unconvincing as hers had been. "Roger and Leo, my all-male duo, will be trying out their scene tonight. I promised I'd go and watch. Wanna join me?"

For the first time since they'd started this meeting, she relaxed. "I would love that. It's been a long time since I've seen that dynamic."

He loved seeing her at ease and was relieved she'd agreed to accompany him so readily. An all-male performance should be safe enough as well. The risk of Roger and Leo triggering memories of Darren were small as far as he could see.

"Oh, Heather, about your stay here..."

His ringtone cut him off at the worst possible time. *Blast.* He could have thrown the phone out of the window. While he listened to the voice talking about things he didn't want to deal with right now but couldn't avoid, he watched Heather gather her stuff and blow him a kiss. He managed to blow one back before he allowed the daily pressures of running a sex club to swallow him again.

Chapter Fourteen

"And then, when Rick fell, face first, into the cowpat" — his face broke into a wide smile — "I thought I'd never stop laughing. Of course, being blind drunk didn't help."

As soon as Jason mentioned the incident, the memories were back. Heather could see the scene in her mind. The short cut back from the pub to their cottages had seemed like a great idea right until the moment Rick had lost his footing and fallen into that mess. Moira, Jason and she had been torn between laughing until they'd cried and trying to help him up. Poor Rick had not been happy.

"Oh, but we did have fun, didn't we?"

She picked up her coffee and looked at the handsome man across the table. There was no sign of his earlier anger and insecurity now. She was still worried about his strange behavior, but decided to let it go for now. The evening was too nice to allow her anxieties to spoil it.

She'd been nervous before she met him for dinner, afraid the evening would be tense, but he'd been relaxed and affectionate. His kiss, when they met, had awoken every nerve ending in her body. She had loved his arm around her, his hand in the small of her back, when they walked to the restaurant. The food had been as delicious as she'd come to expect and she'd enjoyed stealing bites off his plate while he did the same with hers. She'd been reminded of their younger selves, the same playfulness, the same easy banter. All the memories rushing back once they'd started talking about Wexford had taken her by surprise.

"The demonstration doesn't start for another hour or so."

Jason picked up her hand and stroked it while looking

straight into her eyes. The urge to lower hers almost overwhelmed Heather, but she resisted. She wasn't his sub. There had been none of that dynamic involved last night. They hadn't talked about it.

"You're sure you want to watch them tonight?" For the first time that evening, worry clouded his expression.

"I'm sure, Jason. I'm looking forward to it." She smiled.

Two men together could never hurt her. She knew the scene would be beautiful, just as past experience told her watching it wouldn't affect her personally.

"Seeing two men together could never hurt me. The dynamic is exactly the same yet completely different. I'm not sure I can explain it."

The frown on his face told Heather her words hadn't convinced him.

"Don't worry. I don't think there's any risk of me having another breakdown." She thought for a moment. "I think I could watch Hector and Amber again and not fall apart this time. The shock of recognition set me off two nights ago. I've dealt with it now. I'm okay, really."

He looked more relaxed but she knew she still hadn't convinced him.

"Do you promise to safe-word earlier if it gets too much tonight?"

"I do. I won't need to, but if I do, I'll let you know." The light mood was gone and she wanted it back. "I saw there's a band playing in the ballroom tonight?"

"Yes, and they're quite good."

"Would you take me dancing, Jason? I haven't danced in ages."

When his smile returned it was as if a weight had been lifted from her shoulders.

"I love that idea. Come."

Jason took her hand as he helped her up, and kissed her on her lips. "I can't think of anything I would rather do right now than keep you in my arms for the next hour or so."

The ballroom wasn't quite as grand as the name made it sound. It was impressive though. Dim lighting gave the long, wide space an intimate atmosphere, in stark contrast to the bright and airy impression it made during the day when natural light streamed in through the many, large windows. Now, the only bright lights were aimed at the stage and the four-piece band. Heather took a moment to watch the musicians. She liked the double bass, not something you usually saw accompanying a keyboard, drums and guitar. It worked better than she would have expected. The bass gave the music a richer, fuller sound. When the band broke into *Fly Me to the Moon*, shivers ran down her spine. Boy, the man could sing.

"This is wonderful, Jason. You're right. They are good."

She leaned closer into him, loving the feeling of his arms around her. She felt safe and wanted. When he pushed her to the dance floor and turned her so she faced him, she smiled and was delighted to see her happiness returned.

"They're a local band. They play here once a week and are always a success."

He clearly wasn't exaggerating. The dance floor was busy, despite the relatively early hour. His arm came around her and pulled her close. She reached up and put one hand on his neck, just below his hair, enjoying the feel of it tickling her skin. She placed her other hand on his chest, and cherished his steady heartbeat underneath her palm.

He was a good dancer. She could have been floating across the floor. She got lost in the music, Jason's presence and the pressure of his hand on her lower back. Her body responded when he pressed her tighter into him. Just being close, even without any intimate touches, was enough. She smiled as she realized it was quite possible he could feel her nipples harden against his chest. Just as she could feel his cock growing against her belly.

"This is just what I needed."

Heather smiled up at his face. His brown eyes were focused on her and filled with more emotions than she could

122

possibly name. The lust she detected didn't surprise her since she could feel his body's response to her hardening. But there was more. The worry still wasn't completely gone although it did appear to be battling with — she wasn't quite sure what to call it — satisfaction, maybe?

"You feel good in my arms, beautiful."

His smile, at least, was relaxed. And his mouth was oh so hot and soft when it pressed down on hers. She pressed back, wanting more, needing to be closer, and welcomed his tongue when it slipped between her lips.

The music played and they moved around with their lips glued together. She couldn't get enough of the taste of him, his smell or his strong body swallowing her smaller one. One song turned into another, creating a medley for their coming together, a soundtrack to her reawakening.

The realization that she could stay here forever came as a shock. In his arms, floating through a room surrounded by people who were little more than a vaguely outlined background, she felt safe. She wanted to press closer still, except there was no space left between them. She'd crawl into him if she could. The feeling scared as much as it delighted and she refused to investigate those reactions. She would enjoy this evening, this feeling, this sense of coming back alive. Everything else could wait.

"It's time to move on, Heather."

Jason's voice brought her back to the present.

"Move on?"

"The demonstration will be starting in a few minutes. If we're going to watch, we need to go now."

Heather shook her head, unable to believe his words. "We've been dancing for an hour?"

"We have. And I've loved every single minute of it."

Jason couldn't believe how much he'd enjoyed this simple pleasure. Just holding her in his arms — no games, no talk, no sex. Just her body close to his, their endless kisses and her hand stroking his neck. If he could, he'd take her straight to his room, undress her and dance all over again, this time naked. But he'd promised he'd watch tonight and he would.

He kept one arm wrapped around her as he led her out of the ballroom and down the corridor toward the exhibition area.

"I don't want to keep going on about this, but I need to know you'll tell me when it gets too much."

He hated the tiredness creeping into her smile, but he needed the reassurance.

"I will." Her sigh sounded heavy. "Trust me, Jason. I don't want to repeat that experience any more than you do."

"Thank you."

He nodded and started walking again. He'd have to stop this. He couldn't continue to treat her like a child, as if she might break if he didn't keep her together. He knew he wasn't being reasonable but didn't think he'd be able to live with himself if she fell apart again. He shook his head. It was time to let the worries go and concentrate on what was sure to be a spectacular performance. Roger and Leo had a fascinating dynamic between them and never failed to deliver.

Running into Karl surprised him. His manager usually avoided demonstrations unless he expected trouble.

"Everything okay, Karl?"

"Yes."

The man looked flustered, which was as rare as his presence here.

"I thought I'd better acquaint myself with everything connected to the party. I don't like surprises."

Jason shrugged. It didn't make sense. He had people to monitor the dungeon. But his manager was conscientious. He had neither the time nor the inclination to explore this puzzle right now.

The room filled with spectators, Roger and Leo's reputation always guaranteed a good audience. When he found a spot where both of them would have an uninterrupted view of the show, he placed Heather in front of him and pulled her close. The last time he'd only been able to keep his hands on her hips. This time he wrapped his arms around her and placed his chin on her head.

"He's beautiful, Jason."

He looked at the young man who'd caught Heather's attention. Blond curls surrounded his face. The twenty-four year old exuded sex with his lithe but well-defined body.

"His name is Leo. He and Amber are the youngsters here."

He smiled. Despite their youth, they were among the most popular of his employees.

He returned his attention to the center area. Leo had been blindfolded and tied up. Chains attached to the cuffs around his wrists stretched his arms above his head. With his feet secured to the floor, the young sub was the personification of helplessness, and yet nothing in his stance betrayed insecurity or fear while his semi-erect cock indicated his anticipation.

When the crowd turned silent Leo's body tensed.

"That's Roger."

Jason whispered in Heather's ear, trying not to break the total quiet surrounding them. He felt the slight tensing in Heather's body as she watched the black-clad Dom who soundlessly made his way toward the sub waiting for him. For a moment Jason worried. Heather's heavier breathing reassured him. Her tension wasn't the result of fear but a reaction to the sexual atmosphere around her.

"God, he's gorgeous too."

Heather's voice was breathless. He couldn't disagree with her. Dominance radiated from Roger as he approached his sub. Not much taller than Leo, Roger's body betrayed his fondness for exercise and bodybuilding. Well-defined muscles rippled beneath his clothes, leaving a powerful impression. Jason's gaze shifted from Leo, who appeared to be listening for sounds that would betray the Dom's location, to Roger, who'd stopped walking a short distance behind the sub while caressing the paddle in his hand.

As Roger lifted his arm, the crowd collectively held its breath. Leo, sensing the change in atmosphere tensed his body. In the resulting dead quiet, the sound of the paddle connecting with naked flesh filled the room. He heard Heather's soft moan, felt her body press back into his, at that first contact. Jason's reaction was instant. Heat rushed his body, his cock twitched and hardened, his balls felt heavier.

Every single stroke of Roger's paddle elicited a reaction in Heather, as it did in Leo. While the sub in the middle of the room allowed his reaction to be loud and Heather's groans were soft, the similarities between their reactions were undeniable. Both of them thrived on the pain, even if Leo experienced it and Heather had to content herself with watching and maybe imagining.

"You like that?"

"Yes." Her answer was soft and breathless.

"To watch or to experience?" He didn't know why he asked the question. Taking a paddle or any other implement to Heather was out of the question.

"Both."

Even in the dim light he could see the blush creeping up her cheeks. He brought one hand down and squeezed her arse.

"You like having your backside reddened, do you? You enjoy having somebody's marks on you?"

"I do." Her inability to string together longer answers, as if she needed all her concentration to observe the scene in front of her, increased his own excitement.

Leo's cock had long since evolved from semi to full on. Hard, pointing up and straining, with pre-cum glistening in the stage lighting, it betrayed Leo's need to its fullest extent. The man's moans and the pleading sound in his voice underlined Leo's ecstasy. The young sub twisted his body away from and straight into the paddle as it continued to assault his bright red arse.

"You like this, sub?"

Roger's hand was in Leo's curls, pulling his head back, lengthening his beautiful throat. The Dom moved his head toward the elongated neck and he bared his teeth before biting. Leo's scream was filled with pain and heat. Heather's groan in response shot straight to Jason's crotch.

As if they had a mind of their own, Jason's hands pulled up the skirt of Heather's dress. How he loved these tiny knickers. He stroked his hand over the soft skin of her arse and pinched. She tensed and immediately relaxed, pushing her backside into his hand. "Yes."

He had to force himself to keep his attention on Roger and Leo. Heather's arse in his hand, the way she responded to his squeezing and stroking mesmerized him. Roger stroking Leo's cock with his hand while ordering the sub not to come only added fuel to the fire raging inside Jason. Heather's movements against him seemed to suggest the scene affected her the same way it did him. He smiled, and brought his mouth to her neck, nipping her skin with his teeth in a softer imitation of Roger's earlier action.

When Roger picked up a lubricated butt-plug and started pushing it into Leo's arse, Heather groaned loud enough to attract the attention of the people standing closest to them. Jason's body relaxed as it let go of the last remnants of tension he hadn't been aware of holding. She really enjoyed this. There were no signs of distress, only heat and need.

God, the heat. It rushed through his body. He loved this display and couldn't wait for it to be over. He needed to get her to his room, naked. To explore her body, to find out what she wanted, needed, how she would react to everything he could do to her. His mind overflowed with images of Heather tied to his bed, raising her arse to welcome his flogger, moaning as he slipped a finger into her arse.

With a silent curse he stopped himself. He wouldn't allow his thoughts to go beyond sleeping with Heather. He couldn't be trusted to dominate her. He'd lost his touch. He wasn't going to take the risk.

He moved his hand from her arse cheek to the split in

the middle and pressed. Her reaction to the light pressure was immediate. A moan and a slight push back against his finger.

"What do you want, Heather? Tell me." The tone in his voice shocked him.

"You. Everything."

His shock lessened as he reveled in her incoherence. "Watch. We're nearing the end."

Roger's hand continued to stroke Leo's cock as he used his other hand to play with the plug. The sub squirmed and groaned, moving his mouth in an effort to get out the words he couldn't formulate. Jason watched as the Dom whispered in Leo's ear. The sub's moans went straight to Jason's own cock. He couldn't hear the words, but Leo's need shone bright. Heather's whimpers as she watched the sub's exquisite suffering were a delight.

The Dom raised his voice. "Ten strokes, Leo. You're going to count them for me. When you reach ten, you'll come. No sooner and no later. And if you miss one, you won't come at all. Understand?"

"Yes, please, God. Yes, I understand. Please."

Heather's body shook against his, her head resting against his chest and the tip of her tongue visible through her parted lips. Jason drank in the sound of her panting.

"Watch." He leaned forward and whispered in her ear. "Leo's so beautiful when he comes."

He lifted his own gaze back to the scene. Roger matched the movements of his hands, assaulting the sub's arse in the same rhythm as his cock. Leo squirmed, trying to move toward the friction. His groans grew louder and louder as he counted down the numbers. "Ten. Nine. Eight. Seven – I can't. Too much. Please..." Leo's shouts sounded desperate.

"Six. Five. Four. Three. Oh God. Two."

The tension in the room was palpable. The whole audience held their collective breath as Roger stopped his hands for just one second before plunging the plug back into Leo with force. "One!" The sub went rigid as his cock jumped and started pumping. "Yes...oh yes." He wasn't shouting anymore, his voice barely a whisper yet perfectly audible. When he came down from his high and dropped his head, Roger's arms came around the young man and he held him as assistants hurried to release him from his bonds.

Jason's attention flew back to Heather. For a moment he'd been distracted, too caught up in the spectacle. Now he was fully aware of the woman again. She'd all but collapsed against him, panting. He turned her around and looked into her glazed eyes.

"That's how I want to make you feel."

"Yes." Her answer was soft and breathless and completely heartfelt.

Chapter Fifteen

"Strip."

The voice coming from behind took her by surprise. For a moment Heather had no idea where she was or how she'd gotten there. She remembered the men, the beautiful young sub, his orgasm. Her vagina spasmed.

"Heather. Strip for me."

She moved her hands to the top button on the front of her dress, opened it with trembling fingers. She thought back to the moment when she'd more or less collapsed against Jason.

Jason. The voice was his and he was behind her, waiting while she undressed. She tried to make her clumsy fingers go faster, the need to do as he said overwhelming her. The buttons were too tiny, the holes too small. She'd worn the wrong dress. She sighed with relief when the dress was loose enough to slip over her hips to the bedroom floor.

"Pick it up and fold it away."

"Yes." She wanted to turn around and look at him but knew better. Bending forward, she reached for the dress. She could picture what Jason saw right now. Her legs would appear longer than they were in her heels, her muscles were straining and her arse pushed out in his direction.

"Beautiful." He tried to disguise it, but she could hear the excitement in his voice, could feel it enhance her own. "Now your bra. No, don't turn around."

With shaking hands, she released the hooks. Freeing her breasts was both torture and a delight. They were heavy and heated. Her already hard nipples contracted further as air brushed over them. A soft moan escaped her lips.

"Like that, my girl?"

His voice had a teasing note, but she heard something else as well. She had to be wrong. There wouldn't be any insecurity in his voice, surely not.

"I want you to touch yourself and tell me how wet you are."

The movement was automatic. Her hand touched her panties and investigated the dampness.

"Tell me, Heather."

"I'm wet through. I'm so hot and sensitive and…"

"Take them off."

She knew exactly what he wanted and obliged. Hands on her hips, she gripped the slim piece of material and pushed them down, shimmying as she went. She listened for his reactions and a flash of triumph ran through her when she heard his hard intake of breathe. Sure in the knowledge he couldn't see her face, she smiled as she made sure her arse was up in the air when she stepped out of her panties.

"You realize I can see both sides of you, don't you girl?"

"What?"

She glanced up and for the first time noticed the full-length mirror in front of her. She stared at herself. Naked except for her hold-up stockings and her heels she looked… She couldn't deny it. She did look sexy. She looked exactly as she felt — ready, hungry, needy, open.

Shifting her eyes, she glanced at the man behind her. Fully clothed, with his hands behind his back and a closed expression on his face, he looked exactly like the Dom she'd imagined he would be. The Dom he hadn't allowed her to see yet. The thought was enough for her to lower her gaze again.

"That's it. Keep them down." Jason's voice sounded breathless. "I want you to walk to that chair and put your hands on the armrest."

Her movements felt lazy. Slowly, as if her limbs were too heavy, she moved to the chair. She placed her hands as directed and automatically spread her legs to take the strain off the muscles in her thighs.

"God, woman, you're beautiful." Heather loved hearing the appreciation in Jason's voice. How wonderful to be admired again. She'd forgotten how much she loved being looked at. She thrived on people enjoying the sight of her body. And how much better when the man looking at her couldn't quite disguise the heat in his voice.

Heather heard movement behind her, felt his presence close to her needy body. She wanted to look up, catch his image in the mirror, but stopped herself. She took a deep breath and waited. She was in a good place. She was safe. This was who she was. She'd found herself again. Tonight she might lose herself, float away for the first time in two years.

His hand on her arse was soft as he stroked her. "So soft yet so firm. You're body drives me crazy."

His voice. It traveled through her body. From her ears to her nipples and down, teasing her belly, settling in her vagina. She needed something, anything. "Jason. Please."

"That's it. Beg for it." His hand continued stroking her arse. Moving from side to side, his fingers slipped into her crack, touched her tiny hole and moved on again.

"Did you like that, Heather? Did you enjoy seeing the plug entering Leo? Did you imagine it planted inside your own arse?"

"Yes." She wanted to say more. Beg him to give her more. She needed to be claimed and couldn't find the words.

"No toys tonight." His voice took on a teasing tone. "All you're getting is my hands, my cock, my tongue, my body. Think it will be enough?"

His hands, cock, tongue, body. The words sang through her head. God yes it would be enough. It might be too much. She wanted it.

"Answer me. Think I will be enough?"

"Yes...Jason."

She'd almost slipped in the word 'Sir' and wasn't sure what had stopped her. Something deep inside her warned

132

her not to go there.

"You're enough, Jason. I want you. Please, just please."

"Spread those legs wider for me. I need more access."

Her legs shook as she moved them farther apart. The strain on her thighs was unbearable and exquisite at the same time. His hand moved again, making its way down her arse toward the need. When his fingers made contact with the wetness pooling between her legs, she groaned out loud.

"Yes."

The word escaped her as a sigh. She didn't care how desperate she might sound. She wanted him to know how needy she was. She yearned for him to act on it.

His fingers were too light, too soft. She needed friction and he wasn't giving her any.

His breath brushing her ear surprised Heather. His words barely penetrated her fevered mind.

"I saw how you reacted to orgasm denial. You loved it so much I have to give it to you now. You've left me no choice." His voice got lower again. "You're going to wait for my permission."

No. She whimpered, wasn't sure if she had objected out loud or not. She needed to come. She'd explode if she didn't. His fingers were torturing her as they slid between her wet folds, spread her juices and ignored her throbbing clit. She couldn't help herself and rocked her hips until one firm hand stopped her.

"Oh no, you don't. You're going to stand still and take it."

His voice sent shivers down her spine. The combination of heat and control intoxicated her. She gripped the armrest harder, tried to focus on standing still while his hands tortured her with pure pleasure.

Oh God, what was wrong with him? He shouldn't be doing this and yet he couldn't stop himself. He had to find a way to keep himself under control.

You love doing this. You were made to do this. The voice in the back of his mind wouldn't stay quiet. It tempted him to go further, to get out his toys, and find out exactly how much Heather could take. He ignored it. No toys, no pain. Just this. His control over the beautiful, receptive, woman. His voice, his touch, her pleasure and, ultimately, both their satisfaction.

She was wet. He dropped his hand, slid it over the inside of her thigh and rejoiced in the dampness. He'd done that. He'd brought her to these heights despite having written himself off. He brought his hand back up and brushed across her clit. A sharp intake of breath, a low moan and a tensing in her shoulders were his reward. He glanced down at her legs. The muscles were quivering but she stood still, just as he'd demanded. She was so good. *Too good for you.* The voice in his head had changed its tune and these words were much harder to ignore.

He increased the pressure on her clit and listened to her voice. There were no words. He thought he heard fragments of his name, was sure she whispered please once or twice.

"Remember. I don't want you to come."

Her head and her legs were shaking. Her hands were a deadly white from the grip she had on the chair. Her breath came out in one continuous moan. He could feel it when she neared the point of no return. It wouldn't take much more to make her come, with or without his permission. He brought her just a little bit further, watched as her back started to arch and withdrew his hands.

"No. Please. No."

She sounded close to tears.

"Please, Jason. Please, Sir."

He nearly stepped back. *Sir.* He was nobody's Sir. He didn't deserve the title. For a moment he thought she knew what she'd done. Her body stilled and she seemed to be holding her breath.

"Please, Jason. Please don't stop. I need this. I need you."

Her voice contained a trace of uncertainty before it trailed off.

He couldn't stop. Not now. None of this was her fault. He wasn't mean enough to punish her for his shortcomings. He reached for her breasts. They were perfect, slightly bigger than a handful. He stroked the soft skin, skimmed the tips of his fingers around her nipples and felt her body relax again. He loved touching her and would be happy to do it forever.

He brought his face to her neck, inhaled her smell and loved the soft brush of her hair against his cheek. He couldn't resist and licked, just below her ear and enjoyed the shiver it sent through her. Keeping his mouth and teeth busy on her neck and earlobe, he used his fingers to pinch her nipples. They were stiff and pointed. She groaned and moved her arse back, pushing it against his crotch. His cock was rock hard in his pants. He knew he should stop her from moving and punish her for her disobedience, but it felt too good. Just a little bit longer.

"I clearly remember telling you not to move."

He lifted one of his hands and slapped her arse. *Shit. No.* He wasn't doing this. The sharp intake of breath and the low moan betraying her pleasure didn't change anything. He'd promised himself he wouldn't go there. He couldn't go there.

Concentrate on the girl.

He moved his hands back to her breasts and pulled her nipples. "Like the pain, do you, beautiful?" When he pinched her nipples he made sure to use his nails.

"Jason, please. I can't. My legs."

He loved the need in her voice. He would have drawn this sensuous torture out forever, if only he trusted himself. "Please what? Tell me. Ask me for it."

"I want you, Jason. Please, I need you inside me."

He'd thought his cock was as hard as it could get. He'd been wrong. "Want me to fuck you?"

Her breathing quickened again. "Yes, please."

He almost missed her next words.

"Hard. Fuck me hard."

Taking a step back, he took a moment to just look at her. With her legs trembling and her arse up in the air, waiting for his attention, she was so beautiful. He pulled a condom from his pocket before discarding his shoes and trousers. When he was covered, he stepped closer again.

"How do you want me?"

"Hard. Deep."

She sounded as needy as he felt. Deep and hard inside her he could give her without reservations. But this time he wanted to make it last. He wanted it slow and long and, yes, torturous. He wanted to tease both of them. But most of all, he wanted her even more needy, begging, squirming for him. Even if he couldn't get himself to make her submit to him, he wanted to see how far she'd allow him to go, how much she would give him.

He couldn't look at her enough, standing there, shaking with her desperate need for him. She was just the right height in those shoes.

"Bend forward a bit more, Heather. Open yourself up for me."

Her obedience was instant. She moved and her wet cunt almost touched his cock. He put his hands on her hips. A slight push forward had the tip of his cock between her folds. It took all his restraint, but he stopped himself from pushing in all the way.

"I'm going to fuck you, Heather. I'm going to fuck you hard and you're going to continue holding on to your orgasm. You're going to stop yourself from coming until I tell you differently. Think you can do that?"

Jason's cock registered the moment she tensed.

"I, Jason. I'm not..." She relaxed again, a moan escaping her lips. "Yes, yes, I can. Please, just fuck me."

Oh yes, he looked forward to torturing both of them. Excruciatingly slowly, Jason pushed his full length into her warmth. When his balls connected with her body, he stopped and squeezed her hips, reminding her to keep still.

"Feel me, Heather. Do you feel how hard I am for you?

Do you know what you do to me? Just your smell, the way you smile, your soft lips, your teasing tongue. They drive me crazy, make me hard whenever I'm around you."

Her vagina contracted around his cock in reaction to the sound of his voice. Ever so slowly he withdrew his cock until only his tip remained inside her and stopped moving again. Her frustrated groan was music to his ears. He loved all the noises she made and her total lack of shame about making her needs known. With one hard push, he entered her again. No more softly, softly. As soon as he was in, he withdrew. Pushing and pulling hard and furious a few times before coming to a complete stop again. At this rate he'd be driving himself as crazy as he wanted to make her.

"I'm going to move my hands, Heather and you're going to remember to keep still. Just stand there and take everything I give to you."

Heather shook her head from side to side but her answer was a soft and panted "Yes." God, who needed toys or ropes or any other implement if you had a woman this willing to hand over control? His hands found her breasts again and cupped them, squeezing her nipples between his thumbs and index fingers. Her reaction was immediate, a moan and a sharp contraction around his cock. But she didn't try to move her body.

Continuing to tease and torture her beautiful and heavy breasts with his hands, he introduced nails to her nipples before starting to move again. He wasn't sure how long he'd be able to keep going. His plan had been to draw this out, bring her to the edge a few more times only to bring her down again before allowing either of them to come. With his own need building faster than he'd expected, he couldn't wait. He needed that release, needed to hear her, see her, feel her come. One hand came down and found her clit. He rubbed the swollen ball of sensitivity in time with his ever hardening thrusts into her heat.

"Jason, too much. I can't, Jason, please."

Oh how rewarding to hear Heather pleading. It brought

him closer to the edge. He loved hearing her ask, no beg, for what he, only he, could give her. Just a little longer. He didn't want it to stop. He wanted to stay right here all night. Just at this moment, feeling these sensations, hearing her pleas in his ear. This had to be as close to heaven as he could ever hope to come.

Now. He needed to come right...

"Now, Heather. Come with me now."

She was shaking, squeezing him, moving with him. His balls contracted so hard it almost hurt and his release shot through him while Heather's vagina milked his cock with her own uncontrollable contractions. *Heaven*.

When he slipped out of her, Heather all but collapsed. Somewhere he found the strength to pick her up and carry her to his bed. As soon as he'd gotten rid of the condom, he fell down on the bed beside her and gathered her in his arms.

"That was perfect."

Heather's words were only a whisper but held a world of feeling.

"I think orgasmic is the word you're looking for." He smiled. "Sleep, princess."

He smiled at her vague murmurings. As he pulled Heather close, he looked forward to spending another night with Heather in his arms and ignored the feelings of unease growing in the pit of his stomach.

Chapter Sixteen

Light filtered through her closed eyes, creating colors. She didn't want to open them yet, wasn't quite ready for the day to start. She needed to think about something, but she couldn't remember exactly what. Heather stretched her body and groaned. Oh dear, she was stiff. The muscles in her legs hurt.

The images flashed back. Bent over the chair, her hands gripping the armrest, her legs spread. Heat, pleasure and even some pain and oh, God, it had been so good. He'd been right. She remembered the word — if it was a word — *orgasmic*. Last night had been all of that and so much more. Jason.

She opened her eyes and looked to her side. She was alone. Where was he? Why wasn't he in bed with her? The satisfied and relaxed feeling she'd woken up with evaporated to be replaced by a sense of loneliness and worry. Yesterday she'd woken up in his arms and the feeling had been amazing. Not scary or strange, as she'd feared, but right and safe. This waking up alone was both scary and strange.

Heather looked around the bedroom. She really was alone and couldn't hear any noises from the bathroom either. Where had he gone? What did this mean? Her mind drifted back to the night before. It had been so good. She sighed as her body reacted to the memory. Her nipples tightened, a small, pleasurable spasm teased her vagina. And yet, she couldn't put her finger on it, but there had been moments when things hadn't felt quite right. She remembered the doubts flittering through her enjoyment. There'd been something about Jason, as if he'd been holding back. Her mind drifted back even further. There'd been something wrong yesterday afternoon as well. He'd seemed angry, upset. In fact, emotionally, he'd been all over the place yesterday.

Her mood dropped. All the feelings of pleasure and satisfaction left her. Suddenly her body was only sore, her leg muscles screaming. She shook her head as she felt tears burning in her eyes. She wasn't going to cry, had nothing to cry about. All she'd done was sleep with the man, twice. Okay, it had been amazing and life-changing and... She had to stop thinking and find Jason, talk to him. She could be wrong, she probably was.

She looked around again. She needed something to wear. Facing Jason naked, or even in the dress she'd worn last night, would be too hard. Her eyes fell on a bright red housecoat, draped over a chair. She'd no idea where it had come from, but it would do the job.

The bathroom mirror told a story of its own. Staring back at her was a satisfied woman. Her hair was wild, her lips looked bruised. She smiled at her reflection. Whatever happened next, she couldn't deny she'd been well fucked. God, he'd known exactly how to push all her buttons. She'd been shameless and had thrived on it.

She would have loved a long hot shower. Her mind jumped. A very long and very hot shower, with Jason preferably. That wasn't going to happen by the looks of things. She borrowed some toothpaste. A quick brush with her finger, a splash of water on her face — her hair would have to wait until she went back to her own rooms. It would have to do.

Walking back into the bedroom she came face-to-face with herself again. The full-length mirror. Heather's mind flashed back. Her image, shamelessly bent over that chair, her breasts hanging down, her arse in the air and Jason behind her, fully clothed so powerful and so in charge. She stopped. *Had* he been in charge? There'd been moments when he was, she remembered them so well. The way his voice and his demands had made her body react without any physical contact. His fingers pinching her nipples, that one slap on her backside. But there'd also been those other moments, the ones she'd almost managed to ignore last night, when he'd appeared to be holding back, when he'd sounded angry.

What she wouldn't give to be able to talk to Darren for a moment. He would have known. She stopped. Waited. Surely there'd be a stab of pain? A flash of guilt? Nothing. There was a sense of 'if only' but it didn't hurt, not the way she would have expected. She loved her husband with all her heart, would always love him, no matter what happened in the future. But it was as if he'd found a new place in her heart.

She could almost visualize it, Darren moving from all of her heart into a corner of it. A place forever his, where he would stand guard over all the memories they'd created together, where he would be ready to help her when doubt overwhelmed her. She didn't need to talk to him. She knew only too well what he would say. He'd told her before he died, he'd told her in her dreams, and he'd allowed Jason to take his place in her dream recently. She had his blessing. She might not be sure of anything else but didn't doubt he would approve of her actions. If only she had a way of knowing Jason's thoughts. She hated this insecurity and was afraid to go and look for answers.

She shook her head, annoyed with herself for allowing her mind to go into overdrive. Maybe he just hadn't been able to go back to sleep and had gotten up, afraid of waking her. She didn't know him well enough to determine whether or not his behavior last night had been typical. He didn't know her well enough to know what she wanted or needed and might have been conflicted. Her bloody meltdown was bound to have made him weary and careful. Besides, she'd only been here for three days. What did she expect? A declaration of undying love? She had to stop thinking and find Jason. She sighed. Underwear would have been nice but she'd no idea where her clothes had gone. She felt somewhat vulnerable in only this rather short robe. And she had to stop stalling.

She turned away from the mirror, walked to the door and opened it.

The living room appeared to be empty too. She glanced over the breakfast, set out on the table to her right. She couldn't think of anything less appealing than food right now.

A draft of air teased the skin on her bare legs. The doors on her left were open, the balcony bright in the morning sunlight. And there he was. Standing at the railing, gazing at the Atlantic. He seemed lost in thought, with no idea she was here, looking at him, so she took a moment to drink him in.

A small smile touched her lips, despite her anxiety. There hadn't been time to study him in detail. They'd been too fevered together. Sure, he'd had his chance to study her last night. But other than one glance in the mirror while he was still fully dressed, her eyes had been down or closed. He made for a gorgeous picture, especially now, in nothing but a pair of boxers. He was glorious — not very big, but a good head taller than her, with wide shoulders tapering down to a slim waste. His legs were long and well defined — he was a beautiful specimen. His always unruly hair stood up in tufts and made her smile. From the back at least he looked as well fucked as she did. The tiny dart of lust rushing through her body took her by surprise. Even looking at him had her hot and bothered and that was fine, except that it wouldn't be if he'd changed his mind.

She shook her head, determined not to go over all her doubts and fears again. No time like the present to take the bull by the horns. Those clichés existed for a reason. She took a few hesitant steps and stopped on the threshold leading to the balcony.

"Hey there."

The words shook him out of his thoughts and forced him to turn away from the view in front of him.

"Hey there, yourself. Sleep well?"

He sounded like a dork. Why didn't he do what all his instincts told him he should be doing? Why didn't he walk to her, lift her chin and kiss her? He should still have been in bed with her. Should never have left her to wake up alone. God only knew what she might be thinking.

"Yes, very well, thank you."

He hated the insecurity in her voice, detested himself for putting it there.

"I missed you when I woke up."

He looked at her. So beautiful wearing only the housecoat he'd left out for her. He knew she wasn't wearing anything else. He'd sent her clothes to housekeeping himself. She was beautiful and vulnerable. He didn't want to hurt her and was convinced he'd already done so last night. If only he'd been able to restrain himself, to keep the Dom out of their sex.

"I've, ah, ordered some breakfast for us. It's inside but we can have it here if you want."

She tilted her head, as if trying to figure out what he was saying, as if his words hadn't been clear.

"I'm not hungry, Jason. But I'll have a cup of coffee wherever you want to have it."

Grateful for the few moments of respite, he nodded and walked past her into his apartment, careful not to touch Heather. He'd have to talk to her. It wouldn't be fair to let her think she'd done something wrong. But he couldn't tell her everything. He couldn't confess he was afraid she'd see all his failings if they went any further. Afraid she'd lose any respect she might have for him if she ever found out what was wrong with him. Most of all he was afraid voicing his doubts out loud would make them irrevocably true.

Picking up the large breakfast tray, he turned around and walked back. "You'll have to eat something, Heather. It's been a rather tiring night."

Her weak smile proved what he'd already known. He wasn't being funny, and only making her more confused by the minute.

"Listen."

"No."

He recognized the exact moment she made her decision.

"You listen. I don't know what's wrong, Jason, but if you regret what happened last night…" She blinked and looked off into the distance before turning back to him. "Or if what we've shared is enough for you, just let me know."

"No." He wanted to scream the word. He'd no idea how to do this. How could he explain enough to stop her from blaming herself without baring all of his soul to her? "Sit down. I'll try to explain."

"That's not necessary. I'm going home today anyway. I've only been here for three days. You don't owe me an explanation — or anything else."

Her voice was steady, but he could still hear the pain.

Shit. He'd forgotten she was supposed to leave today. She couldn't leave. He'd never be able to fix this, to come up with a workable solution, if she went.

"You're leaving?" Without thinking, he poured them both a cup of coffee and handed her one.

"That has been the plan all along, remember?"

"Yes, of course I remember. I'd hoped you would want to stay on, until after the party at least."

He saw the frown forming and the first signs of real anger replacing the doubt on her face.

"You could have fooled me." Her voice grew harsher. "After all, you couldn't even bring yourself to stay in bed with me this morning. You made me wake up alone after everything we did together last night." She shook her head. "And now you expect me to believe you want me to stay? Really?"

Her face was so expressive. The change from anger back to doubt mesmerized him.

144

"Please tell me you're not playing games with me."

No, he'd been wrong. It wasn't doubt he was seeing, it was pain. He'd hurt her and continued to do so even now. He'd been so afraid of causing her pain and in the process of trying to avoid that, he'd made her feel rejected.

"No. I'm not playing games. I'm sorry I left before you were awake. I just..."

"Just what?"

"Needed to think."

"About what, Jason?"

"About me, you, last night."

He knew he had to give her something, even if he couldn't bring himself to share it all. "I was afraid I'd gone too far last night." The words exploded from his mouth. "I shouldn't have gone as far as I did without talking to you first. I was afraid you'd wake up regretting your surrender to me. I thought you might wake up thinking about Darren and disappointed to find me next to you."

He allowed the silence to settle. Sipping his coffee, he eyed the full Irish breakfast congealing on the table. He had to give her time to think about his words.

"And yet you'd no such doubts when I woke up in your bed yesterday morning."

"That was different." He answered the question before she could ask it. "Our first night together wasn't as intense as last night. I don't know. It felt different to me this morning. I was scared." Every single word he'd said was true. It just wasn't the whole truth. "I want you to stay."

He wanted to add 'please' but knew it wouldn't be fair. He had no right to ask this of her, never mind beg it of her.

He took the cup she held out to him and refilled it. There were so many things he still wanted to say, but he stayed quiet. If he couldn't tell her the whole truth he had to stop here and hope it would be enough.

"I can't stay."

The pain stabbing him shouldn't have surprised him, but it did.

"I only packed for three days." She tried to smile but didn't quite pull it off. "And I will be back in four days anyway." She looked at him and shook her head. "What, you thought I was about to walk out on your party and our contract?"

"No, yes. I wasn't thinking that far ahead."

"You know what, Jason. I'm not convinced you've been thinking at all. You're confusing me."

Her gaze turned to the ocean and he had no problem imagining the turmoil in her mind.

"Okay, I'll be honest with you. These two nights with you have been better than I thought they could possibly be. I didn't think I'd be able to lose myself like that again, not without Darren, and I'm grateful you showed me I still can." She frowned when he opened his mouth to interrupt her. "No, I want you to listen. I always had to go back home today. I didn't come prepared for a two-week stay or for a party. I had hoped we might continue what we started after my return. I thought there was more for us to explore. But I guess I was wrong."

"Heather."

"I'm not done yet." The anger disappeared from her voice. "Listen, I'm grateful you've shown me I'm ready to face the world and life again. I enjoyed my two nights with you and loved submitting to you last night."

His shock at the words must have been visible. Her eyes were filled with questions as she continued.

"But I'm not strong or stable enough to play the will he-won't he game with you. I can't deal with you running hot and cold on me. I know I've been far more honest with you than you're willing to be with me and it hurts."

Sadness swept over her face and tore at his heart.

"So I'm going to go home and use the next four days to try and get my balance back. When I return, the serious work starts. We'll have to be on the top of our game if we're going to make this party work. I'll gather myself together and I promise I'll be the professional you need when I return."

He hated himself. She went out of her way to make this as painless as possible, despite him creating problems everywhere she turned.

"What if I...we...don't want to be just professional when you come back?"

Her sigh seemed to come from her toes. "I don't know. We'll find a way to make it work. We're grown-ups, supposed to be able to control ourselves."

He wanted to object, but knew he'd run out of excuses. She was right.

She stood up, looking deflated.

"I'm going to pack, say goodbye to Amber and drive home. I'll find you before I leave."

He watched as she walked away, admired the beautiful legs as they took her farther from him with every step. His mouth was working, trying to find the words needed to make her stay, but he couldn't make himself verbalize them. *Heather*. He'd ruined it. Not because his fears had come true, but because he'd allowed those fears to stop him from being who he was, who she needed. He was a fool and a coward and he'd no idea how to fix the mess he'd created.

Chapter Seventeen

Pulling off the motorway, Heather breathed a sigh of relief. Nearly home. It had been a long drive, not made any easier by all the thoughts running through her head. Five hours alone with her memories and doubts had not been the best idea. Of course, not leaving would have been worse.

As she turned into Phoenix Park, her thoughts went back to her last hour in The Blowhole. She smiled as she saw the deer off in the distance near the column where half the population of Ireland had gathered years ago to see the Pope. She could do with some divine intervention right now.

Going to say goodbye to Amber before leaving had been a good idea and not only because she'd grown fond of the young woman over the past few days. She ran over their short conversation again. It had been reassuring to hear Amber say Hector had been worried about Jason's behavior for a while.

It helped to know she wasn't to blame for whatever Jason's problem might be. On the other hand, it hurt that he wouldn't just tell her what was wrong. She'd kept no secrets from him. She'd opened up about Darren. She'd had a meltdown in his arms and submitted to him. Had it been unreasonable to expect him to be honest with her in return? Maybe it was unrealistic to expect him to share his deepest feelings after such a short time.

She had no doubts about her decision to come home. She needed some time to sort out her feelings, to try and figure out what she wanted. She hoped it was also what Jason needed.

She remembered what he'd looked like when she'd dropped by his office before leaving. There'd been no fight left in him. He'd tried to talk to her and she'd cut him off. She'd said all she needed to say. The ball was in his court now. He would have to decide if he trusted her enough to open up, wanted her enough to be completely honest. Still, she did regret the short and chaste kiss she'd given him before walking away. It would have been good to feel his arms around her one more, maybe last, time. She felt safe there, with her cheek pressed against his chest, listening to his heartbeat. She'd denied both of them that moment of respite.

Easy or not, it had been the only thing to do. Whatever did or didn't happen next, she liked the man or maybe, if she was honest, more than liked him. She would love to at least stay friends. And that meant not complicating things even further by adding mixed messages of her own to the ones he'd been sending.

She turned into the drive and smiled up at her house. Regardless of how she felt about leaving Jason, coming home was a pleasure. She got out of her car and glanced around the garden before opening the door and stepping inside.

* * * *

A few hours and a long nap later, Heather felt refreshed. She knew better than to worry about things she couldn't change. She couldn't influence Jason and whatever his issues were. She would deal with herself. She needed to get a handle on her own feelings and try to figure out what she wanted from life. Jason was only a small part of what she needed to think about.

Walking into her office, she noticed the blinking light on the phone. She stared at it for a moment. Who would have left her a voice message on that number? Didn't everybody have her mobile number? Sinking into the comfy chair, she picked up the phone and nearly dropped it when she heard the voice.

"Heather."

Her heart stopped.

"You never got back to me after our little talk. I'm disappointed."

Him again. Why couldn't he leave her alone? She didn't need this, not now.

"The offer's still open, of course. But, the longer you wait, the tougher the consequences."

There was a pause, as if he'd been waiting for a reaction, before the arrogant voice continued.

"You know I'm right. You need it. And make no mistake… As long as I want you, nobody else will go near you. I'll make sure of that."

Heather stared at the phone in disbelief. Was he for real? She wouldn't go along with his plans for her, ever.

"Anyway," the voice sounded cruel now, "I suspect we'll be meeting soon. I'm looking forward to it."

Anger surged through her. The self-important, arrogant prick. How dare he? He had to be mad if he thought she would ever turn to him. Even when Darren had still been alive, they'd rarely spent time in his company. She should have been clearer when they'd spoke. She'd do better the next time. She wouldn't leave any room for doubt if he approached her again.

She sighed. He was a distraction. Irritating, but not what she needed to concentrate on right now. He and his arrogance were pulling her away from her real problem. She had to figure out what to do about Jason and how she'd survive having to work with him again in four days' time.

She opened her laptop. She'd write to Darren again.

Darren, my heart

I can't stop writing to you. It doesn't compare to talking with you, but it's the best I have and I need your advice. I'm all over the place. I'm not sure what I feel or how I feel about what I might be feeling.

I thought it would be easier. I didn't think it would be this hard confessing to you that I found myself attracted to Jason over the past few days. There, I've said it. And it's true. He did things to me. He made me feel things I didn't expect to feel again. Just looking at him brought back sensations I hadn't felt since you died. When we got together he took me places I never thought I'd revisit.

I know I promised I wouldn't give up on lust or sex or even love — and I meant it. But now that I'm home, doubts are creeping in. Did you really mean you wanted me to leave you behind? Did you envision me submitting again or did you mean I should allow myself to play occasionally? You were the first and I was sure you would be the last. And yet, with Jason, it was automatic. He spoke and my body reacted before my mind processed his words. It felt good, Darren. I loved submitting again. I mean, I loved submitting to Jason.

And now I'm back home, alone. I left him because I don't know what to make of him. He's hiding something. I don't know if it's big or small, if it's just in his mind or a real issue. All I know is that I'm not strong enough to sit back and hope he'll change his mind at some point in the future. If I allow him to break me I might never put myself back together again.

I told him I'd be back on Monday, and I intend to keep my word. It's business, and you taught me well. But it scares me. I won't be able to lose my attraction to him in just four days. It will be as strong as it was this morning. If he makes a move, will I be able to say no? Should I? He makes me feel things I want to explore, Darren. I think I could fall in love with him given half a chance. I know he could shatter me if I allow him to keep on playing games with me. Tell me what to do. I'm lost again.

* * * *

"Hector." Just what he didn't need. "I'm sorry, but not now. I'm too busy."

Jason waved at his desk before he realized the surface

held nothing. No papers, his computer had gone to stand-by, no other people. Nothing to indicate he'd been doing anything other than staring out of the window. Not that it mattered. His friend didn't give the desk a glance while he walked into the office and dropped into a chair.

"What the fuck is wrong with you, man?"

Whoa. Hector didn't use language like that, didn't go into full attack mode, ever.

With a sinking heart, Jason realized this was it. He wouldn't be able to brush the Dom off, not this time. He'd run out of hiding places.

"You allowed her to walk away. Why?"

Just because he knew it wasn't going to work didn't mean he wouldn't give it a try anyway.

"It's what we agreed, Hector. Heather will be back next week."

"Rubbish." The man shook his head. "I know she was supposed to leave today. What I want to know is why she's staying away for four days if all she needs is fresh clothes? There's a sudden shortage of shops in the West of Ireland?"

Jason felt himself being pushed into a corner and couldn't see any escape routes. "No, of course not. I, Jaysus man, it's personal."

"Yes, you told me you don't want to talk about whatever it is you've been worrying about. And under normal circumstances that would be fine. This isn't normal."

"Of course it's normal. What do you mean it isn't?"

"I saw the two of you together. I saw how she reacted to you when you danced, when you watched Roger and Leo." Hector paused, apparently considering his next words. "And for the first time in over a month, I saw you looking like yourself. You've been acting like a dog without its favorite bone for weeks now. I noticed, Amber noticed. Hell, I think everybody here noticed."

That hurt. He'd thought he'd been able to hide his doubts. He'd known people had been surprised when he'd announced he wouldn't be doing the demonstrations for a while, but had failed to recognize... He stopped himself. He hadn't wanted to recognize that people were surprised and maybe even worried about his behavior. *Shit*.

But what could he do? He couldn't explain what had happened to himself, never mind to anyone else. Trying to explain could cost him everything. He couldn't expect people to work for a Dom no longer able to dominate. They wouldn't trust him anymore. It would create insecurities. He'd lose his business on top of all he'd already lost.

Hector just sat there, looking at him, waiting for him to make up his mind. It was a Dom trick. Jason knew it all too well and didn't appreciate having it used on him. He was restless, needed to move, to get away from the gaze that wouldn't let him go. He pushed out of his chair and started pacing. Up and down his office, five steps, turn, five more steps turn. And those eyes never left him. Sitting back in his chair, his hand underneath his chin, Hector said nothing, didn't move a muscle, just followed him with his eyes, waiting, like a predator stalking its prey.

"I know what you're doing, you bastard. Your tricks won't work on me. I'm not some sub you can dominate into revealing all their secrets."

"No, you're not. But then, are you sure you're still a Dom?"

Jason's heart skipped a few beats. He'd been sure he'd managed to keep his insecurities hidden. Hector was just guessing. He had to be. There was no way he could know. Jason dropped back in his chair and looked at his friend again. He expected to see pity and maybe some amusement or commiseration and found none. He saw concern and interest. He saw a man who wanted to help him, the man he'd been pushing away every time he got too close to the truth. The man across from him was probably one of the few persons he could trust with his secret.

Jason lowered his gaze, perfectly imitating the sub he wasn't, and talked at his desktop.

"You're right. You've hit the nail on the head. I don't

think I'm a Dom anymore. I've lost it. The drive is gone, has been for months now. The past few weeks? Doing those exhibitions only frustrated me. It felt like an act. It wasn't doing anything for me."

He chanced a quick glance at Hector and saw nothing but the man's undivided attention.

"You don't understand, Hector," he spoke as if he'd been interrupted, "I didn't even get excited when I played with those subs. I went through the motions, played a part without ever feeling it. A month ago I decided I couldn't continue. Pretending tore me apart. I knew sooner or later others would catch on to the fact I wasn't in the game anymore. I needed out before I turned myself into a complete joke."

"Jason," Hector's voice was soft and completely non-judgmental, "you must have known withdrawing would attract more attention than pretending ever could."

He hated the man for being so smart and perceptive. Hector wasn't going to let him get away with anything. He knew the Dom wouldn't leave until he'd heard the full story.

"Yes. Of course I did. I lost my drive, not my mind." He really didn't want to go on but forced himself regardless. "It was too painful. Every single time I took one of those subs to the play area, I could feel another piece of me breaking away. It felt like rubbing my nose in my own misery. I'm not a masochist. I just couldn't do it anymore."

"And so you didn't." Hector's voice was calm. "I get that. It may surprise you, but quite a few of us face doubts every now and again. You think I didn't want to run when Amber decided to throw herself at me?" Now it was Hector's turn to look away. "I thought, hell there are days I still think she's too young—too young for me and too young for the commitment she's made. She knew nothing when she met me, was little more than a virgin." He fell silent and seemed lost in his memories. "I tried to keep things simple, vanilla. I spent hours trying to convince myself I could live without the dynamic, that discarding an integral part of me would be better than dragging her into my world.

"What happened?" Jason whispered his question, afraid anything louder would stop Hector's flow.

"Amber happened. She saw right through me and wouldn't stand for it. I think her words were something like, if she couldn't be with all of me she'd rather not be with me at all. She was on the verge of walking away. I'd offered to discard an important part of who I am for her and she threw it back in my face." His face brightened. "God, I love that woman."

Thoughts chased each other through Jason's mind. What had Heather said? That she knew she'd been far more honest with him than he'd been willing to be with her. Those had been the words she'd used to show him her pain. He hadn't been able to tell her, but maybe, if he talked to Hector, confessed it all, he'd be able to work it out, find a way to fix everything he'd broken.

"There's more, Hector."

"I thought there might be. Just tell me, man. I promise, nothing you can say will shock me.

"Losing the drive to dominate was bad enough, but I managed to deal with it."

He saw the look on Hector's face.

"Okay, I fooled myself into believing I could deal with it. But two nights ago, when I allowed Heather to fall apart?"

"What. Tell me, Jason, what did that mean to you?"

"Don't you see? It proved I'd been right to distrust myself. It was bad enough I'd lost the will to dominate. Heather's breakdown showed me my instincts were gone too. I should have seen it coming. I should have been able to recognize the signs and get her out of there before it was too late." He could hear the pain in his own voice, felt tears burning behind his eyes. "Don't you see? Losing my drive has been a blessing. Without it there's no risk of me harming anyone."

He looked at his desktop again. It was still as empty as it

had been when Hector arrived. It would have been easier if there'd been something there to distract him. He wanted to look at the man facing him and couldn't bring himself to do it. He'd said it all. His secrets were out, his fears shared. What sort of damage had he done?

"Jason. Look at me."

He reluctantly raised his gaze and fell into a well of compassion and friendship.

"I've listened to you. I understand everything you say. I get why you believe you've failed."

Relief washed over him. To be understood. To not be thought crazy. It was so much more than he'd expected.

"And I know you couldn't be more wrong."

"What?"

"Tell me what you did when Heather fell apart, Jason."

"I took her away from the crowd into an empty room. I held her in my lap until she was calm again. I apologized for not getting her out earlier and she said…"

"What did she say?"

"She said it wasn't my fault she'd waited too long before letting me know it was too much." Jason shook his head. He might as well have been hearing the words for the first time, even though she'd told him time and again. "She told me not to blame myself for her failure to safe-word early enough."

"So, let me see if I get this. You brought her there because she wanted to go?"

All Jason could do was nod.

"You took her away when she indicated it was too much?"

"Yes."

"You then gave her aftercare, told her you were sorry, listened to her tell you it wasn't your fault and decided to blame yourself anyway?"

He couldn't bring himself to answer again.

"Anybody ever tell you that maybe you're too far up your own arse, Jason?"

For the first time since waking up, he relaxed and smiled.

"No. But I guess they should have." He didn't know if he wanted to kiss Hector or slap himself. "God, I've been such a self-absorbed fool."

And self-destructive. He'd ruined it for no good reason. He'd been so focused on his own misery, he'd pushed away the woman who'd shown him the way back to what he'd thought lost forever. The first woman he'd ever loved. A woman he could love again. *No*, he might as well continue with the honesty. A woman he'd started falling in love with the moment she stepped into his office. The pain was back, sweeping away all the relief he'd felt a moment ago.

"What have I done? I've destroyed it before it had a chance to begin."

He didn't understand Hector's smile. Now, of all times.

"If you'd truly destroyed it I don't think she would have agreed to come back next week. Call her, Jason. Be a man and talk to her. Explain. She's not going to condemn you anymore than I did." He got out of his chair and turned to leave. "And for God's sake, next time you have a problem, will you please just talk to me?"

He would have said thank you. He would have hugged Hector, promised him a pay-rise, the world, anything he wanted, but he couldn't spare the time while he typed a message into his phone.

Chapter Eighteen

I'm sorry. I'm a fool. I need to talk. Can we talk?

Heather stared at her phone in disbelief. She'd only been home a few hours and *now* he wanted to talk? What could he possibly have to say that couldn't have been said this morning? Did she want to set herself up for more confusion, more pain?

I guess. Not on the phone though. Hate phone calls.

Let him work that one out. She'd done her best before she left. She'd given him every opportunity to explain himself and he'd refused. She didn't owe him anything. There was no reason she had to make this easy for him.
Blast. Of course she wanted to talk this out with him. If they didn't, this whole mess would continue to eat at her, make her feel vulnerable just when she thought she might be getting her strength back. Still, it was his move now. She'd wait — the phone pinged — but not for long apparently.

Video call? I'd drive to Dublin but can't leave right now. Please?

Video call? She might be able to cope if she could see him. She hated talking to people she couldn't see — always had. When Darren had still been alive, he'd taken care of all the over-the-phone business. The video wouldn't be as good as being in the same room but, given the situation, being physically close might create more problems than it solved.

Her phone made noises again.

I'll come to Dublin if you want me to. Fuck the business. I need to talk to you.

NO. Stay where you are. We'll video call.

She wasn't sure what to think of the fact he was in such a hurry to talk. He'd said he was sorry and willing to come to Dublin, so maybe he wanted to fix things. On the other hand, he might just want to end their contract in a courteous manner. Maybe she'd pushed him too hard this morning. She wasn't sure. It had been too long since she had had to worry about the dynamics in any sort of relationship.

Two hours from now ok? Have a meeting first.

Two hours from now would be ten.

Ten will be fine. I'll be ready.

Thanks.

Two hours to kill—the idea made her restless. She needed to move. She would drive herself crazy if she spent the next two hours trying to figure out what might be going on in Jason's head.

She left her study and wandered through her home, taking in her surroundings one room at a time. Memories assaulted her and for the first time in eighteen months, she didn't try to squash them down. She relished the pictures forming in her head.

She saw herself cuddled up with Darren on the long L-shaped couch reading or watching TV together. Her fingers trailed over the spines of the numerous books on the shelves as she shuddered at the thought of one day having to move them all. She remembered the parties they had thrown, the times when the house had been filled with happy people, good food and more often than not, steamy

159

encounters.

She moved along, lost in her thoughts until her feet brought her to Darren's old study—the only room in the house she hadn't redecorated at all. Every other room had slowly transformed over time. They were hers now, no longer theirs. Not because she'd been trying to change things but because she'd been living here. In this room she'd made sure to leave everything the way it had always been. Whenever she walked into this study she could almost believe he was still with her or could come back at any moment.

She stepped behind his desk and opened and closed drawers without thinking, until her eyes fell on the envelope. She froze. Her mind stopped wandering. This was why she was here. She hadn't consciously known it, but every step she'd taken since she'd left her own study had brought her closer to this moment.

Her mind flew back and the pictures were so vivid they brought tears to her eyes. Darren in bed, about four months before he died. Both of them had known they were heading for the end and they'd both tried not to let that completely destroy the remaining time.

She'd been out for a few hours. Darren had insisted she spend some time away from his sickbed every day. When she'd come back, he'd told her to sit down by his bed and listen to him. That's when he'd made her promise she wouldn't stop living. He'd told her she was allowed to grieve—but not forever. She remembered the smile on his face when she'd told him she would never love again, never mind submit to somebody else. His response was still fresh in her mind.

"See this letter, my girl. I want you to put it in my desk and leave it there until you're done grieving. Read it when your heart and body have woken up again."

She picked up the envelope and fingered it. Was this that moment? Should she open this last letter now? She'd been tempted to open it so many times in those first months after

Darren died, convinced she'd never reach the stage he'd described and unwilling to risk never reading his last words to her. But she'd been the good girl he would have expected her to be and had left the letter sealed. She had stepped out of her grief now. She'd even submitted to somebody other than Darren.

She looked away. Now that the moment was here, she was reluctant to look at those words. This letter represented Darren's last gift to her. Once she'd read this letter, there would be no more surprises.

She glanced at her watch. Half an hour until her talk with Jason. She'd stay here, in Darren's room. This was her safe place. Whatever happened next, she had the best chance of dealing with the consequences here. Logging herself onto the computer, she knew she was stalling, putting off the inevitable.

Her fingers were shaking when she opened the envelope and her breath caught when she saw the sheet of paper. The letter was short but—tears came to her eyes—handwritten. She stared at the lines filled with blue ink, not even trying to read the words, just drinking in the familiar sight of his nearly illegible writing. She stroked the paper, gliding her fingers over it with reverence. She would have drawn the moment out forever if the need to find out what he'd written hadn't been so overwhelming.

Heather, my one and only,

When you read this I will have been dead for a while. I don't know for how long but I hope you didn't allow too much time to pass before you found your way back to life again. I'm sure you did find your way back though. If you hadn't, you wouldn't be reading these words.

I also hope you found somebody you're attracted to, somebody who wants and needs you, somebody you can submit to.

All I ever wanted is for you to be happy. I hope and like to believe I brought you happiness while I could.

I want you to remember that being able to love again doesn't mean you love me any less, just as me telling you to open your heart to someone else doesn't mean I don't love you. Whatever you do next, wherever you go and whoever you give yourself to, I will always be a part of you. Live, my dear, love. Do it for me, but most of all, do it for you.

Always yours, Darren

When the first tears hit the paper in her hands she shoved the letter away. She didn't want these words blurred. She wiped her cheeks with her hand and sighed. *Oh, Darren.* He'd known her so well. She'd needed this. No, she hadn't felt guilty about her nights with Jason, but whatever reservations she might have had were gone, erased by her husband's final words to her.

With a shock she realized her tears didn't stem from sadness. Yes, she still missed Darren, but she was ready to look beyond him. Her time with Jason had shown her she was still who she'd always been. It was what she had needed to take the next step. Even if her time with Jason was over — she sighed, she could admit to herself now that she hoped it wasn't — she'd always be grateful to him for showing her she could still laugh, enjoy herself and find joy in sharing her body with another.

As if on cue, the computer dinged and a Skype message flared on the screen. Jason...

Shit.

She'd been crying. He could see the wetness on her cheeks. Had he caused her pain again?

He'd planned an opening speech, had it all figured out in his head. He'd apologize and explain, tell her what he'd told Hector and be completely honest.

Just the sight of her and those tear-stained cheeks robbed him of his well-rehearsed words.

"Heather, what's wrong?"

Her smile took him by surprise.

"Nothing. I'm fine — great, in fact."

He waited, hoping she'd tell him more before realizing he'd no right to want that, never mind expect it. Seeing her face-to-face, even if it had to be on a screen, brought home to him how stupid he'd been. He'd been willing to let her walk away just because of his misplaced sense of pride.

"Jason?"

His name snapped him out of his thoughts.

"I'm sure you didn't set this video call up just so you could stare at me."

"No, I didn't. It would have been reason enough though, under different circumstances."

He was grateful when she smiled at him.

"I enjoy flattery as much as the next person, but I need more from you right now."

He snapped out of his fantasies and gathered his thoughts. Okay, he could do this. Heather didn't intimidate him as much as Hector had, and surely the second time would be easier than the first. Jason gathered his courage, took a deep breath and talked.

"Heather, I'm sorry. I'm a fool and a coward and I should not have let you leave without trying to explain what has been going on with me."

She just looked at him, waiting for more.

"I... Shit, this is hard. It started about four months ago..."

He talked. Told her about the moment he'd realized dominating his subs wasn't enjoyable anymore, the day he'd decided pretending would end up killing him and his decision to stop all demonstrations.

"I just couldn't do it anymore. Every time I tried just re-enforced my sense of failure. It hurt too much. My whole sense of self, an integral part of me, seemed to be dissolving before my eyes. I refused to face the pain after a while."

Heather didn't say a word, didn't ask questions, didn't try to interrupt. He saw no surprise or shock in her gaze, never mind the contempt he'd feared. The understanding he did see gave him the courage to continue. The hard part was still to come.

"When you walked into my office, my body reacted for the first time in months. Your lowered gaze that evening heralded the return of all those feelings I'd imagined dead and it scared the shit out of me. I didn't trust that part of me anymore. If it could just disappear, how could I be sure it was real? What if I went with it and it just stopped again?"

He saw Heather open her mouth.

"No, please let me finish."

Her nod was all the encouragement he needed.

"When you broke down after we watched Hector and Amber, I blamed myself. I was convinced I would have recognized the signals if only I were a true Dom. The fact that I'd missed the warning signs proved I wasn't fit to call myself a Dom, never mind ask anybody to submit to me ever again."

The tears in her eyes surprised him. He wanted to ask what they meant but knew if he did, he wouldn't finish what he had to say.

"And then, last night, I couldn't stop myself from making you submit to me. I tried and failed. The urge was too strong. You were so beautiful, so open to suggestion, so responsive."

For a moment he saw the images in his head. Heather bent over his chair, her legs apart, her body waiting for whatever he wanted to do with it.

"It scared me, Heather. I wanted your submission so badly and had myself convinced I'd end up hurting you if you gave it to me. So this morning I decided I had to create a distance between us. If I kept you at arm's length, I couldn't hurt you."

"Any more than you did."

Her voice was soft. Her words hurt as if she'd slapped him. He wished she had hit him. He deserved it.

"Any more than I did. You're right."

"Nobody was to blame for my breakdown, Jason. I've said this before. If anybody made a mistake that night, it was me. Not you. How could you have known? How could you recognize any of my signals when you didn't know me?"

He didn't know why she still didn't sound angry. He'd been ready for an outburst, for her to scream at him, call him stupid, end the connection and yet, here she was, calm and reasonable.

"I know. I know it now. I didn't before. I was too wrapped up in my own misery, in my doubts and anger to listen to what you were saying, never mind think straight. I was too afraid to share my shame with you." *Or anybody else.* "I'm not asking you to understand. I don't expect you to forgive me. I just wanted you to know this whole mess is on me. It never had anything to do with you."

"You thought I wouldn't understand?"

For the first time he heard something other than understanding in her voice.

"How do you think I felt? I didn't think I'd ever be able to submit to anybody again. I couldn't imagine being attracted to another man after Darren and then I saw you. I didn't want to feel what I felt. I denied my desire and need to submit, preferred to lie to myself."

He felt like an even bigger bastard. None of this had even crossed his mind. That ugly little voice in his head tried to worm its way back in. *See, you're not fit to be anybody's Dom.*

"Don't even go there, Jason." Her voice was harsh. "Don't you dare take my words and use them to prove you were right."

How could she possibly know what he'd been thinking? He wanted to ask, but Heather continued before he could.

"What now?"

He hadn't thought that far ahead. He'd only wanted to tell her how sorry he was, explain himself. He'd spent most of the evening trying not to think about what he hoped would happen after he'd said everything he should have told her hours, if not days, before.

"Will you come back, Heather?" He hesitated. "Could we...? I want to fall asleep together and start the next day the way we should have started this morning — with you in my arms."

He listened to the silence, and watched the beautiful woman on his screen, so close and yet so far away. The woman he wanted and might have scared off for good. Her gaze flicked to his eyes before lowering. She appeared to be staring at something in her lap, something that made her smile. When her eyes met his again, something had changed. She looked straight at him and he saw something in her gaze he hadn't dared hope for. When she lowered her gaze again, his heart sang.

"I'd like that."

He could have sworn he heard surprise in her voice as well as gratitude.

"But, Jason. We need to do more talking."

He nodded, too happy to trust his voice right now.

"We're both insecure. We need to tell each other what we feel because I can't go through this again. I'm not strong enough."

She whispered those last words, her eyes on her lap again.

"Look at me."

He was shocked to hear the authority in his voice. He hadn't meant to put it there, but she reacted immediately.

"We'll talk for as long as it takes, and then we'll talk some more. We'll never stop communicating." He hesitated. Should he say this? Of course he should. He'd just promised her he'd be honest. "I would love to promise I'll never do anything to hurt you in the future, but I can't. I can and do promise to tell you if I ever doubt you or me again." In for a penny... He had to say it all. "I know this is new. I know we jumped too far too fast. I've no idea how far we can take this. But I want to find out, with you, together." He wasn't going to demand this. He made his voice soft, allowing all his need to surface. "Please come back before next week. Come back for me, not for the party."

That was it. He'd put his heart and soul on the table. All he could do was wait. No pressure. If she came back it would have to be her choice. The silence lengthened. Her gaze was fixed on her lap again. He couldn't tell what she was thinking, if she even believed him. He wanted to talk, to try to convince her. He needed this uncertainty to end and knew he didn't have the right. This was the price he had to pay for his idiocy. But please, God, please he needed to hear her answer. He'd never forgive himself.

"Okay."

"What?"

Her smile was wide and bright. "Okay, I'll come back. I'll drive up tomorrow."

With a sigh he let out the breath he hadn't known he'd been holding. "Really?"

The expression on her face reflected the relief and hope he felt.

"Absolutely."

Chapter Nineteen

The difference five days could make amazed her. Heather looked at the gates, the drive with the beautiful mansion at its end, the ocean off in the distance and felt none of the apprehension she'd encountered the first time she had stood here. Everything looked the same, up to and including the little rainbows lighting up the air above the Atlantic, and yet everything had changed. She wasn't the same. Today she didn't hesitate, didn't even get out of her car. She pressed the button and waited. The gates opened immediately. She was expected and she was welcomed.

The change was subtle yet huge. She was nervous today, just as she'd been the first time, but the feelings didn't compare. Today she felt anticipation rather than worry. There was no doubt she wanted to be here. She wasn't second-guessing her decision to come. These nerves felt like bright butterflies partying in her stomach and increased as the distance between her and the parking area decreased. In a few minutes she'd see Jason again. Jason who'd asked her to come back, who'd opened up to her, apologized and wanted her here, with him. Heather thought she should try and get the silly grin off her face but it might as well have been painted on.

She got out of her car and nearly floated up the steps and through the doorway until she found herself face-to-face with...Karl. The grin slowly faded as worry tried to replace the butterflies in her belly. She'd been so sure Jason would be waiting for her, ready to scoop her up into his arms.

"Hiya, Karl."

"Heather, it's good to have you back."

"It is?" She couldn't bring herself to do it. She wasn't going to ask Karl why Jason wasn't here. She looked around at the guests walking through the lobby.

"If you leave me your keys I'll have someone take care of your luggage."

As Karl handed her keys to a rather beautiful young man, Heather glanced around again. *Where are you, Jason? Why are you doing this to me?* Questions came and went unanswered. Flashes of their conversation the night before ran through her mind. Had she misinterpreted everything? She was certain she hadn't. She knew Jason wanted her here as much as she wanted to be here. And yet, he hadn't come to welcome her back. She shook herself, disgusted at her own insecurity. She knew better. It wasn't as if he had the time to spend a day in the lobby waiting for her.

Karl's eyes on her were kind and understanding. "Just follow me, if you don't mind."

"Karl, where's...?" Again she stopped herself from asking the question. "Never mind. I'm sure I'll find out soon enough."

She followed the big man down the hallway, past the bar, the restaurant and the ballroom. The entrance to the play areas came and went in a blur and still she had no idea where they might be going.

He stopped at the patio doors. "Do you remember the way to the pergola?"

She thought for a moment. It had been dark the one and only time she'd been there. She glanced around the large gardens and nodded. "I think so."

"Good. I'll let you get on with it then." His smile was filled with warmth and encouragement. "Have a nice evening, Heather."

God, she hoped the evening would be nice. So far her return had been rather disappointing. She'd been so sure Jason would be the first person she'd see, that he would be as eager to reconnect and make sure everything they had said last night still held true, as she was.

169

As she made her way down the twisting path, she admired the gardens again. Whoever had designed them was a genius because they didn't look planned at all. She imagined a giant standing in the middle of the grounds, tossing seeds into the air, allowing them to land wherever they wanted. There appeared to be no rhyme or reason to the combinations of flowers and plants, but the end result took her breath away.

She rounded a corner and faced the entrance to the pergola. It was as beautiful as it had been the first time she'd seen it. She glanced into the little house completely built from flowers and saw the small table, the ice bucket, two glasses and... "Jason."

A huge smile lit up his face. "Heather, beautiful, you're back."

She couldn't bring herself to take the last few steps. *God he's gorgeous.*

"Are you okay? What's wrong?"

She'd been staring and wasn't sure for how long. "I'm fine. It's just that I expected to see you when I arrived." She felt silly now. She'd been worrying while he'd gone out of his way to create this romantic welcome back surprise for her. "Don't mind me." She was tempted to leave it there, but they had promised to be honest with each other. "I guess I'm more insecure than I thought I was."

She grimaced as Jason groaned.

"Shit. I got it wrong again, didn't I?"

She shook her head. "No, Jason, this one is completely on me."

"No, you don't get to claim this. I should have thought this through. I could have created this set-up and still have met you in the lobby." He looked away for a second. "I wanted to meet you here. For it to be just the two of us." He took the three steps still separating them and touched her face. "I wanted to welcome you back in private." He moved his face closer to hers and softly kissed her mouth. "I didn't want witnesses or bystanders for this moment.

170

Just us, nobody else."

"Jason." She touched his cheek, enjoying the soft sting of his stubble against her fingers. She glanced around and noticed the plates with bite-size treats, the candles and, as if there weren't enough of them around, the flowers spread over the table. "It's perfect. This is perfect."

"Come." Taking her hand he pulled her into the flower-built structure. Sitting down, he lifted her onto his lap and wrapped his arms around her. He touched her face, traced her lips, stroked through her hair and she lost herself in the sensations. She'd expected a stormy reunion, a rushed coming together of two people hungry for each other and only now realized she needed this sweet, slow reconnection so much more. The last remnants of tension left her. Resting her head against his chest she closed her eyes. She kept them shut as he lifted her chin and kissed her.

"I can't believe how close I came to ruining this."

His voice was soft, almost a whisper, but she recognized the remorse.

"It wasn't just you."

She'd been thinking about this during the drive from Dublin. It would have been easy to blame him and his pride for everything they'd put each other through. Easy, but not fair.

"We rushed into this, Jason, both of us. We never stopped to think, never mind talk."

"I know, but I should have—"

"No." Maybe it was rude to interrupt him, but she wasn't about to allow him to do this again. "You should have nothing. You didn't force me to kiss you, or sleep with you or even to submit to you."

"But I knew you were only coming out of your mourning."

"Maybe. But how I deal with my past was, and is, my responsibility."

She watched as emotions swept across his face. She recognized worry, and a hint of anger followed by a tenderness so vivid she could almost feel it surround her.

171

The determination finally settling on his face told her the discussion wasn't finished by a long shot.

"Listen." They both said the word at the same time and burst out laughing. When she calmed down, Heather continued, "Just let me say one more thing then I will listen, I promise."

Jason nodded his head.

"Everything I did—coming here, watching Hector and Amber, kissing you, sleeping with you, submitting to you... I did all those things because I wanted, needed to. Those were my decisions. Maybe I didn't think all of them through as well as I should have. Maybe I should have known myself better and postponed watching a scene until I'd been here a while longer. But I didn't and it was something I had to experience. I shouldn't be involved in organizing your party if I can't deal with what is such a big and essential part of it."

This was harder than she'd thought. She wasn't quite sure how to say what she thought and felt, what words to use. "And I'm glad I did it, Jason." She smiled when he frowned at her. "I needed that shock to my system to get me out of the rut I'd fallen into.

She stared down and smiled when she noticed herself twisting her wedding ring around her finger. A glance at Jason told her he'd noticed her nervous tick. In an effort to distract both of them, she picked one of the flowers from the table and stroked the petals.

"If it hadn't been for the shock of seeing Hector and Amber, if I hadn't gone through the pain that night"—she sighed—"and if it hadn't been for you holding me through the aftermath, I don't know if or when I would have started feeling and living again."

* * * *

Confusion reigned supreme in Jason's head. He looked at her face, trying to determine if it was his turn to speak yet, and felt some of the tension in his body dissolve when he saw her smile. He had to search for the words. This wasn't the speech he'd been preparing in his head all day. He'd been ready to take responsibility, apologize again and promise to pay more attention to her from now on. He was ready for a talk about boundaries, limits and safe-words. They still needed to have that talk. Later.

"Even if I accept I wasn't responsible for your breakdown"—he saw her frown at the word 'even' but decided to ignore it—"it still leaves the fact I missed the signs. No matter what you say, I'll always feel I should have paid more attention to you and should have seen it coming."

Heather opened her mouth and closed it again.

"It's okay, what do you want to say?"

He could see her weigh her words before answering.

"I think you're being too hard on yourself."

She looked at the flower in her hands and his gaze followed hers. She'd torn off all the petals.

"You just didn't know me well enough to pick up on whatever signals there may have been." She hesitated. "Chances are you still don't."

He thought about it. Part of him wanted to jump on her words, abdicate responsibility and stop feeling guilty at last. But it wasn't as simple as she made it sound. "It's part of what a Dom's supposed to do, Heather—is supposed to be able to do."

"No." She was emphatic. "You're a Dom, not a mind reader or clairvoyant."

She stopped talking again and looked at his face, as if it could tell her what she should and shouldn't say.

"Even with Darren, even after years together, there were times when he didn't read me quite right."

She whispered those last words. Jason had no idea what the confession might have cost her and had no intention of asking. He put his hand in her hair and kissed her, slow and deep. His lips tasted hers, caressing them, no hurry, no demands, just soft contact.

"Okay." He broke the kiss because he needed to talk before they took things any further. "We'll leave that in the past, where it belongs. I'll never feel good about what happened, no matter what you say, but I'll try not to beat myself up over it anymore." He treasured her grateful smile. "But we do need to talk about where we go from here and how we go about it. I'm not risking a repeat."

"Fair enough." She relaxed on his lap as she spoke. "What do you want to know?"

Typical. As she relaxed he could feel himself tensing. So much depended on her answer to his next question.

"You submitted to me — because you wanted to or because you had to?"

"Both, I think."

"What do you mean?"

"I mean" — a shy smile appeared on her face, making her look a lot younger than her thirty-eight years — "that my instinct was to submit to you from the moment I walked into your office."

She looked into his face and he recognized the exact moment she decided to just tell it all.

"It started small, with the need to lower my eyes. But it got stronger every time we were together. Whenever your voice changed in a certain way, my gaze would go down and it wasn't long before I had to force my knees to stay straight." She looked down, as if to underscore everything she'd said. "The urge to get down on my knees and present myself was strong, Jason."

"But you didn't?"

"No, I didn't, because I wasn't your sub. I don't kneel for anyone except the man I've agreed to submit to." Her gaze drifted away toward the garden outside the pergola where darkness had settled. "I've never submitted to anyone besides Darren."

It blew him away. Heat raced through his veins. He felt triumphant, proud and humbled all at the same time.

Heather, this amazing, strong and independent woman, had never submitted to anyone except her husband but had felt the need with him and had done so on their last night together.

"And what do you want to happen now?"

He had to force himself to breathe. He wasn't sure what answer he wanted. He longed for her submission. He'd come to accept the need over the past twenty-four hours. But he still wasn't convinced throwing themselves straight into the deep end of the dynamic would do either of them any favors.

"I want to explore this with you." Heather's gaze flew up to his and she looked into his eyes. Now they were reaching the crux of it. "But I think I need to take it slow, like a natural progression."

He could tell she wanted to look away and had to force herself to continue looking him in the eye.

She continued. "I don't want contracts or checklists or anything formal."

"Heather." He looked away. "You know better than that."

"It's too formal, too much like a commitment, a permanent arrangement."

Something in her voice forced him to look back at her.

"I trust you, Jason. I know you'd never harm me."

He couldn't help himself and laughed an anything but happy laugh. "I'm glad one of us does."

He regretted the laugh and the words as soon as they left his mouth. Whatever the intention behind his little joke had been, it wasn't the hurt-filled look on her face now.

"You didn't hurt me when I submitted to you. Why do you think you'll do so next time?" She sounded exasperated. "Why can't we explore this together? Feel our way into it? See if it works before getting all formal about it?"

"Because," he suppressed the fear and frustration he felt, "I'm just not sure I trust myself enough." It was painful to admit but true. No matter what Hector had said, regardless of Heather's words he wasn't convinced he had the instincts for anything that didn't involve strict boundaries.

"But I do."

Her words were soft and sliced their way through his anger, lessened his fear and filled his heart with something he didn't want to explore right now. He sighed.

"What are your safe words? I know about black."

His mind flew back to the moment that had been haunting him for days and he heard it again, the desperation in her voice as she had thrown the word at him, *"black, black, black."* The word was etched into his brain.

"What about when you're not sure about what I'm doing?"

Her smile was filled with relief. "Gray."

Black and gray, they could work with those. "And what about when everything is good?"

"It used to be 'white'."

"Used to be?"

Heather smiled and nodded her head. "Yes. Black, gray and white. It's a natural progression. Similar to the traditional one but personalized."

"But now you don't want 'white' anymore?"

He thought he understood. Of course she didn't want a constant reminder of her times with Darren while she submitted to him.

"No." Her eyes lifted and shone with something he couldn't name.

"No, my word will be 'rainbows'."

"Rainbows?"

"Yes. They've been everywhere since I arrived here. They've been floating over the Atlantic. There were thousands of little rainbows at the blowhole when you took me there. I see them every time I look out of my window." She touched his cheek. "Because I took them as a positive sign when I first arrived here. Because seeing them makes me happy, just as coming to The Blowhole has brought so much unexpected happiness."

His heart lifted. Her decision had nothing to do with

Darren. Rainbows would be *their* word. "Rainbows. I like the idea. I want to give you all the rainbows."

It was time to make the decision. He wanted this. He wanted her submission. He longed to see her on her knees, waiting for his command, offering herself up to him. He felt no need to take things to the extreme. If he kept a close eye, checked on her state of mind, they might be able to explore where this would take them without the formalities. For now.

"Okay. We'll take baby steps as we figure it out. If you promise to use your safe words as soon as you think you need them."

Her nod, combined with the smile spreading across her face, reassured him and he continued.

"We'll take our time while we discover each other's comfort zones. We'll pretend we're both novices, experiencing new sensations for the first time."

Maybe it would be better that way. If he knew all her limits, it would be too tempting to just rush in and discover how far he might be able to push her. This way both of them would have the time and opportunity to discover what worked between *them* and what didn't. He nodded his head, confirming his decision both to himself and to Heather.

"But first, we eat." It had to be his imagination, but he could have sworn he noticed a load falling off her and was certain she felt lighter on his lap. "And, we'll have a general talk about likes and dislikes while we do so."

She turned to face him. He waited and kept his gaze on hers as she moved her mouth toward his. He felt rather than heard the words when their lips met.

"Thank you."

Chapter Twenty

Heather tried to empty her mind but couldn't stop the thoughts buzzing through her head. It had been so long. She took a deep breath in on a count of four, held it and let it out again, on another count of four. She wanted to look around, see if he was in the bedroom with her but forced her eyes closed instead. Deep breath in, hold, slow breath out.

Her mind drifted back to her reunion with Jason. She'd stayed in his lap after their talk and they'd fed each other small bites of the treats he'd welcomed her with while talking. Initially the conversation had been innocent, but it had quickly turned more heated.

When they'd eaten all but the last crumbs, Jason's voice had started to change, growing deeper. His words combined with the lower pitch of his voice had made her legs weak and her heart speed up.

"When you submit to me tonight, it won't be an accident. I'll demand it because that is who I am and what I do. You will give it to me because you need to."

"Yes."

His words had left her breathless, even before he'd started torturing her with slow strokes, small bites and soft kisses. The touches had woken up nerve endings all over her body. Just when she thought she couldn't keep herself from begging for more, he'd brought her here, to his bedroom, and had told her to strip and kneel.

She wanted this and yet it was so strange to find herself on her knees, completely naked, waiting for a man she'd been in lust with twenty years ago, a man who wasn't Darren.

Another deep breath.

It felt strange and yet it was completely natural. She'd listened to his instructions and done exactly as she'd been told. She'd stripped and put all her clothes away before walking to the center of his bedroom and kneeling. Her arse rested on her feet, her hands were on her thighs her head bowed. It felt like coming home after a long journey. Her body remembered this, as did her muscles. Even her breathing was just as she recalled, wanting to speed up unless she paid attention and kept it under control.

How long had she been waiting? Seconds, minutes, longer? The need to say his name grew stronger. Deep breath in, hold, slow breath out. Relax the shoulders, allow instinct to take over, shut the mind off and concentrate on your body.

She felt, rather than heard, him move behind her. She wanted to look up, open her eyes and watch him as he approached her. Instead, she kept her eyes closed and forced herself to concentrate on her breathing.

"So beautiful."

His hand on her head was like a benediction. His voice a blessing.

"Tonight you're mine."

His voice rushed through her body, claiming her. She could feel herself yielding. It was a process she was consciously aware of. Her muscles relaxed, her deep breathing became automatic, her nipples tensed and heat flowed into her vagina.

She kept her eyes closed as he slowly walked around her. His hand, still on her head, keeping her grounded.

"Lift your chin."

His voice was soft and full of command. She heard the words and lifted her head toward the sound.

"Open those beautiful eyes for me."

She was reluctant to leave the darkness but couldn't refuse his wish. He stood in front of her, his black jeans accentuating his powerful legs. She drank all of him in. His

179

bare chest, muscled and covered with a light dusting of nearly black hair, his neck, his mouth and his brown eyes, large and filled with a stormy light, staring straight into hers.

"No. Don't look down. Keep looking into my eyes."

She hadn't been aware of the urge to lower her gaze again until he mentioned not doing so. She kept her eyes open and felt herself falling into his.

His hand tightened in her hair, pulling her head, stretching her neck, keeping her captive between his hand and his stare.

"That's my girl. Give it to me. I want it all."

Yes, all. Take it all. Everything. Please.

The words jumped through her head, the depth of her need taking her by surprise. He bowed down and kissed her, hard and demanding. His tongue pushed through her slightly parted lips and attacked hers. She took it, moved with it. Stroke for stroke she absorbed his heat and hunger and answered with her own. His sharp intake of breath when he pulled his lips away was her reward. *This.* How had she lived so long without these sensations? How had she thought she might survive without these feelings, this surrender?

His stare was still burning into her eyes. His voice low and soft.

"I've been dreaming about this. There's so much I want to do to you, with you." His thumb stroked over her lips. "I want to explore your hot body, discover your limits and take you there." When he pushed his thumb into her mouth she sucked it in, rolled her tongue around it and relished in the deep sigh he responded with.

"Yes, baby, suck it for me. Show me what your mouth is capable of."

His voice was controlled, soft and yet she could hear the heat beneath his words. He kept his thumb in her mouth as he pushed her head to his crotch with his other hand.

"Feel what you do to me."

His cock was hard against her cheek, the material of his trousers straining. She couldn't stop herself from rubbing against the stiffness like a cat. The hold on her hair tightened, forcing her to stop moving.

"Not until I say so, girl."

He pulled his thumb out of her mouth and she mourned its loss. She wanted... No, she *needed* to taste him. She craved his touch. Her body glowed. It radiated heat and created a yearning she remembered but hadn't experienced in a long time.

He kept his hand on her head as he walked around her again, stopping when he stood behind her. She felt the material of his trousers against her heated skin as he crouched down. She missed his touch the moment he lifted his hand off her head and sighed when both his hands found her breasts. She wanted to lean back, feel his naked chest against her back, have those little hairs tickle her skin but knew better than to move without his permission.

"So soft."

His voice was a whisper in her ear, a sensual flow of air across her cheek. Fingers brushed her nipples and the voice was back. "So hard." Followed by, "So sensitive" as he squeezed his fingers together, trapping her erect buds between them. Heather heard her groan as if it came from somebody else's mouth. All she knew were those hands, the fingers stroking and pinching her. From pleasure to pain and back again, like a wave carrying her away from her thoughts.

Her breathing grew harder, her mouth opened and panting noises escaped. A need to ask, to beg for more, gripped her. She wasn't sure why she didn't speak. He hadn't told her to be quiet. She wanted to experience, needed to surrender. Heat moved through her body, from her breasts to her vagina. She felt open, exposed, wet and beautiful. She only desired to make him happy. Nothing more and nothing less.

"What are you murmuring?"

His question shocked her. She hadn't been aware of making sounds. She thought she'd been quiet.

"Tell me, girl. I want to know what you feel."

Her mind spun. She knew the answer to this question if only she could find her tongue.

"Rainbows. I feel rainbows."

"That's my girl."

She heard the triumph in his voice and rejoiced in it. His hands continued their tortuous attack on her breasts. Soft strokes, painful pinches, hard pulls followed by more tender caresses. She lost herself in the sensations and had to force herself to concentrate when his voice returned.

"I want you to crawl to the bed, Heather. Keep your perfect arse in the air for me to admire."

She missed his hands even before they left her breasts. With something sounding like a sob, she dropped her hands to the ground and lifted her arse off her feet. She looked at the bed, just a few meters away and started toward it. Hand, knee, hand, knee. She felt her pussy contract under his gaze. She was lost in her feelings. She'd been found and brought home. She was herself again.

Jason had to stop himself from growling. He wanted to throw his head back and howl at the moon and beat his chest with his fists. Tears were burning in his eyes. The sight in front of him had to be the most beautiful thing he'd ever seen. Heather crawling, toward the bed, her arse in the air as he'd demanded. The inside of her thighs glistening in the faint light.

He followed her, keeping his eyes on those beautiful white globes, loosening his trousers as he went. He was so hard it was almost painful. He couldn't wait to push himself inside, fuck her until she screamed then fuck her some more. But wait he would.

He was in control. He could feel it flowing through his veins. This was who he was, who he was meant to be and she, Heather, might just... He cut off the thought, not the time to go there. Too much, too soon, wrong moment.

She stopped when she reached his bed and patiently waited for him. He could hear her breathing, loud and irregular. He admired her form and her control. She didn't move, just stayed there, beside the bed. She didn't look around, didn't talk.

He walked around her, close enough to have his jeans brush against her flushed skin and enjoyed the shiver running over her body. So responsive. It was obvious Darren had trained her well. The stab of pain took him by surprise. It could have been him if only he'd been less scared and impatient twenty years ago.

He shook himself. Useless regrets. He should be grateful to Darren for all he'd taught her and relish this opportunity to reap the benefits.

He sat down on the bed and lifted her chin. "I want you on my lap, belly down, arse up. Now."

Her eyes were huge, her pupils dilated. She moaned softly as she got off her knees and moved herself. He grabbed her middle as she settled herself on his lap, pulling her close to his stomach. She was loose and pliable, allowing herself to be positioned by him as if she had no muscles of her own.

Her arse was firm yet soft to his touch. When he raised his hand, her arse muscles tightened in anticipation of a spanking he wasn't quite ready to dole out yet. He loved keeping her guessing, treasured the heady combination of anticipation and frustration she exuded. He tapped her arse, moving from one side to the next, teasing her with barely there sensations holding a promise of what might be coming. Her moan was music to his ears.

"What's wrong, beautiful? Not happy?" She shook her head but didn't answer. Two quick and hard spanks rewarded him with a loud yelp followed by enthusiastic squirming.

"When I ask a question, I want an answer." He made his voice deeper and saw her instant reaction when her body tensed up for a moment.

183

"More." It wasn't even loud enough to be called a whisper but he'd heard her.

"More what?"

"Harder, please."

She had to work for the words. He loved how deep she'd gone before he'd properly started. "Harder please what?"

He needed to hear her say it and wondered how long it would take her to figure out what he required.

"Harder. More. Spanking. Hands. Please."

Desperation crept into her voice and he loved it. She wasn't saying what he wanted to hear though so he tapped her arse a few times again.

"Please, Ja..." She fell quiet. "Please, Sir. Please give me more."

He could have come then and there, just on the sound of her saying that one, simple, three-lettered word. *Sir*. This time the title felt right. He had no doubts tonight. He was in control. He *was* Sir.

"That's my girl."

Now she'd deserved the spanking. He found a rhythm and kept it. Up and down his hand went, covering all of her arse, the top of her thighs, the tender skin between her arse and legs. His eyes were glued to her sensitive skin. He'd smack and a red glow immediately appeared. Each subsequent slap deepened the glow and elicited a louder response. Her groans went straight to his groin. He loved hearing the sounds she made, and needed to bring her to the point where she'd be screaming.

"Stay still." He kept his voice low and soft but the response was instant. The movements she'd only started a moment ago stopped. She lay there awaiting his ministrations, her hands squeezed into fists and her breathing labored.

"Where are you, Heather?"

"Rainbows, all the rainbows."

Her answer was breathless and sounded more like a plea for more than an answer to his question. His hand stung and Jason grinned. Probably nowhere near as much as her arse, but it was time to change the game. Her breathing became ever more erratic. He could feel her moisture through his jeans. Her moans sounded like music and her fists were deadly white. He knew she had to be fighting herself, battling against the almost irresistible urge to move. As her breathing changed again, he watched her body tense under his hand.

"Did I mention you're not allowed to come?"

The frustrated groan was delightful. She shook her head and whimpered.

"What's that? I can't hear you, girl."

"Please. Please. Please, Sir." The words kept on tumbling out of her mouth.

He stroked her glowing arse, the heat transferring to his hand as he went. He brushed over the back of her legs and trailed his fingers up, toward the wet and yearning place between her thighs.

"Yes." It was a sigh more than a word when his fingers slipped between her folds, getting soaked with her juices. He cock throbbed as he lifted his fingers to his mouth and tasted her. "Oh, you're delicious, beautiful."

He laughed at her frustrated groans before returning his fingers to her vagina and stroking with purpose, dipping his fingers in until he could feel her muscles gripping them before withdrawing again. He made a point of avoiding her clit. If he went there, she'd come, with or without his permission, and he wanted it to happen on his command.

"Tell me what you want, Heather. You won't get it unless you ask me for it."

He felt her body strain against his legs, heard her try to gather her breath.

"Answer me, girl." He whispered his demand into her ear before taking the lobe between his teeth and biting while he continued to torture her vagina.

"Please, Sir. Make me come. Take me. Please." She took several deep breaths and groaned as he bit her ear again. "God, please, I can't. Please, just fuck me" — desperation rang in her voice—"Sir, please."

He smiled knowing she couldn't see it. This was who he was, who he was meant to be. He'd been a fool to believe otherwise. This was right. Heather's submission, his dominance. This was how it should be.

He lifted her up and placed her on the bed. "Open your eyes, girl. Look at me."

Her eyes fluttered, opened and closed again before she managed to keep them open and focus on him.

"Yes, like that. I want your eyes on me while I fuck you. I want to read the need in your eyes."

"Please." The moan sounded plaintive.

Her attention shifted to his cock as he dropped his jeans and she licked her lips while she watched him stroke himself with languid movements.

He reached for a condom and ripped the foil package. Her eyes darkened even more as he pushed the condom over the head and down his throbbing shaft. She licked her lips again and for a second he was sorry he hadn't made her use her clever mouth on him.

Her gaze was glued to his hand as he teased both of them with slow and deliberate strokes of his cock. "I could come like this. Just looking at your beautiful naked body, all flushed with need. At my mercy."

Her eyes were filled with something close to panic when she stared up, before returning her attention to the hand on his cock.

"This what you want, girl?"

Her gaze met his again as she nodded her head.

"Tell me. I want to hear your voice, hear you ask for it."

"Please, Sir. I want you inside me. I need you, please."

"See that wasn't so hard." He kept his face straight as he lowered himself to her waiting body, pushing her legs further apart as he went.

The tip of his cock reached her heat. It was all he could do not to push in hard and fast, take her and give both of them what they were yearning for. He wanted to make it last, drag out the teasing. He needed to discover how far he could push her before she lost it.

"No, don't close your eyes. Look at me while I take you. Watch me tease you."

Her struggle was obvious. Her eyes blinked, trying to focus on his although he wasn't sure at all they were seeing him.

"I want to see your feelings in your eyes. I want you to see mine."

The tip of his cock was still the only part of him inside her. He felt her muscles contracting around it, trying to draw him in deeper. He wanted to laugh out loud when she narrowed her eyes at him and hissed.

"Jason."

His frown was enough.

"Sir, please, I can't. I need."

He pushed deeper into her.

"I know exactly what you need, beautiful. And if you're good, you might even get it." Pushing deeper, he saw her green eyes darken. Her need screamed at him in silence with such force it took all his restraint not to let go.

"Feel me as I take you, possess you."

God she was hot and wet and tight. When his balls connected with her arse, he rested, and brought his mouth to hers. His tongue pushed through her lips and withdrew as his cock would do to her pussy in a few moments, giving her a taste of what to expect. Her reaction was instant. She lifted her bum, trying to get closer to him.

"Did I give you permission to move, girl?"

She shook her head. "No, but please, Sir."

He withdrew until all but his tip was free and pushed back, hard. Her groan went straight to his balls, her need translating into an almost irresistible urge to drive both of them home.

"I. Know. Exactly. What. You. Need." Every word accentuated by his cock pushing deep inside her. He wasn't going to be able to make this last as long as he'd hoped. It had been too long, his control was too fragile.

"Ride with me, Heather. Give me all of you."

Her reaction was instant, her body exploded. She moved against him, meeting him move for move, driving him harder.

"Sir, please. So close. Please."

Yes, so close. He could feel himself losing it, falling into her eyes, needing to let go.

Heather first. He had to see her face as she came for him. Moving most of his weight to his left arm he moved his right hand to her clit and rubbed. "Come for me, Heather. Give it to me. Now."

And she went. Her eyes blinked, her mouth worked in a silent scream as she convulsed around his cock, squeezing him, milking. *Not enough.* He wanted more from her. He was nearly there but managed to hang on to the last vestiges of control. He needed to see her give him everything before he followed. He drove into her harder, keeping the pressure on her clit constant. Her back arched, her head moved restlessly, her breathing heavy and loud. *Too much.* Her body, her gift to him and her heat convulsed around his cock.

It was a relief to let go of control and fly with her. "Heather!" He heard the scream and knew somewhere in the back of his mind it was his voice, but he was lost. Lost in her body, lost in his release and lost in the knowledge he never wanted to lose this.

It was all he could do not to collapse on top of her. He managed to get rid of the condom, grateful for the bin next to his bed, before wrapping her in his arms.

"So good, so beautiful, so brave."

He saw the effort it took for her to open her eyes and look at him. Her smile was small but filled with something he didn't want to name in case he was reading her wrong. "Thank you."

The whispered words worked their way into his heart, filling him with warmth and comfort. This was how it was supposed to be. He'd found the missing link and now that he'd discovered it, he couldn't bear the thought of losing it again.

Tomorrow. He'd work it out in the morning. For now he just wanted to sleep with this beauty in his arms.

"Sleep, my girl. I'm here." He thought for a moment before he added, "And I'll still be here in the morning."

Chapter Twenty-One

Heather lifted her face and closed her eyes. The tree behind her back was a rough, solid presence, grounding her while she felt as if she might take flight. Bright sunlight filtering through the canopy of leaves above her played tricks on her senses. She allowed her mind to drift. She had some time before the meeting and needed this peace and quiet to sort through her thoughts and feelings.

She'd been relieved when Jason had told her he had some work he needed to take care of. It scared her how badly she wanted to be near him. She wasn't sure she was ready for her body's reactions to his slightest touch.

Jason, Sir. Last night had been so natural. After those first few minutes on her own, it had taken her no time to get lost in his touch, his voice and his dominance. Her body and mind remembered the sensations. Her thoughts had floated away and her words disappeared. She'd been reduced to skin and sensations, to feelings and emotions stronger than she was comfortable with.

His voice resonated in her head. *"That's my girl."* But she wasn't, his girl, was she? Did she want to be? Did he want her to be 'his girl'? She shook her head and smiled as the tree's bark scratched her head.

Of course she'd been *his girl* in the moment. She'd submitted to him which had made her his for those hours. But his claim hadn't sounded temporary. Her delight when she'd heard the words hadn't been limited to that moment either. It scared her.

She'd never submitted to anyone before Darren, hadn't even known about the existence of BDSM or what it entailed before she met him. She sighed. And they'd been exclusive. Until Jason, she'd only ever given all of herself to one man. It shouldn't have been this easy to submit again, it shouldn't feel this natural. But it had and it did, and she'd have to find a way of dealing with the fact.

While Jason didn't physically resemble Darren at all, he had a lot of the qualities she'd adored in her husband. And yet she didn't think those similarities were the reason her need to be with him was growing stronger. Her breath faltered. Where had that thought come from? When had her wanting the intimacy turned into a need to be with Jason?

She stared into the distance in an effort to stop her fevered mind from asking her questions she couldn't answer. Couples walked through the garden and others were swimming or sunning near the pond. She felt peaceful in these beautiful surroundings. The Blowhole with its majestic manor and the lush and peaceful grounds was like a small piece of paradise on earth right now. Everything around her was quiet and soothing and yet her mind refused to fall in line.

She closed her eyes and allowed memories of the night before to surface. She'd gone so deep. There were parts of last night's scene she still couldn't recall. She hadn't expected him to have that much control over her after such a short time. Delight at having found a way back to this lost part of herself battled with a sense of too much too soon.

She opened her eyes and looked at the pond again and watched people swimming, splashing each other and laughing. Heather smiled.

Waking up in Jason's arms this morning had been sublime. It had felt natural. There hadn't been a moment's doubt. She'd known whose embrace it was, whose erection she felt pressing into her arse, as soon as she'd opened her eyes. And yet...she had all these conflicting feelings she didn't know what to do with.

"Hey, mind if I join you?"

She had to squint her eyes in the bright light before she

recognized the girl. "Not at all, Amber. It's lovely to see you."

"I know." The redhead smiled. "I'm so happy you're back." Amber stared at the pool, apparently lost in thought. "I'm not sure I should say this but we worried when you left so suddenly." The girl's smile grew wider. "Well, I worried. Hector went ballistic."

"Hector went ballistic? Why?" Heather turned to the woman next to her. "I can't imagine Hector being anything but calm and collected. I don't understand. Why would he react so strongly?"

Amber shook her head. "I'm not sure. I told him about our talk and what you said about Jason before you left—how he didn't seem to know what he wanted." The girl's eyes grew distant for a moment as she remembered the conversation. "Hector went rigid, murmured something sounding like *the bloody eejit* and walked away." The distant look was replaced by a smile when she continued, "When he came back he was a different man, relaxed and happy. He wouldn't tell me exactly what happened. Only that sometimes even the smartest people are incredibly stupid."

Heather smiled. "Remind me to give your man a huge hug next time I see him."

The surprise on Amber's face made her laugh.

"I'm sure I'd still be in Dublin if it hadn't been for Hector talking sense into Jason." She thought about it for a moment. "I'd love to tell you the whole story, Amber, but that wouldn't be fair to Jason."

Amber's understanding nod filled her with relief. "I don't need to know the details, Heather. I'm just glad you're back." A naughty grin crept over the girl's face. "It's good to see you look so satisfied."

She felt the color creep up her cheeks. It hadn't occurred to her people might be able to see how she'd spent the night just by looking at her. "Is it that obvious?"

"To me it is." Amber smiled. "Don't be embarrassed. There's nothing better in the world than a good night submitting to a man who knows what he's doing."

Their simultaneous sighs made them both laugh.

Heather looked away. If only it were that easy. She wanted to just enjoy the memories of last night, allow her body to remember the sensations and relive them. She didn't want to be second-guessing herself and her feelings.

"Heather, you're frowning. What's wrong? Do you regret coming back?"

The lightness was gone from Amber's voice, replaced by concern and worry.

"Last night was wonderful, Amber." Heather shook her head. "Almost too good, if I'm honest. I'm all confused now. Don't know what I'm feeling or how I feel about what I may or may not be feeling. Am I even making sense?"

She looked into Amber's blue eyes and found understanding.

"Yes, I get that." Amber nodded her head. "I can't even imagine having to go on without Hector." She thought for a moment and hesitated. "Just tell me if I'm out of order. But—" She hesitated again. "Are you insecure about what you might be feeling or are you suffering from guilt because you're having feelings at all?"

"I..." God, she was perceptive. "Amber, I'm not sure. Both I guess."

Heather felt the frown form on her face and saw the worry in her friend's eyes.

"The guilt is stupid anyway. Darren more or less ordered me not to close my heart off." She hadn't known she needed to open up like this, but she felt better with every word. "I'm also afraid."

There, she'd said it. Heather felt as if some of the weight she'd been barely aware of carrying was lifted off her shoulders.

"What if I have these feelings and they're not returned? I'm not sure I'm strong enough to deal with the loss of anyone I've grown attached to again." She shook her head. "I mean, there's no way Jason's feelings are anything like mine. Look at him. Look at this place. He's spoiled for choice. Why would he need or want me with all my baggage?"

Her words took Heather by surprise. She hadn't allowed her thoughts to dig this deep. She still didn't want to admit that what she felt for Jason was more than some form of animalistic attraction.

Amber's laughter surprised her.

"I'm sorry, Heather, but have you looked at Jason's face when he's with you? It is as if the rest of us cease to exist. When he's with you, you're all he sees."

The jolt of joy Heather felt was as scary as it was delightful. "Really?"

"From the moment I first saw you with him." Amber smiled. "And remember the state I was in at the time — I've had no doubt that you were what Jason needed." She grew serious. "I told you. Jason had been out of sorts for quite a while before you arrived. As soon as you were here, he started turning back into the man he used to be."

They both turned to the pond and smiled as a pair of swimming trunks went flying through the air.

"As I said, Hector hasn't told me any details about his discussion with Jason. But I saw it. He seemed to have lost something and whatever it was, he found it again when you arrived here."

Heather nodded. She did know what Jason had thought he'd lost. She wasn't going to share his secrets with Amber any more than Hector had, but those words made perfect sense. Could the rest be true as well? Could his feelings possibly mirror the ones she could feel herself developing for him? She glanced at her watch and realized she had a meeting to attend. Relief at the forced interruption flooded her. She wasn't ready to delve much deeper into the intricacies of whatever she and Jason might be feeling for each other.

"Sorry, Amber, I have to go. Thank you so much for finding me. I didn't know it, but I needed somebody to talk to, a friend."

A big grin appeared on the girl's face as she gripped Heather's hand and squeezed it. "Yes. Friends."

＊ ＊ ＊ ＊

Jason looked at his notes. They were getting there. All the agenda points had been worked through, last minute issues resolved and final decisions made, which meant they'd arrived at the trickiest part of this meeting.

"Now then, is there anything I need to be aware of or worried about as far as our guests are concerned?" He caught the quick glance between Heather and Hector. "I don't think I've met any of these people before, so I'm depending on your familiarity with the Irish scene to help me out here."

He turned to Heather and lifted an eyebrow. "Anything you want to share?" He shifted his gaze. "Or you, Hector?"

The anxious glances between the two of them made him nervous. He registered Hector's small nod in Heather's direction before she faced him and answered.

"A name has been added to the guest list since the last time I saw it." She frowned as she looked at the paper in front of her. "A name I would have preferred not to see." Her gaze shifted to Hector in what appeared to be a silent plea.

"Rogan." Hector frowned. "He could cause all sorts of trouble. He sees himself as the king of the BDSM world and so far, nobody has had the courage to disabuse him of that notion."

Jason frowned. "I can't see you taking shit from anybody?"

"No, I don't, but I've never found myself in a situation where he felt the need to exert his supposed power over me. And I prefer to not go looking for trouble."

"But you think he'll bring trouble to The Blowhole?" Jason asked.

"He'll want to make sure he doesn't lose his position and

yes," Hector answered Jason's unasked question, "he will see you and your club as competition."

Jason thought about it for a moment. He'd come across situations like the one Hector had described several times in America. This *uber-dom syndrome* was far too common and almost always led to trouble. The last thing he needed was a guest under the illusion he could take over proceedings. In Jason's experience, such an attitude usually hid a rather insecure personality but that knowledge wouldn't help him if the man — Rogan — decided to cause trouble. He needed more information.

"So what should I expect from him?"

If he knew what he was up against, hopefully he'd be able to ward problems off before they actually started.

Another worried glance between Heather and Hector. Whatever came next, Jason knew he wouldn't like it.

"He'll jump on any weakness he finds — perceived or otherwise." Hector took a deep breath. "Which is why you can't afford to not put on a performance this weekend."

Jason looked at Heather who stared right back at him.

"He's right. You're going to have to put on a show. Rogan will take it as a sign of weakness if you don't, and use it to put people off coming here." She smiled as if trying to apologize for something she couldn't change if she wanted to. "You don't have a choice. You have to pick a sub and put on the best exhibition you are capable of."

Just for a second the thought flew through his mind. What if he could do it with Heather? Then he let it go. Of course not. She'd only just returned to the dynamic. She wasn't ready and they didn't know each other well enough.

He could feel the eyes of the other Doms on him. None of them had any idea why he'd been so reluctant to do his share lately, and he'd no intention of telling them.

"Okay. I don't like being pressured into this, but if the success of the weekend depends on it, I will of course do my part." He sighed. "Hector, please tell Souris I'll be playing with her. I'll meet with her tomorrow afternoon to work out the details."

Hector's relieved nod told Jason he'd made the right... No, scratch that, the only decision.

"Anything else?"

"Rogan will be trying to catch you out, trip you up, no matter what you do."

He didn't like the worried look on Hector's face.

"The man is a pain and a control freak. All of us will have to keep an eye on him. It's only for two days, so it should be possible to control the situation."

God, he didn't like the sound of this at all. He'd thought he had most problems covered, and now this. He didn't like playing power games with other Doms. Strutting around like a self-important hard-man just to keep up an image was not his usual style. Having to pretend to be someone he wasn't would be exhausting, not to mention frustrating.

"Fine. We all know to keep an eye on him then. At the first sign of trouble, talk to me, Hector or Karl. We'll deal with any problems.

Jason looked around the table. "Anything else?" God he hoped not. This Rogan situation was enough to cause a major headache. "Grand. We'll stick to the plan and hopefully we'll be congratulating ourselves on a successful weekend come Monday. Thank you."

He watched as his senior staff gathered their papers and got up to leave. "Heather, could you stay for a minute?" Her nod and smile lifted some of the tension gripping his shoulders.

As soon as they were alone, he stalked over to her. There must have been something in his face because she retreated, until the back of her legs hit his desk.

"Jason, what are you doing?"

"There's something you haven't told me."

"I—" Heather faltered and looked away.

"Tell me."

"He came by my house some time ago."

"Rogan did?"

"Yes." Anger flashed across her face. "And told me it was time for me to submit again and then he claimed me."

"He what?" Jason couldn't believe his ears.

"He trains subs and mentors new Doms. There are few lifestylers in Dublin he hasn't had under his thumb. Over the years it has created the illusion the Dublin community only functions because he organizes it. He expects people to fall in line when he wants something. And, to be fair, most people do. It has become a habit."

Jason's mind spun. "So, you're his now?"

Heather glared at him. "Of course not. I told him to f-off, and swore I would never submit to him." She paused. "I thought it had been enough. But when I got home there was a voicemail waiting for me. He restated his claim." Anger flared across her face again. "He said he'd see me soon enough. I didn't think he meant here, because his name hadn't been on the original list."

"Were you going to tell me any of this if I hadn't asked?"

Heather opened her mouth to answer and closed it again, dropping her gaze to the ring she was twisting around her finger. "Probably not." Her eyes met his in a silent plea for understanding. "I would have dealt with it. He's my problem, not yours."

"Like hell he isn't." It took some restraint not to shout. "We promised each other there wouldn't be any more secrets. I need you to talk to me."

She stared at the floor as she nodded. "I know. I'm sorry."

He sighed. He didn't want to make her feel insecure. They would deal with this Rogan situation as it happened. For now, all he wanted was to see Heather happy again. He smiled.

"I think we'll have to come up with a scenario for situations like this."

"Scenario? What do you mean?"

He knew she wasn't sure whether he was serious or not and he liked it. "One where I get to punish you whenever you break our rules."

He walked to the door and turned the lock. He opened his trousers as he moved back to her. "Something like you're now going to get on your knees and use that smart mouth of yours to show me how sorry you are."

His heart lifted when he saw her reaction. Heather's mouth opened, her eyes got darker and her breathing was suddenly audible. She lowered her gaze until her eyes rested on his hand, stroking his rigid cock. He didn't think she realized she'd just licked her lips. It was hot and he could feel his body's reaction in his hand.

He kept on stroking himself with slow, deliberate movements as she lowered herself to the floor, her gaze fixed on his hand. As soon as he stood before her, she moved her head and kissed the tip of his cock. She licked her way around the head before parting her lips and taking him in. When her tongue explored the little hole, he couldn't suppress a deep sigh. "God, yes."

She continued her explorations, her tongue now finding and teasing the stretched strip of skin underneath. He couldn't help himself and pushed his cock further into her mouth. A heavy breath escaped him when she started sucking.

The suction intensified as she bobbed her head, taking his dick deeper every time. He put his hand on the back of her head. Aroused as he was, he still wasn't inclined to allow her to control this. On each movement of her mouth down his cock he pushed her farther than she wanted to go. His cock touched the back of her mouth and he kept her there until he felt the slight gagging movement. When he relaxed his hold she pulled back, only to push forward again, taking him deep, sucking him hard. He could feel his balls tightening. He wasn't going to last long, not in her sumptuous mouth.

"Yes, that's it. Take me deep."

Her gaze lifted and she stared into his eyes. She intensified her movements, pumping her mouth up and down his cock. God, she was good.

She raised an eyebrow as one of her hands found his balls and squeezed. In the back of his mind he knew he probably shouldn't let her get away with showing such initiative, but it felt too good.

"Yes, Heather."

He bit back the shout wanting to escape as his orgasm roared through his body but couldn't stop the groans as she sucked his cock until every last drop of cum had disappeared down her throat. *Jaysus, this woman.*

Reaching for her hand, he helped her to her feet. He grabbed her head and brought his mouth down to hers, savoring the taste of him on her lips and tongue.

"Good girl. I like it when somebody can take their punishment with grace." When she lowered her gaze, his heart soared. "Tell me, Heather. Did you like sucking me? Did it make you hot?"

Not that he needed her answer. The red flush on her face and chest combined with the heavy breathing told him all he needed to know, but he wanted to hear her say it.

"Yes, Sir, very hot."

He'd never get enough of hearing her call him Sir. "Too bad we're out of time. Remember, we're having Hector and Amber for dinner tonight." He stroked her arse, squeezed it and delighted in the sigh escaping her lips. "I may or may not take care of your needs later.

Heather's frustrated groan was the sweetest sound he'd heard in a long time.

Chapter Twenty-Two

"That was delicious." With a sigh, Hector leaned back in his chair. "I think it may have been the best tiramisu I've ever tasted."

He wetted his finger and picked the last specks of crumb and sauce off his plate. With a soft groan he sucked the treat off his finger, glancing at the others as they burst out laughing.

"What? Good food is a close second to mind-blowing sex."

"Thank you." Heather had a huge grin on her face but also a slight blush.

"You made this?"

"I did." Heather smiled. "I have a thing about desserts. I love creating them almost as much as I love eating them."

"Please tell me you'll teach Amber how to make this. If I never eat anything else, I'll be a happy man."

"Of course, if Amber wants to learn."

She glanced at the redhead, who nodded her head enthusiastically. She'd enjoy spending an afternoon cooking with Amber. Sharing the result of their efforts with these two men afterwards would be even better.

"Irish coffee, anyone?"

Jason's suggestion met with unanimous approval and Heather watched him as he got up and walked to the counter separating the kitchen from the rest of the living space. She loved looking at him. He was such a beautiful man. Tall and muscled, he radiated both strength and gracefulness. She adored the unruliness of his dark hair. The little specks of gray took nothing away from the picture. If anything they made him more attractive, more refined looking.

He placed four glasses on the counter and put a spoonful of dark brown sugar in each. The Jameson's glowed golden in the low light. As soon as the hot coffee hit the alcohol, the powerful smell of hot whiskey filled the room and Heather felt her mouth water. Soft cream on top and the Irish coffees were done.

This evening had been filled with light-hearted fun. She'd been afraid they'd spend the evening bellyaching about the weekend and Rogan, but they hadn't talked about anything specific at all. Friendly chat, jokes and playful teasing had kept things relaxed and comfortable. She'd missed this. It had been too long since she'd just enjoyed time with friends. She was ready to join the rest of the world again. The party would be the perfect opportunity to reconnect with people she'd neglected for far too long.

Oh. She'd been so lost in her thoughts she hadn't noticed Jason's return to the table or the moment he put her glass in front of her. His hand on her thigh, brushing her skin and moving up brought her back to the present in a flash. It also re-enforced all the pent-up lust still lingering after their encounter in his office. When his finger brushed against her panties she couldn't suppress a shudder. She glanced at his face and saw the wicked grin. He knew exactly what he did to her, building her need, driving her crazy. His wink seemed to indicate he also realized she loved it. The tension in her body and the constant wetness between her legs thrilled her. How could something this frustrating feel so good?

"I'm sorry?" She'd completely missed Hector's question.

"I was asking" — his grin was knowing — "what kept you and Jason apart the first time you met?"

Heather turned her head and looked at Jason. Did he want her to answer this question? Do it himself? The slight nod of his head gave her permission.

"I'm not sure." She thought back. Twenty years ago. She'd been so innocent back then. "No, I do know. At least,

I know what made me keep my distance."

She glanced at Jason again. He smiled, apparently happy for her to continue.

"I was too young back then. I knew next to nothing about sex and intimacy." Talking about it brought the feelings back. "I was attracted to Jason from the moment I first saw him, but he was too intense, too dangerous for me. I don't know how or why, but I knew I wouldn't be able to be who or what he needed."

Soft laughter escaped before she could stop it. The three questioning faces made it clear she'd have to explain.

"I knew I'd made the right decision when I heard him and Moira one afternoon. It was toward the end of our holiday. I'd left Rick in town and returned alone, hoping to take a nap. When I walked into our cottage I heard noises coming from Moira's room. They were intriguing."

Jason's hand got more active on her leg, his fingers drawing circles on her skin, brushing against her underwear with more force, increasing her need.

"Go on, Heather."

"It scared me at first. I heard slaps and Moira made all sorts of noises I couldn't identify."

The memory got more vivid as she talked. At first she'd thought Moira might be in trouble. It had sounded like Jason might be abusing her. She'd been half way across the room, fully prepared to burst in on them and put a stop to whatever Jason might be doing, when she'd heard Moira begging for more.

"The need in her voice made me stop and just listen. I knew I should turn around and leave but couldn't make my feet move. The combination of slaps and moans held me captive."

They had more than intrigued her if she was honest. They'd made her hot. She'd been surprised when her nipples hardened as a result of the sounds. She'd felt her vagina get wet and swollen and hadn't been able to stop herself from touching the ever increasing heat. She'd been wet and hot before of course, but never like this. The moment she'd touched herself a need had been awakened. The need had grown and refused to be ignored as she'd listened to Moira begging to be fucked. Heather had continued touching herself as Jason gave Moira exactly what she wanted. She'd rubbed her clit until her own moans mingled with Moira's. The combination of the sounds from the bedroom, the danger of being discovered and her growing need, had brought her to a quick and hard orgasm.

She had no intention of sharing that particular detail right now.

"I needed to meet Darren and explore my sexuality with him before I could even begin to understand what I'd been listening to and why it had such an effect on me." She thought for a moment. "I wasn't ready for anything as extreme and adventurous at the time and I'm sure Jason knew that."

It was a relief when Hector and Amber's scrutiny switched from her to Jason. And she was rather curious to find out what it had been like for him.

"She's right."

The look of disappointment on Jason's face took her by surprise.

"I was attracted to Heather from the first moment I saw her but knew she wasn't ready for everything I wanted and needed. Moira, on the other hand? Let's just say the girl was up for anything."

For a moment his gaze turned distant, as if he could see things invisible to the others.

"I wasn't sure what I wanted back then, but knew it was more than a sweet summer romance, more than Heather would be able to give me."

The smile he directed at her was filled with so much affection it made her heart jump.

"It's hard to believe now, but back then she was innocence personified. The afternoon we spent kissing, enjoyable as it was, confirmed that." His face turned thoughtful. "If I'd known how things would turn out for her, I might have pushed. But I didn't know and that's probably just as well. I was too inexperienced. I could have spoiled the experience for her, might have put her off for life."

She saw the question in his eyes and answered before thinking about it.

"Chances are, you would have. I didn't just jump into BDSM with Darren. We were together for months before he introduced the idea to me."

She smiled at the memory. "We'd played some games before he got more serious about instructing me. He'd given me some books to read and we'd recreate scenarios from those stories. We were together for a year before we became serious about dominance and submission."

By then she'd been ready for it. She'd wanted nothing more than to give her heart, her body, her mind and her soul to Darren. She had, and she'd received his in return. Her heart clenched. It wasn't the pain of loss, not exactly. No, she mourned something special she'd never get back in the exact same form although she now knew she hadn't completely lost it either.

"You okay?" Jason's voice was filled with concern.

"Yes, I am." She smiled at him. "It's a strong and precious memory. I'm still getting used to the idea that I will never have that connection with Darren again."

She saw the concern on his face and searched desperately for the words to explain what she meant.

"But I realize how blessed I am to have those memories. And I'm blessed I'm now discovering that losing Darren didn't mean losing the opportunity to create new ones as well."

"You wouldn't know what happened to Moira, would you?"

She was grateful Jason changed the subject. All the soul-searching was getting tiresome.

"I do. She went to Australia not long afterwards. We lost contact for a while but recently found each other again on Facebook. She's been in a committed relationship for the past fifteen years." Heather smirked. "Would you be surprised to hear both she and her partner are switches?"

Jason shook his head. "Not surprised at all. She was constantly trying to wrestle control away from me in Wexford."

The sound of a chair scraping across the floor put an end to their almost private reminiscence.

"I think it's time for me to get my sub back home." Hector smiled as he held out his hand to Amber and helped her out of her chair. "I think we'll get some practice in before our performances this weekend. What do you say, girl?"

Heather could see the heat flaring in Amber's eyes and felt a similar response in her own body.

"Ready when you are, Sir. After all" — Amber grinned — "practice makes perfect."

Pure adoration glowed in Hector's eyes. "Since you're perfection personified, my darling, maybe we should stop calling it practice."

The blush looked charming on Amber although she couldn't keep the naughty tone out of her voice. "I don't care what you call it, Sir. But please don't ever stop."

Laughter filled the room. This had been a perfect evening. Jason had started her on the road back to herself. She'd found friends in Amber and Hector. For the first time in eighteen months, Heather believed life didn't just go on, it also provided unexpected but very welcome surprises.

* * * *

"Are you sure you're all right?" He looked at her face. Despite his plans to keep the evening light, the conversation had gotten deep and personal. He worried it might have been too much for Heather. He was fine with the way their sexual relationship was developing, although fine didn't quite capture the depth of his feelings. He wasn't sure how to deal with her memories though. He had no idea if being reminded of her past with the man she'd loved and lost made things easier or harder for Heather

"Yes, I'm sure. I don't mind being reminded of Darren and my life with him, Jason. They're good memories and I'll always have them." Her smile was bright.

"I'm lucky to have so many things to treasure in my past. And now, with you"—her touch was soft against his cheek—"I'm blessed to have this opportunity to discover delight all over again."

She shook her head as if surprised by her own words.

"I'm more than all right, Jason. With you I'm good, happy."

He studied her face, not quite able to believe it could be as easy as she made it sound. He didn't see any doubt. She lowered her gaze as he stared at her but not before he'd recognized the need in her eyes, her willingness to submit. He lifted her chin and forced her to look at him.

"Good because I want you."

Hunger flared in her eyes.

"What?" He wanted to hear her say it, ask for it.

"I want you too, Sir."

There it was again. One little word was all it took to push him forward. He smiled as he remembered how he'd left her all hot and bothered earlier. *God*, that had been a rush. Her mouth on his cock had been heaven but leaving her all needy afterwards and her unquestioning acceptance of his decision, had felt like coming home.

"Feeling needy, girl?"

She tried to drop her gaze again but he forced her chin up and enjoyed the blush creeping up her cheeks. He knew she was hot for him, of course. He'd been touching her leg and panties for at least an hour and had found and cherished the wetness. Still, he needed to hear her say it.

"Very needy, Sir."

"For what?" He whispered the question.

"For you, Sir." Her answer was just as soft.

"Good girl."

He took her hand and led her past his bedroom to the door at the end of the hallway.

"Through there is my private dungeon." He studied her face but saw nothing to indicate fear or hesitation. "You think you're ready to play in there?"

He heard her breathing change, saw her pupils darken. Her lips moved but no sound escaped.

"What's that?"

The answer was rushed and breathy. "Yes, Sir, I'm ready."

He wanted to laugh and cheer but kept his face smooth. "That's my girl. I want you to go inside, undress and wait for me. I'll join you when I'm ready."

Jason let go of her hand and watched as she opened the door, looked around his well-equipped playroom and walked in, before turning and entering his bedroom. Tonight he'd allow himself to go into full Dom mode. All the signs indicated she wanted to submit to him as badly as he wanted her to surrender. If he was right, tonight would be a magical experience for both of them.

He smiled wryly when he opened his wardrobe. All his Dom attire had somehow ended up on the far left of the rail. It had been over a month since he'd last donned his leathers and they'd literally gotten pushed to the sidelines. Not anymore though. His fingers trailed over the trousers, enjoying the feel of leather. Well-worn and good quality, they were soft to the touch. He picked his favorite pair with buttons on the fly rather than a zip. *Great fun when fingers get clumsy and my cock is hard.*

Pulling the trousers up felt like coming home after a long absence. Just the sensation of the cool material against his legs and the grip it had on his buttocks when he closed the buttons had his cock hardening. He thought about Heather. How would she react to him in his leathers? How had she decided to wait for him? Would she be kneeling? Was she nervous? Had he made her wait long enough? He wanted her anticipating his arrival. Seeing her slightly on edge would be good.

Jason wasn't worried she'd have second thoughts. He was sure she needed and wanted this as much as he did. But it had been a while for her and allowing her to get too nervous while waiting wouldn't serve any purpose.

He glanced at himself in the mirror and smiled. *Oh yes, I'm back.* He was ready. He wanted this. He needed this with Heather. Tonight both of them were going to fly.

He forced himself to take his time walking back to his dungeon, to have patience as he opened the door. His breath caught. God, she was beautiful. She looked like she belonged here. Naked, on her knees in the middle of the room, with her legs apart, her hands on her thighs and her gaze on the floor, she had become submission personified. He saw the slight tensing of her muscles as the door hit the wall and admired her restraint when she didn't look up or flinch.

Staying silent, he walked across the room. His pant leg brushed her arm when he walked past her. Her shudder sent a thrill of delight through his body. His dungeon wasn't overly equipped. After all, he had everything a Dom could wish for a few floors down. He opened a drawer in the large oak cabinet, made from the same wood as the bench he had plans for and the four-poster bed, and selected his favorite items.

He turned around and took the time to just look at the beauty kneeling in the middle of his dungeon. Her skin glowed in the soft light dispersed by the multitude of tiny bulbs in the ceiling. She hadn't moved at all. Her back was straight—the honey-colored curls streaming down toward her glorious buttocks.

He walked back, stopping behind Heather, and put his chosen items on the small table, just out of her sight, before circling around her, admiring every inch of her body. She stayed still. Her head didn't move to track him as he walked. Her body was relaxed. He stopped walking when he was behind her again and listened to her heavy breathing.

"Beautiful girl."

He stroked her hair, using his fingers to massage her scalp and loved the sound of her breath catching.

"Tell me. Did you like waiting for me? Did you imagine what I might do to you tonight? Did it make you hot?" He waited. "Answer me, beautiful. Nodding your head is not enough." He paused before fisting his fingers and pulling her head back by her soft hair. "When I ask you a question, I want an answer. Unless I tell you differently, I never want you to be quiet. Do you understand?"

Her gasp when he emphasized his question with another tug on her hair went straight to his already rock-hard cock.

"Yes, Sir. I understand." She swallowed. "And yes, I'm hot and curious and—" She hesitated. "Also nervous."

"That's my girl. Now tell me, why are you nervous?"

He completely understood why she shook her head. It had to be difficult to articulate everything going through her mind right now, to verbalize all her feelings.

"I'm not sure. It's been so long. I don't know what to expect."

Her voice trailed off and he had to strain to hear the rest.

"I want it so badly it scares me."

He crouched down behind her, catching her body between his thighs. "What do you want, Heather?" He whispered the question because he didn't want her to know how desperately he wanted to hear the answer.

"I don't know. Everything." The words rushed out of her mouth. "I want to lose myself. I need to surrender."

He noticed the hesitation. "Tell me everything, Heather. No holding back."

She had to force the words. "I want you. I need to surrender to you."

Triumph and exhilaration filled him. "Yes, you do. And you will. Tonight you're *mine*."

Jason picked up the blindfold. It was soft and completely lightproof. She would be lost in the dark.

"Let's see how much you really trust me." He covered her eyes and secured the mask. Her sharp intake of breath was his reward. "How do you feel, Heather?"

"Good, Sir. Rainbows."

"I love your rainbows, girl, but don't forget your other words. Use them if it gets too much. There's no hurry and I need to be sure you'll stop me when I go too far."

"I will, Sir. Black or gray. I promise."

The muscles in his thighs were starting to complain but he wasn't ready to get up yet. He squeezed her shoulders, searching for any tension. Her body relaxed under his hands and a low moan escaped her. He explored her naked skin, shoulders, arms, her tummy and up until he found her beautiful full breasts. They were made for him, a perfect fit for his hands. Cupping both of them, he softly squeezed the nipples between his thumbs and index fingers. The reaction was instant. Her nipples hardened, her back arched, pushing her upper body into his chest and her breasts more firmly into his hands. Using his nails, he pinched the stiff nipples. Her groan was all the invitation he needed.

"So sensitive."

He attached nipple clamps to the hard buds and tightened them, listening closely to her breathing for clues. He loved this. Discovering what and how much a sub could take had to be one of the best parts of this dynamic.

He wanted to put his hand between her legs, discover exactly what his ministrations were doing to her but waited. He would take her exactly where she wanted to go first. He'd make her lose herself so she could find herself again in his arms.

When he got up, Heather's body swayed. Jason stepped in front of her and picked up the chain connecting the two clamps.

"On your feet, girl."

A slight pull on the chain had her gasping and rushing to her feet as best she could while blindfolded. So beautiful. So helpless. Completely at his mercy.

"Walk."

Keeping the chain tight enough to create a constant pull

on her nipples, he directed her toward a slim bench. It was a shame to let go of the chain and Heather's soft groan showed she felt the same way. Still, it wouldn't be for long.

Pushing her down, he positioned her until she straddled the bench, which was high enough to force her up on her toes. He attached her wrists to the ties at the end of the bench before attaching the chain between her clamps to the cuffs. Any extra sensation in her nipples would now be self-inflicted. He grinned. If she stayed still, this was as bad as it would get. If she moved though... His grin widened, safe in the knowledge she couldn't see his face. How much she moved would be a great indication of how much she could take.

"How does that feel, beautiful?"

"It's good, Sir."

"Cuffs too tight? Clamps?"

"No, they're good. I'm good. I'm..." Her voice trailed away, words escaping her.

"That's my girl." He made a point of lowering his voice. "Now we're ready."

Stepping back he admired the beautiful and inviting picture in front of him. Blindfolded and cuffed, she truly was his to do with as he pleased. His hand moved to his crotch as if it had a mind of its own. He stroked himself through the leather. God he was hard. He wanted to take his time, draw it out, make her beg and yet, every time he saw her naked, the need to just enter her was overwhelming. *Restraint.* Taking her would be so much better once he'd reddened her arse.

He stroked the inviting buttocks, adding a few slaps for good measure and indulged himself in the sight of her squirming. The yelp escaping her when her movement pulled on her nipples satisfied a need deep inside him. He stroked her arse again, trailing his fingers over the soft, pink skin before pushing a finger into the split between her buttocks. Her low groan when he rubbed over the tight little hole answered a question he hadn't asked. He picked up the lube with his free hand and squeezed.

The resistance he encountered when his slick thumb pushed down might as well have been an invitation.

"Tell me you want it, Heather. Ask me for it."

"Please, just please."

"Please what, girl. You have to be specific."

"Please, Sir. Your finger. My arse."

"Want my fingers in your arse?"

"Oh, God, yes."

She screamed the words as his thumb broke through the resistance and entered the tight space between her buttocks. Her arse moved to meet his finger and another scream escaped her lips as the movement tightened the chain attached to her nipples. He couldn't stop himself from grinning as he worked her arse. The sounds erupting from her mouth were incoherent, didn't even resemble words. He watched her constant struggle between needing to move along with his finger in her arse and the urge to avoid the consequent pull on her nipples. His cock throbbed in his trousers, pleading with him to be released. He was sure the groan he heard when he withdrew his thumb was caused by disappointment. Little did she know. She wouldn't be empty for long. He grabbed the last item from the table and covered it in lube. He'd picked a medium sized one. Not too small because she was experienced, but not too big either. It had been a while, after all.

He wished he could see her face as he pushed the plug into her tight hole. He could imagine it though. He watched the muscles in her arse clench and relax in quick succession as he slowly but steadily pushed the plug deeper. He could visualize the changes as they had to be flying across her face, the heat in her eyes, her mouth open, her tongue licking her lips while she tried to catch her breath. He could hear her breathing stopping and starting, as if she had to remind herself of her need for oxygen.

The fattest part of the plug disappeared into her depths and her muscles clenched around the stem.

"It's your job to keep it in place, Heather."

A total lack of response had him lift his hand and slap her arse a few times.

"Answer me, Heather. Are you going to keep this plug inside for me?"

A few more slaps, a deep intake of breath and a strangled reply.

"Yes, Sir. Anything."

He needed to be inside her. He couldn't wait much longer. He walked around the bench and faced her, looking down at her beautifully bound body. He admired her for trying to lift her head but wasn't surprised she couldn't.

"Listen to me, girl." A slight nod of her head indicated she'd heard him.

"Do you want me inside you?"

Another nod, but this time he wanted more from her.

"I can't hear you. Don't you want me?"

"I do. Please, Sir. I do. I need you." Sheer desperation rang in her voice.

"Wriggle your fingers for me."

Her body went completely still as she processed his request, before she moved her fingers. He studied her hands. They weren't discolored and movement appeared to be no problem. Well, he smiled, wriggling wasn't. He'd find out how well they moved soon enough.

"If you want me to fuck you, you're going to have to release me."

This time she did manage to lift her head. Her groan thrilled him. He moved closer, bringing his fly within reach of her fingers.

"Open those buttons, girl. Go find what you want."

Her trembling fingers against his hyper-sensitive cock were the best kind of torture, despite the leather still covering him. He watched her fingers as they blindly searched for the first button and fought with it, trying to push it through the hole and finding the job much harder than it should be.

She made it past the first button and the second before running into trouble at the third.

"You're half way there, beautiful. Don't you want me?"

Her frustrated moans turned into sobs as her fingers fought with the leather.

"That's it. Just one more and I'll take you."

Sobs and whimpers escaped her mouth. Soft whispers of *please, please, please* rang through the air. He saw her tears before she managed to release the last button on his fly.

"Good girl. Now take it out."

His cock was dark and hard and throbbing just inches away from her mouth. Pre-cum glistened at the tip. He took a condom from his back pocket while he moved his dick across her opened mouth.

"Taste me."

Her moan when her tongue encountered his erection was almost enough to set him off. Stepping back he ripped the foil and pushed the protection over his length. He trailed his hand over her back and buttocks as he walked around the bench. His fingers moved to her vagina for the first time since he'd tied her up and found her open, wet and ready.

"What do you want?"

"You, Sir. Please. Fuck me. Take me. I need."

"What do you need, girl?"

"You. I need to come. Please."

Sobs replaced her words as her body started to wriggle in front of him. He knew it had to cause pain in her nipples and yet she didn't stop. Her voice might have failed her but her whole body had taken over the job of begging him for his attention.

He pushed his tip against her cunt and only just managed to suppress a groan. God he wanted her. He needed to be inside her, deep and hard but forced himself to push forward an inch at a time.

"You're so tight with the plug. Feel how I fill you."

"Yeeesss." She hissed the word.

He stopped moving the moment he had fully entered her.

He looked at the plug and twisted it. Her vagina contracted around his cock, squeezing him even harder. It nearly became his undoing. If he didn't move now, he'd come without properly fucking her.

Bending forward, he found the chain attached to her breasts and grabbed it. He pulled almost all the way out before plunging into her again. His body took over and all restraint evaporated as he fucked her hard. He knew every hard push forced her clit against the soft material of the bench. He could feel her clenching around him.

"Not yet. Don't come until I tell you to."

Sobs, cries and moans were her only response. He was so close. Just a little bit longer, he just wanted to hear it one more time.

"Please. Sir. Please."

"Yes. Now, Heather. Give it to me now."

As her body exploded around him, he grabbed the plug and slowly pulled it out. Her pussy squeezed and relaxed, milking his cock as he drove her on, extending her orgasm for as long as he could. He dropped the plug to the floor as his balls contracted. He heard a roar. For a long moment he was lost.

He only barely managed to stay on his feet. Jason wasn't quite sure where he found the strength but he took a step back and discarded the condom before turning his attention to the now motionless woman in front of him. Bending his body over hers he moved his hands to her nipples.

"Deep breath, Heather."

He released both clamps at the same time. The scream he'd expected didn't come. Her breath stalled for a moment and her body tightened before she went limp and silent again.

Suddenly worried by her lack of reaction he walked around the bench and untied her hands, which dropped down. She didn't try to move, didn't lift her head, didn't even shake her hands. Her body was still and suddenly looked too small and fragile.

Lifting her chin, he looked at her face. Her mouth was

slack, her eyes were open but didn't appear to be seeing anything. He lifted her up and carried her to the big four-poster bed in the middle of the room. Laying her down on her back, he crawled next to her, pulling her into his arms. He listened to her breathing, felt her heart's steady beat underneath his hand.

"Come back to me, beautiful. You were so good. You're magnificent. Come back to me now."

All his insecurities returned in a flash. Had he gone too far? Had he pushed too hard? Shit, he hadn't asked her about her state of mind in ages. He could have kicked himself. What was the point in having safe words if he didn't ask her for them? Maybe he'd been right all along. He just wasn't up to this anymore. He'd lost it somewhere along the way. Hector and Heather were wrong. He wasn't a Dom. He was a big failure.

"Jason?"

The soft whisper loosened something in his chest he hadn't known was tied up.

"I'm here, baby. Are you okay?"

He looked at her eyes as she struggled to focus on his. The small smile forming on her lips giving him the reassurance he needed.

"Oh yes. I flew. You made me fly, Jason. I was there, among the rainbows." The smile grew wider. "And it was heavenly."

Chapter Twenty-Three

She guessed it could have been worse. In fact, up until a few hours ago things had been running more smoothly than she'd dared hope. About half the invitees had arrived yesterday, from late afternoon until well into the evening. Catching up with those familiar faces had been great. She'd been worrying about nothing. There had been no awkward moments, no difficult questions. People had been happy to see her again, nothing more and nothing less.

Far more importantly, so far, everybody she'd spoken to had sounded impressed with The Blowhole, delighted with their accommodation and positive about everything Jason's club had to offer. Hector and Amber's demonstration the previous evening had gone down a treat. It had been the same one she'd seen the night of her breakdown, but this time she'd been able to fully enjoy it.

She grinned at the face staring back at her in the mirror. The time she and Jason had spent together in his room afterwards had been even more enjoyable. She couldn't quite believe how easy submitting to Jason had turned out to be. It was as if the connection between her body and her mind shut down the moment he put his hands on her. As soon as his voice changed tone, free will disappeared until all she was left with was the undeniable urge to please him. She wasn't quite ready to admit it out loud, but if she was honest with herself — and if she couldn't be honest with herself, who could she be honest with? — it felt natural to submit to this man.

She stretched out on her bed and smiled. It was good to have some time on her own now. Lunch, on the terrace in the sunshine, had gone well. Even Rogan had seemed to enjoy himself.

Rogan. Just thinking of the man made her frown. He and his sub had been the last guests to arrive late this morning. She was sure it was part of a well thought out plan to intimidate Jason before he even met him. And Rogan had made his presence felt from the moment he stepped through the front door. He'd barely given his surroundings a second glance, as if they weren't worth his attention. Jason, on the other hand, had gotten the full force of his scrutiny. Rogan had taken his time to look Jason over from head to toe before welcoming him to the Irish fetish community, as if Rogan were the host and Jason the guest. She'd watched Jason closely as his face went blank. She'd been proud of him for taking the moral high ground. Thanking Rogan for his words and welcoming him to The Blowhole had been a small victory. If Rogan had expected to come up against a pushover, he knew better now.

All sense of victory had fled when Rogan had turned to her and asked her if she'd come to her senses. She'd felt Jason tense beside her and had said a small prayer he'd keep his mouth shut and allow her to deal with it. She vividly recalled every single word of their short and not altogether friendly conversation.

"Well, girl, I told you I'd see you soon enough. Have you come to your senses yet?"

She'd glared at him before answering.

"There was never anything wrong with my senses, Rogan."

His frown when she used his name rather than any title he might have been hoping for, had given her a jolt of pure pleasure. Unfortunately it hadn't been enough to disabuse him of his delusions.

"I don't know about that, sub." He'd made sure to stress that last word. *"But I can wait. Sooner or later you'll realize what you are and what you need. When you do, you'll come crawling to me. My leniency will depend on how much time has passed. Remember who I am. Without me, you have no way back."*

Gratitude for Jason filled her again. She didn't know where he'd found the restraint, but he'd stayed calm while he pointed out to the arrogant so-and-so that now was neither the time nor the place for this particular conversation, before finding someone to show Rogan to his room.

Jason had been fit to be tied by the time they found a moment on their own. He'd suggested sending Rogan straight back to Dublin and had only reconsidered after she'd reminded him of Rogan's position in the Dublin community. If Rogan left and the rest of the Dublin crowd followed him back to the East Coast, the whole weekend would end before it properly started and Jason's opportunity to establish The Blowhole as a viable club would be gone. Even with those arguments it had taken a while and a lot of persuading before Jason had agreed to let Rogan stay. At the time they'd both taken comfort from the presence of his sub. They had taken it as proof that Rogan was prepared, at least for now, to leave Heather alone. The feeling had been short lived. They'd since discovered the girl wasn't *his* sub but rather another one of his trainees.

Heather shook her head and banished the memories. She needed to keep her mind on the here and now. The meeting of the Doms was about to start and would go on for a while longer, followed by Leo and Roger's demonstration. Then, after dinner, it would be Jason's turn. He still wasn't happy about it but had resigned himself to the idea. A smile spread across Heather's face again. She couldn't wait to see him in action. She knew, with absolute certainty, it would be fantastic, even if her lover had his doubts.

Loud knocking on the door shook Heather out of her musings.

"Heather, are you there? Open the door, Heather."

Amber's voice was frantic. Heather couldn't shake the feeling of pending doom. She'd never seen the girl anything other than happy and carefree.

"Amber?"

One look at the young sub's face confirmed her suspicions,

something was definitely wrong.

"I just got a text from Hector." Amber's blue eyes were filled with worry. "That Dom we were all warned about? Rogan? He's decided all subs should join their Doms at the end of the meeting. Hector's text told me to get ready and talk to you. We need to…"

Heather turned around and walked away from the door, tuning out Amber's voice as thoughts rushed through her head. She understood Hector and Amber's worry. They saw this as a challenge to Jason's authority. As far as she was concerned, it was a golden opportunity to kill two birds with one stone. Rogan had just handed her the perfect way to get him off her case for good.

Heather turned around and smiled at Amber. "It's not a problem. I'll go."

Amber's face was a mixture of relief and confusion. "You'll go? Are you sure? You haven't committed to Jason. You would do that for him?"

"I've been submitting to him for the past ten days." Heather smiled. "And I know Rogan. I don't like the man. It will be my pleasure to spoil whatever his agenda is."

Oh yes. It would piss him off. He'd be disappointed when a submissive showed up for Jason, since he didn't expect one. He'd be livid to see her — the woman he'd been trying to claim — on her knees at Jason's feet.

"How long have we got to get ready?"

"Only about half an hour." The girl still looked worried.

"It will be okay, Amber. I know what I'm doing. I'll meet you at the back door in twenty-five minutes. We'll go there together."

"Okay. If you're sure."

The young sub visibly relaxed when Heather nodded.

Heather stared at the door Amber had just closed. She could do this. She'd been here before. Not with Jason, but still. She just had to be quick about her preparations. She smirked. Which was just as well since it wouldn't leave her time to worry about what she was about to do.

She stalked into the bathroom and got to work. Heavier make-up, bigger eyes, her hair straightened to within an inch of its life. She took a minute to study her reflection. She hadn't seen this version of herself in two years and wasn't quite sure how she felt about being forced into this reunion. She didn't mind going the full distance for Jason.

The thought stopped her for a moment. She *really* didn't mind. In fact, she looked forward to him seeing her like this. She couldn't wait to kneel at his feet in public, even if she would have preferred to do it on her own terms, at a time of her choosing. And she didn't have time for these reflections. Less than ten minutes left before she had to meet Amber.

Opening the wardrobe, she smiled. She'd felt foolish when she'd packed her sexier outfits when she returned to The Blowhole. Now she didn't feel silly at all. The green, no-bra-required, mini dress was exactly what she needed. Her G-string matched the dress and the pattern on her heels was the same color. The mirror told her all she needed to know. She looked sexy. The dress hugged and accentuated her curves. The deep V-neck covered little besides her nipples and the dress was so short parts of her arse would be exposed once she knelt down. She just needed one final touch.

She allowed the feeling of sorrow to run through her for just a moment. She hadn't worn this for a long time. She remembered when Darren had bought it for her and could still hear his words.

"I'll never collar you, Heather. You're my wife. You're wearing my ring. I know you're mine. You'll only wear this when we're meeting people who don't know us."

Her fingers rubbed the soft material of the green collar, allowing her mind to travel back to the times when Darren had secured it around her neck.

When she looked into the mirror she grinned. Darren would have gotten a kick out of her doing this. He'd detested Rogan and he would have liked Jason if he'd ever met him. This was the sort of idea he would have come up with. He'd always enjoyed outsmarting others and she knew, without a doubt, he would have been proud of her for making this decision.

"*I love you, Darren.*" She whispered the words. "*I'll always love you, but I'm ready to follow your advice. I'm moving on.*"

Heather couldn't help laughing when she met Amber at the back door.

"Were you watching me when I picked my clothes?"

The redhead looked glorious in a dress the exact same tint of red as her hair. It was also the same style as Heather's, for the second time since they'd met.

Amber visibly relaxed when she saw Heather. "You are beautiful."

"As are you." Heather smiled. "Come on, let's go. We don't want to be late."

A line of subs waited outside the room the Doms had been meeting in for over an hour now. Heather allowed her gaze to drift over all of them and marveled at the similarities. All male subs were wearing tight black leather trousers and little else besides their collars. The females all wore different versions of the same dress. She allowed her gaze to linger on the young girl who'd arrived with Rogan. She couldn't put her finger on it, but something about the girl felt off, as if she didn't belong. Heather couldn't help feeling sorry for her. It was so clear she was nervous. If she was a day over twenty, Heather would eat her panties. Heather let it go. Whatever the problem was, it wasn't her business. She had other things to worry about.

Karl opening the door interrupted Heather's thoughts and she hurried to take her place at the end of the line. The manager's voice was loud and clear.

"You're to come in one at a time and make your way to your Dom."

She saw the surprise on his face when he recognized her and she smiled at him. As the line began to move, she straightened her back, lifted her head and looked down.

She could do this.

* * * *

Jason had to work hard to keep the frown off his face. As luck would have it, every single Dom and Domme in this room had a committed sub to kneel at their feet. It wasn't the end of the world, but he didn't like the idea of standing out as the only person left on his own once this procession was over. Rogan wanted to undermine him, that much was clear. And while he'd no desire to fight Rogan for his perceived position in the Irish BDSM community, he didn't want to give the man an easy opportunity to steer potential clients away from The Blowhole either.

Part of him was proud anybody would see him as a threat to their authority — perceived or otherwise — but Jason hated having to concede this round to the man he had taken an instant dislike to. A dislike that had turned into something far stronger as soon as he'd addressed Heather. Jason still wished he'd spoken up there and then. It had felt wrong not to jump in and defend the woman, but there was no official commitment. She submitted to him, yes, but she wasn't *his* submissive. He'd known she wouldn't thank him if he'd interfered, and their talk afterwards had proven him right. Even being sure he'd done what she'd wanted him to do didn't make him feel any better about not having been able to speak up for her.

He watched as one by one the subs entered the room. The envy he felt every time a sub knelt at his or her Dom's feet surprised him. He'd never wanted a committed sub. Once, years ago, he'd collared a girl, only to discover six months later that he wasn't made for an exclusive relationship. Right now though, or rather, since Heather had entered his life...

This wasn't the moment to think about Heather or what he wanted with her, from her.

Jason resented the smirk Rogan sent his way when the

young trainee sub knelt at her Dom's feet.

The room filled up. Just a few Doms were still waiting for their subs. Of course, one of them would still be waiting after the door closed again. It ate at him. Not just because he hated Rogan for making him the odd Dom out. He wanted what the others had. The bond and intimacy he'd always thought he didn't need, were suddenly something he craved.

Amber walked through the door and moved across the room, displaying all her natural grace. When she knelt at Hector's feet, she winked at her Master before glancing at him. Anger flashed through Jason. Did the girl not realize the seriousness of the situation? And why on earth hadn't Karl closed the door yet? He turned toward the door, opened his mouth to order his manager into action and stopped breathing.

She was beautiful. Her hair fell straight down her back. The green dress displayed her beauty to its fullest advantage. And around her neck, he didn't believe what he saw, a collar? She didn't look up, didn't glance to her left or right, just put one foot in front of the other until she reached his chair.

"Sir."

The whisper barely reached his ears as she knelt down and rested her head against his knee.

It hit him like a bullet. He loved her. He'd been trying to deny it for days, but he knew. This woman, strong and independent, yet willing to submit to him. She was clever. She was more than his equal and happy to sit at his feet.

"Heather?" Rogan's voice was cold and filled with disbelief. "You're kneeling at this man's feet?" The Dom all but pushed his sub to the floor as he jumped from his chair. "You turn me down when I offer you my dominance and submit to *him*?"

Jason put his hand on Heather's neck, fully expecting to feel tension and not finding it. Her smile when she looked up at him lifted his heart. She wasn't sacrificing herself. She did this because she wanted to.

"I'm talking to you, sub."

Rogan's voice broke through his thoughts, but Jason didn't miss the lift of Heather's eyebrow before he turned to face the Dom who stalked toward them.

"What would Darren say if he saw you now? You think he'd like to see you prostituting yourself for this wannabe?"

Rogan's gaze flew around the room, looking for support and finding nothing but embarrassment from those who knew him and anger from everybody else.

Heather still hadn't acknowledged Rogan. He admired the way she'd completely ignored the man's remarks, as if they weren't directed at her.

"May I, Sir?" Her voice was soft and confident.

"Of course, beautiful. On you go."

Admiration flooded him as Heather stood up and turned to face Rogan, who was almost on top of them now.

"Darren," she said, her voice cold and calm, "would congratulate me for finding a good Dom to submit to." She paused to consider her next words. "You seem to be forgetting that submission is a gift, not a right. I could only submit to a man I trust completely. You are not that man — could never be him."

Anger and admiration fought a battle in Jason's head. Heather took his breath away. Her calm and her certainty in the face of this angry and, Jason couldn't deny it, rather intimidating Dom, were beautiful to behold. He wanted to grab and kiss her, claim her in front of all these witnesses. But he held back. This was her moment. He had to deal with Rogan though. This madness had to stop. If Rogan couldn't accept Heather would never be his, he'd have to leave. It was that simple.

Jason watched closely as emotions chased each other across Rogan's face. Surprise transformed into fury before a cold and deadly calm settled on Rogan's features.

"You can't talk to me like that. You're a sub. Didn't Darren teach you to show proper respect to your betters?"

The smile on Heather's face was made of steel. "To my betters?" She smirked. "Darren taught me there is no such thing as my betters. He told me to show respect to those who deserve it. People have to earn my respect before I'll grant it. And you..." Fury shone from her eyes. "You lost any respect I may have had for you when you decided you could claim me."

Rogan's face twisted in anger. "Be careful what you say, girl. You may have knelt at his feet" — Rogan threw a contemptuous glare in Jason's direction — "but I know you didn't formally submit to him. That's not his collar. I've seen it before. No self-respecting Dom would allow his sub to wear another man's collar. When this weekend is over and you come back to Dublin, you'll be alone. And after this performance, you'll stay alone. None of us would touch you with a bargepole."

"That's enough." Jason jumped in before Heather could respond. "Rogan, we need to talk. Either here, with an audience, or just the three of us. It's up to you. I won't have you behave like this in my club, especially not toward the woman who knelt at my feet. Make your choice."

"What? You're going to throw me out?" Rogan glared at Jason. "You come to Ireland, open a club and expect all of us to just accept you? I've earned my position. I've trained and mentored most of these people. You're nothing."

Without taking his eyes off Rogan, Jason was aware of people leaving the room. Some stared at him and Rogan, while others seemed to go out of their way to ignore them. Jason's heart sank. This was the sort of situation he'd hoped to avoid. Here he was in a battle of wills with the self-proclaimed leader of the Irish BDSM community. He didn't want that position. He wasn't interested in power. This weekend's only purpose was to introduce his club to potential Irish customers. Somehow he had to get back on track.

He waited until the last of the Doms had left with their subs before turning to Rogan. Grasping what little patience he had left, Jason took a deep breath.

"No. I'm not kicking you out. I'd like to, but it wouldn't serve any purpose. I've no idea why you see me as a threat. I'm not. All I want is to run my resort successfully. I believe I've got something good, something special here. I thought you and the other lifestylers in Ireland might be interested, might want to spend time here. I'm not after you position, whatever that may be."

Rogan's expression showed nothing except disbelief and distrust.

"If you want to stay, you're more than welcome to."

The distrust on Rogan's face turned into surprise.

"On one condition."

"I knew it." Rogan sneered. "Of course there is a condition. Tell me. What's your price?"

"You're going to leave Heather alone." Jason reached out and wrapped his arm around the woman who would never cease to amaze him. "She's made it perfectly clear she is not interested in your offer."

Jason had to stop himself for a moment. *Offer my arse.* The Dublin Dom had tried to order her into submission.

"If you're half as good a Dom as you claim to be, you know submission is a gift. We don't claim it. Our submissives grant us the honor of their submission if they so desire and on their terms."

Jason looked at Rogan's face, trying to determine whether anything he'd said had gotten through to the man. He thought some of the anger had disappeared from the man's eyes but couldn't be sure. When Rogan turned his head and fixed his gaze on Heather, every muscle in Jason's body tensed.

"What gives you the right to talk for her?" Rogan's words still sounded hostile but most of the fury had disappeared from his voice. "She may have knelt at your feet, but I know she isn't yours any more than she is mine. Show me a contract between the two of you and I'll step back."

Heather pressed her body closer to his and Jason knew,

without looking at her, that she wanted to jump into the conversation. He squeezed her softly and hoped she'd understand he wanted her to stay quiet for a little while longer.

"You're right. I haven't formally collared her. But she chose to kneel at my feet. That on its own gives me the right. But even if that wasn't the case, this is my club. I expect my guests to respect each other and my staff, regardless of their standing. Safe, sane and consensual. You know those rules as well as I do. There is nothing consensual about trying to bully someone into submitting. And I won't allow behavior like that in my club."

Rogan's gaze shifted to Heather again. "You've made your choice then? You're sure you don't want everything I can offer you?"

Jason couldn't stop himself from worrying. Common sense told him what Heather's answer would be, but a small part of him was convinced Heather might be better off walking away from him.

"Yes, Rogan, I've made my choice." Heather's voice was soft and calm. "I told you when you first approached me. I have no desire to submit to you. I don't want to fight with you either, so please, just accept what I'm saying and don't ask me again. I'd like to think Jason and I organized a wonderful weekend. Stay. Enjoy it. And reserve your judgment of Jason's character and resort until Sunday."

Silence settled in the room as Rogan contemplated Heather's words. Jason stared at him in an effort to determine what might be going on in the man's head. It wasn't about the weekend anymore. He couldn't bring himself to worry about the future of his resort. All that mattered was Heather and her peace of mind. If Rogan couldn't agree to leave Heather alone, Jason would tell him to leave. If that meant the whole of the Dublin crowd left with him, so be it.

Rogan's features relaxed. He didn't look happy, but the anger had disappeared completely to be replaced with a look Jason would have liked to call admiration if he didn't think that was too optimistic.

"Fair enough. I won't approach you again. It's a shame though." The Dom's mouth curved into a wry smile. "You've just displayed all the reasons I wanted you to submit to me. I've admired you for a long time. Whoever you end up submitting to, whether it's him"—he nodded his head in Jason's direction—"or someone else, he'll be a lucky man."

For the first time since Rogan's outburst, Jason relaxed, only for the tension to return when Rogan turned to him.

"Thank you for giving me the option to stay. I'm not sure I would have done the same, in your position. I'll take you up on it. And I look forward to fully exploring your facilities."

Jason waited until Rogan had left the room before pulling Heather into his arms and devouring her mouth.

"You were magnificent." He emphasized his words with another kiss. "But now we need to talk." Jason looked at the collar around Heather's neck and stroked it. "You've got some explaining to do."

Chapter Twenty-Four

"Let me look at you." Jason's voice felt like a caress across her skin. He held her hands, standing two arm lengths away, while he slowly looked her over from tip to toe. His gaze came to rest on her neck. "A collar?"

"What's wrong? You don't like my collar?"

He dropped one of her hands and stepped closer to touch the velvet around her neck. "I love your collar, but..."

Suddenly she got it.

"It's not Darren's collar, Jason." She smiled. "Well, in a way it is, but Darren never collared me. He didn't think he needed to. He said the wedding ring was the only collar he needed on me. We only used this when we played in public."

His eyes had drifted to her left hand as soon as she said the word 'wedding ring' and she knew he only noticed it now. "You took your ring off." He whispered the statement but she could hear the question he wasn't prepared to ask.

"I did."

She was lost for words. She hadn't articulated the decision for herself and had no idea how to explain it to anyone else. Wearing the ring while kneeling at Jason's feet in public hadn't felt right. She'd known Rogan would jump on the ring if he saw it on her finger. Even without the ring, he'd wasted no time before throwing Darren in her face. Those were good reasons for taking the ring off, and they were true. But there was more. There was this feeling, tugging at her. A feeling she hadn't allowed herself to examine too closely because it confused and scared her. Her thoughts tumbled through her head as she allowed Jason to lead her to the couch and pull her onto his lap.

"You what? Tell me, Heather. Why did you take it off?"

She heard something in Jason's voice she hadn't heard before, something hovering between hope and fear. He pulled her close.

"What's going on in your head, beautiful? Talk to me."

She forced herself to relax, allowing her head to rest against his shoulder while savoring his presence and the soft strokes of his hands over her skin.

"Part of it was to not give Rogan any more ammunition."

She saw the disappointment as it flashed across his face and closed her eyes. This was difficult.

"Heather." His voice had changed. "I shouldn't have to explain to you how important honesty is. I would have thought we're both all too aware of the need for communication after the mess I created with my silence."

Where were the words when she needed them? She didn't know how to say this. She wasn't sure what was going on in her head, in her heart. Even if she found a way to articulate her feelings, how would he react? Things were moving too fast. She couldn't keep up with herself. Her mind was spinning and she couldn't catch her breath.

"Breathe, Heather."

Jason's voice sounded muffled, as if it came from far away.

"Listen to me, girl. Look at me."

She opened her eyes and forced herself to look up until she met the concern in his.

"I just want you to tell me what you're thinking, feeling. There are no wrong answers. You can't disappoint me." His thumb stroked her bottom lip. "All I want is for you to be happy. If you allow, I would love to make you happy. But you have to talk to me."

The truth. Nothing but the truth. It would be hard, but if she just opened her mouth and allowed the words to come, she might be able to manage it. No over thinking it. She'd just speak the words and trust they would make sense. To her and to Jason.

"Things are happening so fast, Jason. It scares me. You awakened something inside me when I walked into your office after arriving here—something I thought was dead and buried. I tried denying it and when denial didn't work, I tried playing it down. But I was hurting when I drove back to Dublin. It was more painful than it should have been. And returning was too close to coming home." She looked around the room. Jason's apartment, Jason's furniture, Jason's lap. "This isn't my home. Why does it feel like I belong here?"

"You do?"

The sense of wonder in Jason's voice was almost immediately replaced by a certainty she could also read in his features.

"Because you do. I want you to belong here, to belong with me, to me."

It should have made things easier. Jason wanted her. Not just for this weekend, not just because of the party but for longer and more. So why was she still afraid? Why wasn't his need for her enough to reassure her?

"Don't you think we're going too fast? Doesn't it scare you? It scares the shit out of me. It's been less than two weeks since our second first kiss." She hadn't meant to be funny but couldn't help but smile with him. "I..." She took a deep breath, unable to believe she was about to verbalize this thought she hadn't even allowed into her head until now. "I could fall for you." She looked into his eyes again and forced herself to keep her gaze steady. "I *am* falling for you. And I'm afraid. I don't think I can risk my heart again. I don't want to feel the pain again."

Everything inside screamed at her to look away, get up and walk to the other side of the room, get away from this man who made her feel things she'd never expected to feel again.

"What if I give in to these feelings and urges and it all goes wrong? You told me you don't do committed relationships.

I don't do casual affairs. How are we ever going to make this work?"

He opened his mouth, ready to give her an answer she didn't want to hear yet.

"No, let me finish while I have the courage. Submitting to you feels natural. Everything inside me reacts to your presence. Your voice makes my heart flutter, your touch awakens my skin and your dominance touches my soul. It shouldn't be possible after such a short time and yet I yearn for you when you're not near me. Don't you see? If I'm this dependent on you after only two weeks, what will happen to me if I stay?"

The truth and nothing but the truth, God help her.

"I put the collar on to send a message to Rogan, sure. But more than anything I put it around my neck because it felt right, because I wanted to show all of them, me and you — most of all you — that I've chosen you as the man I want and need to submit to. I can't tell you anything else. That's my truth. So if it is too much, too soon, more than you want or need please tell me now, get it done and over with so I can leave and try to patch myself back together before I completely lose myself."

She wants me. The realization jumped around in his head, skipped to his heart and took his breath away. She wanted to be here, with him. His Blowhole felt like home to the only woman who had ever made him seriously think about commitment. How had he gotten this lucky? He'd gotten a second chance after the complete fuck up he'd created earlier. She could have thrown his lack of communication back in his face and he wouldn't have blamed her. If she'd refused to answer his questions he would have had no right to insist, not after the way he'd behaved. But she hadn't. Her struggle had been so clear on her face, in her body language and still she'd found the courage to tell him the truth. She'd shown him all her cards, had put all her feelings on the table with no guarantees he'd be gentle with them. She'd given him more than he had the right to ask of her and now it was up to him to repay her trust and prove she'd made the right decision. He had to find the right words. But first had to create the time.

He knew it would worry her but he had to take care of this first. Reaching for his phone, he picked a number and hoped his smile would reassure her for now.

"Hector. Change of plan. Something's come up and I need to do my demonstration tomorrow."

He kept his gaze on Heather as he listened to Hector's response. He touched her face, her cheeks, her mouth and worried when it wasn't enough to get rid of the frown on her forehead.

"No, nothing you need to worry about, but I would be grateful if you and Amber could do your second one tonight. Oh, and could you let Souris know? Thank you. I'll be staying in my apartment for the time being."

He saw the surprise in her eyes as he put down his phone. "Why?"

"Because this is more important, Heather. You are more important."

He pulled her closer. "You've made me so happy." The lump in his throat took him by surprise. "I hoped you might feel some of the connection I feel to you. And I've been telling myself I don't have the right to hope for such a miracle, never mind expect it. Not after the way I've treated you. Not with us only having met again two weeks ago. Especially not since it hasn't been very long since you lost Darren."

"Jason."

"No, it's my turn now. I have all these things I want to say to you. I just don't know how to say them. Twenty years ago, I said that if I ever got married it would be to a woman like you. I said those words although I'd rejected you that summer because I thought my needs would be too much for you. I was too young, too inexperienced, too impatient and too bloody selfish to take a risk. But even then I knew what I'd said no to. I knew the day would come when I'd regret that decision and still I made it. When you walked into my office and subsequently lowered your eyes? It was as if someone had decided to give me a second chance. And still I was stupid enough to risk it all again. Most people don't get second chances. I did and managed to almost ruin it."

The sound of rain against the window interrupted his thoughts. It wasn't supposed to rain. The forecast had been good enough for them to plan a barbeque. He glared at the sky and saw it was probably nothing but a short summer shower. He lifted Heather off his lap and got up, taking her hand. "Come."

Opening the balcony door he walked out into the rain with her, allowing the soft, warm drops to fall on them.

"This feels like my third chance. I'm not going to ruin it again. I want you, Heather. I want you at my feet, in my bed, as a part of my life. I would love to share my world with you. It would make me happy if you saw this" — he waved his hand around — "all of this as home."

He saw the smile on her face and followed her gaze. Hundreds of tiny rainbows floated above the Atlantic.

"Our rainbows, Heather. Let them be the sign we need." He hesitated. Would it be too much too soon? Could he, should he say this? Now? "The truth hit me when you knelt at my feet."

The words disappeared, he couldn't go on.

"What truth?"

Heather was calm again as she studied his face. Her ability to know exactly what he needed amazed him. She turned her back to him and leaned her head against her chest. "Tell me, Jason. I gave you all of my thoughts and feelings. It's only fair you do the same."

"When you knelt and rested your head against my knee, all doubt was gone. Everything I'd been trying to deny for days was there, staring me in the face, daring me to look away."

It felt so good. He loved the way she fitted against his body, the smell of her hair just under his nose. He wrapped his arms around her and pulled her closer. He couldn't bring himself to say the words out loud so he whispered them.

"I love you, Heather."

He wanted to go on but those four words had taken his strength away.

He braced himself, sure she would laugh, or tell him not to be ridiculous. He expected her to tell him he couldn't possibly have those feelings after such a short time. He wouldn't be surprised if this shocked her straight out of his life again. Her silence was worse. Surely she was trying to find a kind way of telling him she didn't share his feelings, and didn't think she ever would.

The seconds dragging by felt like hours. Heather still felt the same in his arms. She hadn't tensed up, didn't try to get away from him but she didn't say anything either. He needed a response and wasn't sure he wanted to hear it.

"Really?" Her voice was soft, and when she turned around her face seemed to glow. "You love me? Really?"

Her smile restored his ability to breathe.

"I do. I mean I know it's soon for such grand statements and I've been trying to tell myself I couldn't possibly have such strong feelings for you after such a short time together. But Heather, I've never felt like this before. It scares me and makes me feel whole for the first time in my life." He rushed on. "I know you don't feel the same. That's okay. I just want you with me. If you stay then maybe one day you'll…"

She put her finger over his lips.

"Shhh. You talk too much. I've fallen for you, Jason. I could never give myself to a man the way I have to you if I didn't have feelings for him. I've been trying to ignore it but I know myself well enough to be certain that I couldn't have submitted to you if I hadn't been emotionally invested. Like I said, it scares me. I've lost one love, I'm not sure I'd survive losing another."

She got on her toes and kissed him.

"I'm falling in love with you, Jason. I want to explore those feelings. I want to know what we can be together. If you love me, I think I can take the risk."

Too much happiness swamped him. The lump was back in his throat. He couldn't have spoken if somebody forced him. Looking at her beautiful, happy face he lowered his mouth to hers, pulling her closer as he pushed his tongue between her lips, forcing her to join him in a dance of tongues to seal the deal.

The kiss went on. Her tongue answering all his heated questions. It was enough. Who needed toys, commands, obedience, even sex when you could have this togetherness, the joy of intimacy and the promise of a future? The only reason he broke away was because he needed to know.

"Will you stay? When the weekend is over and the guests have gone, will you give us the opportunity to find out who we are together?"

"Yes."

He glanced over her shoulder. The clouds had almost drifted away and the rain was getting lighter. He stared for a moment and allowed the magic of the moment to fill him.

"Remember what you said about the little rainbows?"

"I do." Her smile was bright. "I took them as a sign that coming here was the right decision for me."

"Look."

He turned her around and showed her the most perfect rainbow he'd ever seen. It stretched from one side of the bay to the other, the colors so bright he thought he might be able to touch them.

"There's ours." He whispered the words in her ear as he told her his truth. "That's our sign in the sky. Our rainbow, promising us light, love and a future. Together."

Chapter Twenty-Five

Heather looked around the room. The place was packed. They'd picked the largest space available for this exhibition and still she couldn't help feeling there wasn't room for one more body. Of course they hadn't expected everybody to stay this long. They'd assumed most guests would leave earlier today. The Blowhole was miles away from anywhere and even those who didn't have to go all the way to Dublin or even farther, had a long drive ahead of them. But curiosity about Jason, she smiled, *Master Jay*, had kept them all here.

He'd surprised her. She'd expected Rogan to have one or two other tricks up his sleeve, but not only had the man been on his best behavior, he had given the impression he was enjoying himself.

"This should be interesting. Let's see if the Master can live up to his title."

Rogan's voice broke through Heather's thoughts. Her body tensed. Maybe she'd been overly optimistic when she'd thought the worst was behind them. If Rogan interrupted Jason during this particular scene, the consequences would be horrific. She thought about turning around and confronting him before deciding against it. She'd listen. If she thought he'd actually cause trouble, she'd act.

"Looks like the show is about to begin."

Rogan lowered his voice as a stark-naked Souris was escorted to the middle of the room by two dungeon assistants. They placed the raven-haired beauty underneath the cuffs hanging from the ceiling and secured her hands. Once her feet were locked in place as well, the girl stood on her toes with her legs spread and very little wriggle room.

"I'm surprised he's using a club sub when he has a woman kneeling as his feet."

If she'd had any doubts about Rogan's intentions, they evaporated now. It was no accident he'd ended up standing behind her. He wanted her to hear his words, was trying to provoke a reaction she wasn't inclined to provide.

A collective intake of breath told her Jason had entered the room as well. Her heart filled with something she still wasn't quite comfortable naming. He looked stunning in black leather trousers and a simple but tight fitting black T-shirt. His looks weren't what had caused the audience's reaction though. He held the reason for their stunned silence firmly in his right hand.

She'd watched him practice with the bullwhip over the past few days and had been amazed by his accuracy. Of course she hadn't seen him with Souris yet. As curious as she'd been, she'd decided to wait until he was ready. What she had seen while he went through his moves in the dungeon had taken her breath away. She'd never been on the receiving end of one of those, but with his skill, she could imagine she might, maybe, some day in the future.

"A bullwhip."

She heard the reluctant admiration in Rogan's voice and couldn't stop herself from grinning.

"I sure hope he knows what he's doing. A bullwhip is a dangerous weapon."

The man just couldn't leave well enough alone, but she wasn't going to take the bait. He'd find out soon enough how accomplished Jason was with his chosen instrument.

"Rogan, just stop." Whoever Rogan had been talking to had apparently also had enough of his negativity. "You asked all of us to find fault with this club and its owner. It's just not here to be found. The man appears to know what he's doing. The resort is great. I for one am looking forward to coming back here with my sub and exploring everything we didn't have time for this weekend."

Heather was glad she had her back to the men behind her. She'd no hope of repressing the smirk appearing on her face.

Jason circled the sub as Heather's thoughts went back to the talk she'd had with the sub Rogan had brought with him. She hadn't been able to shake the feeling something wasn't quite right with the girl and she'd been afraid Rogan might be mistreating her. She'd been relieved to discover that wasn't the case. If she'd read the situation right, the girl either wasn't a natural submissive or was pushing herself too hard. Heather had suggested as much, but the girl had denied it. If she'd known the girl better or if she'd had more time she might have pressed her point, explained more about the dynamic and the fact it only worked for those who were able to surrender. As it was, she'd have to trust the girl would figure it out for herself. Heather could think of a host of reasons why anyone might wish to be somebody's submissive. Unfortunately, just wanting it wasn't enough. It had to be an ingrained need as well. She'd ended the conversation by telling the girl there was no shame in leaving the lifestyle. It was all she could do under the circumstances. Evicting both Rogan and the girl from her thoughts, Heather turned her full attention to the man who'd become an important part of her life in just a few weeks.

Jason stopped walking and stood in front of Souris, staring at her. You could have heard a pin drop in the room. He didn't even have to raise his voice when he spoke.

"You want this, sub?" He raised his hand, putting the whip right in front of the girl's eyes.

"Yes please, Master Jay." The answer was breathless and soft.

"Do you deserve it?"

"That's for you to decide, Master."

"Yes." He smirked. "I decide if you deserve it. How much of it you deserve and how hard I'll be hitting you. And why

241

is it my decision?"

"Because you're the Master."

He stepped around her and paced the distance before turning and facing her naked, unmarked, back. "Because I'm the Master."

He took a moment. It never hurt to allow a build-up of anticipation in both the sub and the audience. Both reacted so much better once they were on edge. He found Heather in the audience and stiffened. He didn't like Rogan's presence just behind Heather. Was the man trying his luck one last time? He wanted to stalk over and pull her away. He looked again. Rogan's presence didn't appear to bother her. Her focus was on him and Souris.

He couldn't afford to get distracted. It was too easy to do real damage with this whip. His focus returned to the girl waiting for his attention and he flicked his wrist. The whip sang and snapped but didn't touch any flesh. Not yet. Lack of contact didn't stop the girl from moaning though.

He walked back to Souris and stopped right behind her, pulling her head back by her hair. "Thirty strikes and you're counting them for me." A sharp intake of breath was his reward. "If you're very good, I may allow you to come before we're done here."

Back in position, he lifted his arm and went to work. He found his rhythm immediately, as if it hadn't been months since he'd last whipped a sub, almost as long since his last exhibition. He couldn't believe he'd ever thought he could live without this. Having Heather on the receiving end of his whip would have been even better but he could wait. One day it would be Heather. After tonight he wouldn't be doing scenes with anybody other than the woman he loved. The woman who'd given him back everything he'd thought lost for good.

"Fifteen." The girl moaned the numbers exactly as he wanted her to. He looked at her beautiful, no longer unmarked, back and buttocks. Bright red stripes flared across her skin, one or two welts were starting to rise. He walked back to her and stroked her whipped skin.

"Halfway there, sub. How're you doing?"

"Good, Sir."

He slipped his hands between her legs and found her wet and open. "Very good indeed. Get ready to start counting again."

The whip felt like an extension of his arm, the movements natural. Her screams and moans made him hard. The thought of Heather watching him drove his need even higher.

"Twenty-eight. Twenty-nine."

He lowered the whip again.

"The last one, sub. You're doing well. Good enough, maybe, for an orgasm."

Souris' moan was drowned out by the gasp from the audience. He smiled. After all, he was an expert.

He pulled his arm back and threw one last, underhanded, lash at the sub. The tail of the whip flew low over the ground, between her legs and made contact with her pussy. He couldn't see it but he knew he'd hit her right on her clit. The girl's cries turned into moans as he stepped close and stroked her tortured clit. It took no time at all. He made contact and the girl tensed and came, shaking in her bindings, almost crying in relief.

He dropped his whip and gestured to his assistants before wrapping his arms around the girl and holding her while the two men released her legs. As soon as her hands were freed, Souris collapsed against his chest.

"Thank you, Sir." The words were whispered and welcome. He was back.

"Take good care of her." Jason allowed one of the assistants to lift her up and carry her away. "She's earned it."

As soon as he was sure Souris' aftercare was being applied according to his instructions, he sought Heather in the crowd. She'd turned around and was talking to Rogan and some other men. He wished he could see her face. Was she all right? If Rogan turned out to be pressuring her again, he'd kick the man out. If that meant he'd destroy all the goodwill this weekend had created for The Blowhole, so be it. Words began to reach his ears as he got closer.

"I'm glad you enjoyed it."

Heather sounded happy. "Master Jay is rather magnificent with his whip, isn't he?"

His heart swelled when he recognized the pride in her voice. *Master Jay.* The words took on a whole new meaning in her mouth and made blood rush to his already hard cock.

"I'm surprised you weren't involved in the scene, Heather."

Rogan's voice didn't sound hostile, but his words made Jason angry regardless. He opened his mouth to put the Dom straight, but Heather beat him to it.

"Not that it's any of your business, Rogan." Heather's voice had taken on a steely tone. "But we always intended to offer our guests the best of everything this weekend. I've been out of circulation for too long to participate in anything that extreme right now. Who knows, maybe if you come back in the future, you might find me on the receiving end of that whip."

Images formed in Jason's mind as soon as he heard Heather's words. He could see it. Heather bound and helpless, while he marked her back and buttocks.

Jason took the last few steps and stopped behind Heather. "We would be delighted to have you visit us again."

He looked Rogan straight in the eye, searching for malice.

"Oh, I will. In fact I plan on booking a weekend before leaving today." One of the other Dublin Doms jumped in. "You've got a spectacular place here. My girl is going to be very happy if I bring her back here. She hasn't stopped singing The Blowhole's praises."

"Thank you." Jason gave the man a quick smile before returning his attention to Rogan. The man was staring back at him and appeared to be making up his mind about something. Maybe he imagined it, but Jason thought he saw Rogan's shoulders relax.

"He's right. You've created something special here." Reluctance was audible in Rogan's voice. "I may come back. I don't know yet. I've not quite figured out what your presence in Ireland means for the rest of us."

Rogan hadn't said the words, but Jason could hear them. He'd meant for *me*.

Jason thought for a moment. He didn't want to be this man's enemy. He was fairly sure the man's opinion about him or his resort wouldn't deter other people from coming, but he didn't like the idea of animosity in what was a small and usually close-knit community.

"Why does it have to mean anything?" Jason waited, but Rogan didn't reply. "All I want is to run my club and offer a safe environment to those who want to play their sexual games. Nothing more and nothing less. I'm not looking to expand or branch out." Jason looked around for a moment and returned his gaze to Rogan. "What you see is what you get. That goes for me and for my resort. It doesn't affect you in anyway, except that it gives you another place to play."

Rogan nodded and turned his head to look at Heather. He kept his gaze fixed on her while he spoke.

"Fair enough. I don't need or want to fight with you. It may not be in the immediate future, but yes, I can see myself coming back too." Rogan continued to stare at Heather for a few long seconds, before turning to Jason. "Thank you for this weekend. It's been an experience. I'd better round up my sub and hit the road. It's a long, long way to Dublin."

For the first time since the festivities had started, Jason saw a genuine smile on Rogan's face. He got it now. The man's worry about what he saw as his elevated position and what difference Jason's presence might make, wasn't the real issue. Rogan really was interested in Heather— not as a trophy and not because he felt entitled to her. He wanted her for the same reason Jason wanted her, because she'd awakened feelings in them. This gracious admission of defeat probably hurt Rogan more than he'd ever admit. Jason wasn't about to rub it in.

"Thanks." Jason held out his hand and was grateful when Rogan took and shook it. "I'm looking forward to your future visit. We'll make it something special."

Jason waited until Rogan had disappeared from view before pulling Heather close for a long kiss. He poured all the heat from the scene as well as the relief he felt now that the weekend had ended on a high note, into the woman in his arms. "Want you."

He felt her need, could smell it. Her whispered "yes" brought him to full arousal.

Epilogue

"What do you need, sub?"

The voice sent shivers down her spine. Six months after she'd decided to stay, his voice was still all she needed to melt. He would use his special, deeper tone and her mind started to float. Even now, in this setting, she could feel it. Everybody was here. Jason had closed The Blowhole for the weekend so he could claim her in front of all these people who had turned into so much more than 'just' staff.

Her nipples tightened, her pussy contracted and her breathing got heavier. She knew her voice would give her away and was proud of it.

"You, Sir. All of you. Always."

Yes, always. Whatever doubts she might have had last summer, were gone now. She knew she'd found her place. She was sure she belonged here, with Jason, at his feet when he ordered her there, shoulder to shoulder as they managed The Blowhole.

"And what do you offer in return?"

She was sure nobody else had noticed it, but she had. His voice wasn't as stern and controlled as he would like it to be. For once he wasn't in complete control of his inner Dom. Joy filled her. The effect she had on this man would never cease to amaze her.

"All of me, Sir. Today, tomorrow and forever. My love, my devotion, my submission, my body, my mind, my heart and my soul."

It was harder than usual to keep her gaze lowered. She wanted to look at him. Search his eyes to see if the emotions rushing through her were mirrored there. She needed to know what he thought of her outfit. She'd hesitated before settling on the white corset-dress. Was white too much? Would he understand what her choice meant?

"Do you accept mine in return? My love, my devotion, my dominance, my body, my mind, my heart and my soul? Today, tomorrow and forever?"

God, yes. She still couldn't understand how she'd gotten this lucky. To find a perfect partner once was special. To find one again was more than she'd believed possible. There'd been no second thoughts. Of course they'd had their moments but she'd never considered leaving. The house in Dublin was up for sale. And, much to her surprise, she didn't mind. She'd been happy there with Darren but that part of her life was over and she didn't need the house to hang on to her memories. They were safe in a secure part of her heart, where they'd live forever, while Jason and she created new ones of their own.

"I do, Sir. And I'll treasure them as I treasure you."

She heard him approach and resisted the temptation to look. She wanted this moment to be perfect. His shoes entered her field of vision, his lower legs in leather trousers. Her Dom stopped in front of her. His hand was on her head, stroking her hair.

"Look at me, Heather."

The love glowing in his eyes still took her by surprise. He'd been quick to recognize his feelings for her. It had taken her longer. She couldn't remember the exact moment she'd admitted she loved him too. Maybe the feeling had been there from the start, just as it had been for Jason. It made sense she'd needed more time to accept the feeling. There'd been a few weeks when she'd worried her feelings for him might be less strong than his for her. Jason had laughed when she'd shared her fear. "I love enough for both of us," he'd told her. "I know you're mine, even if you're not sure yet. Your eyes and your body don't lie."

His eyes didn't lie either. She could lose herself in them.

"Are you ready to accept my collar?"

She hadn't expected to hear nerves in his voice. Did he think she'd change her mind? Now?

"I am, Sir. I'm ready to accept your collar. I want to be yours."

"Look."

The sight took her breath away. Tears sprang into her eyes. She looked from the collar to his eyes and back again. She'd never seen a collar like this. It appeared to be made of something like chain mail and… She couldn't believe her eyes. Every chain had a colored bead inserted.

"You got me a rainbow."

He twisted the collar, revealing the little golden ring attached to it.

"My wedding ring?"

Tears were streaming down her face. If she'd had any doubts about this decision, they would have disappeared now. This man knew her so well. He got how she worked, knew her love for Darren took nothing away from her feelings for him. He'd accepted and wanted all of her, past, present and future. And they were his. She was his. She'd spend the rest of her life next to him and be grateful for the precious gift he was. Every single moment.

Her tears worried him until he saw her smile. She was fine. They were good. He'd made the right decision. He still couldn't believe his luck. He'd known they were good together from the moment she'd decided to stay. Just as he'd been sure she wouldn't leave him any time soon. But he hadn't known if she'd ever be ready to commit again. She'd done it once and losing her man had nearly broken her. He wouldn't have blamed her if she'd refused to take the risk again and. Yet here she was, dedicating herself to him and accepting him in return. He was the luckiest man in the world.

"Yes. Your wedding ring. I hope you don't mind."

It had been a risk, taking the ring from her jewelry box. She hadn't put it back on her finger after that weekend. For a while she'd worn it on a chain around her neck then it had disappeared completely. He'd never asked about it and she'd never told him why she'd made the decision. The ring hadn't bothered him. He'd no problem with her past. He was sure he would have liked her Darren if he'd ever met him and felt nothing but gratitude for the man who'd seen and developed in Heather that which he'd been too blind to recognize when he was younger. Whatever way he looked at it, the conclusion was always the same. If it hadn't been for Darren, she would never have ended up here with him.

"No, I don't mind at all."

Tears were still glistening in her eyes.

"But, are you sure you want a constant reminder of my past attached to the collar you've picked for me?"

He smiled. They were breaking protocol now. They'd planned the whole scene. Like a wedding ceremony but different. Of course she hadn't known about his ideas for her collar. Just as he had been kept in the dark about her outfit. He couldn't believe their ideas had been this similar. The ring, even if it wasn't his, and her white dress. This might not be an official marriage, but it was as close as they'd get without the paperwork.

"Heather, the past made you who you are. If it wasn't for your past, we wouldn't be here together. I want all of you and that includes the past."

He bent his knees and got down, bringing his face close to hers. This was just for them.

"I know you love Darren, that you'll always love Darren. I also know you love me and hope you will love me for the rest of our lives. Your love isn't fickle. It is a gift you give forever. I want your gift. I'm proud you think I'm worthy of it and can only hope I won't betray your trust."

"Sir. Jason, I have no doubts. My love is yours to keep. Your love is more than I expected to find. You are my rainbow. I'll be proud to wear yours."

Something slotted into place when he put the collar around her neck. When the little lock clicked shut, he knew more than just a collar had been secured. This was the woman who'd shown him who he truly was, and now she would be around to remind him every single day of his life. At last, at the age of forty-three, he'd arrived where he was supposed to be, living the life he was supposed to live with the woman who was supposed to be his.

Taking her hand, he helped her up and captured her mouth for a long and deep kiss. He laughed at the excited yelp when he gave her arse a firm smack. Looking around at his friends, employees and colleagues he couldn't suppress his triumphant grin.

"Let the party begin."

SCENES FROM
ADELAIDE ROAD

HELENA STONE

HE'LL HAVE TO FIND THE COURAGE HE NEVER KNEW HE HAD

Scenes from Adelaide Road

Excerpt

Chapter One

I took one step forward before retreating again. The wall against my back grounded me, taking some of my panic away. I stared across the street at the door, the bouncers and the slow trickle of people entering the club. I had waited for this moment, dreamed about it for months but now it had arrived I couldn't find the courage to take the last fifteen steps separating me from the threshold.

I forced myself to breathe slowly while I counted up to ten and down to zero again. My body was on high alert, thoughts rushed through my mind and worry cramped my stomach. This was ridiculous. I only wanted to enter a club, discover what it was like on the inside in order to satisfy my curiosity. Here in Dublin, I had no reason to be afraid — there was no one to tell me what I could and couldn't do, and, most importantly, nobody to frown upon me and who

I was.

I was free at last, but I might as well still be shackled to my father and his rules for all the good it did me. I could hear the contemptuous words my dad used to spew at me whenever I'd attempted to create a social life for myself as if he stood next to me. *'Don't make a fool of yourself. Surely by now you've figured out people don't want to be around you. Nobody likes a loser.'* I had hoped the distance between us would diminish his power over my thoughts. I'd been wrong.

Across the road, two more men entered the club. They exchanged a few words with the bouncers and a burst of laughter reached my ears. I studied them. They looked just like me — nothing made them stand out as special or remarkable. Tight jeans, even tighter T-shirts, and loafers. Nothing about their appearance distinguished them from the people who walked past the club on their way to different venues. Nothing, apart from the fact that some of them had been holding hands and others had their arms wrapped around each other, or hands stuffed into each other's back pockets. Nothing, except that couples entering this club were either all male or all female.

That stood out like a red flag in a black-and-white movie. I couldn't imagine ever seeing that back home. The sight filled me with a longing so deep it hurt. I closed my eyes for a moment and allowed the soft June breeze to wash over me. I wanted to believe I could be one of those men one day. Nineteen years of being told I was nothing — not good enough, a disappointment as well as a disgrace — had me convinced my dream would always be that, a futile fantasy.

Time passed and I just stood there. I had to make up my mind — either bite the bullet, cross the road and enter the club or go back home. There would be no shame in going back to my house. I'd only arrived in Dublin two days ago. I didn't have to hurry or force myself. This city was home now. I could visit this club and others like it whenever I wanted, or rather, whenever I found the courage. I half turned to start the short walk home before stopping myself. *No.* If I chickened out now I might never be brave enough to take the first step. Before I could change my mind again I stepped away from the wall, crossed the street and walked up to the door.

"Sorry, mate, we'll need to see your ID."

The bouncer sounded kind enough, but his words still left me fuming inside as I pulled my wallet out of my pocket and handed my age card over. Looking like a sixteen year old when my nineteenth birthday was months behind me sucked.

"Thanks. That's grand. Enjoy your night." The bouncers stepped aside and allowed me to enter the place I'd been longing and dreading to visit in equal measure.

What had I done? Why had I not gone home? Every instinct screamed at me to turn around and walk out again. I glimpsed bright lights, dark corners and a bar along the left hand wall before I lowered my gaze to the floor. I'd seen enough to know the place was relatively empty. A few bodies moved on the dance floor in the middle of the club and some people sat at the tables surrounding it. The music was loud and the beat traveled through my body, making my eardrums vibrate. I didn't look up while I made my way to the far end of the bar where I picked the empty stool next to the wall.

The marble-like surface of the bar wasn't interesting enough for all the attention I paid it, but I couldn't bring myself to look up, never mind study my surroundings. I waited for someone to come and tell me I wasn't welcome. It had happened whenever I'd found the courage to go out in the past and I couldn't believe the same wouldn't happen here. The setting had changed, but I was still the same as I'd always been.

"What can I get ya?" The bartender appeared out of nowhere, or maybe he'd been there all along.

"Bacardi and Coke, please." I whispered the words and wasn't surprised when I had to repeat them so he could hear me over the noise. I took advantage of the bartender having forced me to look up and studied my surroundings while I waited for my drink. The place was dimly lit and divided into various areas. On the far side, couches and coffee tables created comfortable looking seating areas. Near the door, where people were now entering in a steady flow, and at the opposite end of the large space, I saw high tables without seats. The dance floor in the middle of the room sparkled under the spotlights and steadily filled up with swaying bodies.

The bartender had moved back to the center of the bar to fix my drink and talked to a man while he did so, nodding his head when the man stopped talking. Despite the fear churning through my stomach, curiosity took over. Something about the customer with dark hair caught my attention. He was little more than a silhouette but I couldn't pull my gaze away from him until he turned his head and looked straight at me. *Shit.* Muttering the soft curse, I diverted my attention back to the marble top of the bar and traced a dark line with my finger while trying to get my breathing under control. So much for staying inconspicuous while checking out the club. I fought the urge to look back up and establish whether or not the man was still looking at me. *Don't attract attention to yourself.* The voice screamed in my head and I acknowledged its wisdom.

When my drink appeared in front of me on the bar, I paid for it without looking up or acknowledging the barman. I nearly spilled the rum and Coke as I picked it up. The combination of bubbles and alcohol hit the back of my throat as I drained half the cocktail in one gulp. Tears sprang to my eyes and I swallowed hard to keep from coughing. I couldn't do this. Admitting defeat was easier than forcing myself to be braver than I'd ever be. I'd finish my drink and go home. Being alone wasn't easy but I preferred it over the fear and tension keeping me on a knife's edge right now. Maybe once I'd lived in Dublin a while longer, after I'd gotten a better feel for the place, this would be easier. After all there was no hurry. I'd no intention of ever going back home. I had a new place to live and the rest of my life to explore it.

My heart stopped jumping in my chest and my breathing slowed down as soon as I made my decision. My hand was almost steady when I reached for my glass again.

"Are you keeping this seat for anyone?"

I banged my head against the wall next to me as the barely audible voice addressed me. The shock of pain made me careless and without stopping to think, I looked up into the face of a beautiful man before immediately looking away again. Of course it was the same man I'd been staring at only a moment ago. I could feel color rising up my cheeks, as a cold sweat broke out across my brow. I numbly shook my head and returned my gaze to the half-full glass in front of me.

I felt more than saw him sit down and could feel his gaze travel over my body. A voice in my head screamed at me to forget about the drink and just leave. I couldn't do this. God only knew who he was, what he wanted. Why did he seek me out when only a few stools along the bar were occupied? I'd thought it might be safe to come here. I shouldn't feel threatened. But what if I was wrong? What if there was no safe place for me? What if I hadn't been singled out for the reason I'd always assumed but because I sent out this subconscious message, inviting people to bully me? I had never been able to figure out why my father detested me, why people looked down on me or why others got a kick out of hurting me, but it had been the one constant in my life. I'd no reason to believe it would be different here in Dublin.

"Is this your first time here?"

His voice was still barely discernible but I couldn't detect any hostility in it. I nodded my head, unable to find my voice and grabbed my glass. Two deep swallows was all it took to finish what remained of my drink. I placed my hands on the bar, ready to push off and leave. Before I could raise myself, his hand landed on my arm.

"Don't tell me you're leaving already. I saw you come in—you've only just arrived."

For a moment, curiosity overtook fear and I turned my head to really study him. He looked even better close up than he had from a distance. Black hair fell in unruly locks around his face, his fringe nearly hitting his dark eyes. His cheekbones stood out and created an interesting pattern of light and shadow on his face. I allowed my gaze to rest on his full, smiling lips for a moment before looking away again.

"What are you drinking?" he asked when the barman walked over and stopped in front of us.

"Bacardi and Coke. But, I'm leaving." I turned away and stood up. His hand on my arm stopped me in my tracks.

"Don't. Not on my account. If you'd rather be on your own I'll go sit somewhere else."

I looked at him again, trying to figure out what he wanted from me. The words to send him on his way were on the tip of my tongue, but I swallowed them back. I'd made myself walk into this club in the hope of meeting people who'd accept me without conditions. Telling the first person to talk to me to fuck off would not help me in my search for friends.

"I'm sorry." Even while I apologized I looked around half expecting to see a group of his friends behind him, ready to pounce on me without warning, but he appeared to be as alone as I was. "I'd like another Bacardi and Coke if the offer's still open."

He rewarded me with a huge grin. "I was right, wasn't I? You haven't been here before."

"Yes." I nodded. "Is it that obvious?" My mouth curved in a weaker version of his contagious grin, despite the doubts swirling through my head.

"Only to someone paying attention." His voice sounded warm and unthreatening. "I saw you walk in and recognized the way you behaved." He smiled a bit self-consciously.

"It's not that long ago since I entered this club for the first time. It can be scary, especially when you're on your own." He paused and a slight frown appeared on his face. "I'm Aidan, by the way. Can't believe I didn't introduce myself first."

"I'm Lennart." I held out my hand. After Aidan looked at it for a second he grabbed and shook it. A blush crept up my cheeks again. Trust me to go all formal and polite and make the situation awkward, again.

"You don't sound local." Aidan smiled. "A new arrival to the fair city, are you?"

I couldn't help returning his infectious smile. "Very new. I only came to Dublin two days ago."

"And you like it?"

"I think so." His question made me think. I hadn't actually considered what I thought about Dublin, too caught up in the relief I felt now I was away from the place I'd grown to hate over the nineteen years of my life. "I haven't seen a lot of it yet."

"And on your second night here you decided to explore the local talent?"

The lopsided grin on his face combined with a quick wink did nothing to decrease my anxiety levels. "I wasn't thinking about talent." The defensive note in my voice made me cringe. "Where I'm from there are no clubs like this. I didn't know what to imagine."

"That's a shame." His smile took on a different quality, one I couldn't identify although it made me feel both insecure and flattered.

The club had gotten a lot busier while we talked and people were starting to press in on us, trying to get the bartenders' attention. I tried to stay calm but couldn't stop myself from nervously glancing over my shoulder as tension settled in my muscles and my breathing became shallow.

"You wanna go and find a seat over there?" Aidan pointed at the seating area I'd noticed earlier. "It's getting a bit cramped here, and it's only going to get worse."

I nodded my consent and followed Aidan as he made his way around to the far side of the club, grateful he didn't try to cross the dance floor and the sea of moving and grinding bodies. The club was packed now and I took advantage of the fact we were moving to drink in my surroundings. I'm not sure what I'd expected before I walked in, but I couldn't have imagined what I saw in my wildest dreams. I'm not stupid. I've always known I wasn't the only one of my kind. But to see such numbers of people just like me enjoying themselves without fear of repercussions and without feeling the need to hide, boggled my mind.

Chapter Two

I barely noticed the chairs we sat down on, transfixed as I was on the crowded dance floor. Men danced with men, women with women and nobody batted an eyelid. For a moment I allowed my imagination to run amok and pictured myself in the middle of that crowd. Even in my fantasies I wasn't quite brave enough to visualize somebody dancing with me, but it would be wonderful to just let go for once, forget about all my fears and insecurities for the duration of one or two songs.

"I'm sorry?" I'd been so lost in my thoughts I'd missed Aidan's question.

"I asked if you like what you see?" He smiled. "It's probably a stupid question. I can tell you're fascinated."

I cringed and looked away from the dance floor, embarrassed at having been caught out. "I can't get my head around people being as comfortable as everybody here seems to be. I wasn't aware of other gay people back home. I mean, there must have been others, but whoever they were they kept their sexuality well hidden."

Aidan's attention was focused on me as if we weren't in the middle of a loud and busy club. Encouraged, I told him more about the life I'd left behind in Bally-Go-Backwards.

"Our town is tiny. Everybody knows everybody and their business and, I don't know, there was this unwritten law that people shouldn't stand out—attract attention to themselves. So I tried to fit in, be like the others, but people knew. For as long as I can remember they always looked down on me, shut me out..." I allowed the sentence to trail off. I didn't want to burden this man I'd only just met—somebody I hoped might turn into a friend—with all my years of trying to survive in a hostile environment. I wanted him to like, not pity, me. Some of the details I didn't share must have been obvious regardless. Something changed in his face as he listened.

"I didn't realize how lucky I was growing up here." Aidan's voice was pensive. "Not that it's all been smooth sailing..." He didn't finish his sentence either and his expression seemed to harden for a moment. He shrugged and the easy smile returned. "But it's all good now, isn't it? You don't have to go back to where you came from, do you?"

For the first time that evening the smile on my face came straight from my heart. "No, I don't ever have to go back. The town, the people who live there, my father—all of them can go to hell as far as I'm concerned. If I never see that place again it will be too soon."

"Even your parents?" Aidan asked.

"Just my father, my mother died before my second birthday. But yes, my father is the one person I really hope to never see again." I recognized the combination of sadness and surprise on his face and added. "It's a long and not particularly happy story. I won't go into it. Trust me, though, I won't be missing him and I doubt he's even noticed my absence."

My last statement almost made me laugh out loud. My father hadn't even offered me a lift to the train station when I left. He'd stood in the hall and watched me go. My father had still been furious things hadn't turned out the way he'd hoped. His parting words still rang in my ears. *'Enjoy it while it lasts, boy, because it won't. And don't even think about turning to me when it all goes wrong. Once this door closes behind you, it stays closed.'* No, he wouldn't miss me at all, although I imagined my father cursing my name every day for the foreseeable future.

"I'm sorry. I didn't mean to spoil your evening." I addressed the frown which had formed on Aidan's face. I couldn't believe it had happened again. I'd met Aidan all of an hour ago and I had already managed to alienate him. It had to be some special talent of mine. *How to alienate people and never make friends,* I should write the book.

"What? No." Aidan stared at me. "You didn't spoil anything. I just have a hard time getting my head around parents who abandon their own children."

We both stared at the dancing crowd for a moment before he continued. "Besides, you're here now. You can start a new life on your own terms. It's time to start having fun, don't you think?"

Fun? I'm not sure I'd recognize fun if it jumped up and hit me in the face. My inner critic reared its ugly head again. When I answered Aidan my voice was harder than it had been, as I attempted to drown out the internal dialogue.

"I am having fun. I didn't think I would but I really am. Thank you." I cringed inwardly. Did I have to make myself sound as needy as I just did? If Aidan noticed he was too polite to comment on it.

"You wanna dance?"

Every muscle in my body tensed at his suggestion. Imagining myself on the dance floor was one thing. To actually get up and move among the swaying crowd took far more confidence than I had.

Aidan didn't give me a chance to say no. He got out of his chair and held out his hand. When I grabbed it he pulled me up and held on to my hand as he led the way to the middle of the floor.

The acoustics in the club were phenomenal. The difference between the volume levels on the dance floor and where we'd been sitting took me by surprise. Now, in the middle of the fray, the rhythm took hold of my body. I felt the heavy bass vibrating in the floor and traveling up my legs. I should have been too self-conscious to dance but I couldn't resist the combination of beat and moving bodies. Almost against my will, my body swayed along with the rhythm. Pride filled me when a huge grin spread across Aidan's face as he watched me crawl out of my shell. His hand, still holding mine, gave me the confidence to let go of my inhibitions for a minute.

I stopped thinking as I lost myself in the music. My usual shyness disappeared, the cynical voice in my head couldn't be heard over the beat. Even Aidan letting go of my hand and throwing himself into the music couldn't put a dent in my newfound confidence. This was what I'd hoped for when I moved to Dublin, this sense of freedom, the permission to be myself, and the opportunity to stop worrying about what impression I might be making on those around me.

"You move beautifully."

Aidan's voice only barely reached my ears but his words made me glow. We circled each other as we danced. I almost froze when Aidan got very close behind me and ground his crotch into my arse.

"Relax. It's all good. Everybody here is just like you and me. Look."

I did look. Between the smoke machines and the blinding lights, it wasn't easy to see anybody in detail, which reassured me. If I couldn't see them, they couldn't see me. But what I did see showed me Aidan's grinding was as innocent as interactions on this dance floor got. A lot of couples might have been having full on sex if it weren't for the clothes they wore. Groins pressed into arses, hands explored the outlines of cocks and tonsil tennis appeared to be the taste of the day. And that was just the men. The female couples I spotted had no more inhibitions than their male counterparts. It was an exhilarating experience and my body couldn't help but respond. The stirring in my pants as blood found its way to my cock felt both delicious and uncomfortable. Part of me couldn't help but be afraid people might notice and make fun of me even while common sense told me I did not stand out in this crowd.

Songs ended and others started and our bodies moved. I'd never felt this good in my life. The sense of freedom was intoxicating. I remembered how I'd wanted to walk away from this club and Aidan. Gratitude for whatever it had been that had made me stay, filled me. My new life was turning out much better than I could have hoped.

The music changed. The beat all but disappeared as a much slower song started. I'd taken one step back toward where we'd been sitting when Aidan grabbed my shoulder and pulled me close. "Don't walk away. This is where it gets real good."

Not that I had much of a choice. With one hand holding the back of my neck and another just above my arse, I couldn't have walked away without violently dislodging myself from his hold. No matter how much the closeness scared me, I didn't want it to end and lose the opportunity to discover what it felt like to hold somebody's body close to mine.

When he pulled me closer I went. A sigh escaped me when our chests connected. With Aidan slightly taller than me, my nose ended up against his neck, just below his ear and I inhaled his aroma. Sweat combined with something earthy I couldn't name, captivated me. I closed my eyes and surrendered to the heady combination of music and Aidan. Our crotches touched and the realization my cock wasn't the only one reacting to our closeness sent a rush through me. He moved his hips and I followed his movements. Our bodies rubbing off each other brought me pleasure and frustration in equal measure.

"I told you it would be good."

Even with the music as loud as it was I could hear the heat in Aidan's voice.

"I didn't know." The words escaped my mouth before I could think about them.

"Didn't know how it would feel to dance with a man?"

I had no idea how to answer Aidan's question. I couldn't tell him I didn't know what it might be like to do anything with a man, dancing, kissing, touching. I had no experience with any of it so I just shook my head and kept quiet.

"Hey, look at me." Aidan's voice was so soft I had to strain to hear him. "Enjoy. It doesn't matter if it's a first for you. All of us had to start somewhere at some time."

I didn't know whether to be grateful or scared that he saw right through me. How could he possibly know my thoughts and feelings? We'd only just met. He didn't know me any better than I knew him and yet he seemed to have a very clear picture of who and what I was. I looked at him and saw something in his eyes that took my breath away. His heated gaze flicked from my eyes to my mouth and back again before he moved closer and pressed his lips against mine for a moment.

My body tensed and stopped moving. My heart thundered in my chest and my breathing sped up. I pulled back with enough force to break Aidan's hold and stepped away. My gaze flew around the club until I'd located the exit. I strode toward it without looking at anybody, panic driving me forward. I vaguely heard my name and ignored it. I needed to get outside, away from all these people, away from the new experiences and away from all these feelings I didn't know how to deal with.

I'm not sure I took a single breath while pushing my way toward the door. Only when I was safely on the footpath in front of the club did I allow myself to inhale a lung full of fresh air. My relief at being away from the situation that had triggered all my anxieties was short lived. As soon as my heartbeat slowed down again the full implication of what I'd just done hit me. I'd run away from a man who might have been a friend. I turned my back on somebody who'd had the patience to put up with my unsociable behavior.

That's why you're alone. You don't deserve friends. My internal tormentor didn't waste a moment, and for once I didn't try to argue with him. He was probably right. Aidan had given me a soft kiss, nothing more. Why had I panicked? I shrugged the question off. It didn't matter. I had well and truly ruined whatever might have been with my childish behavior. I didn't turn around to look back at the club where I'd known a few happy hours, before walking away.

"Wait. Lennart. Wait."

Running footsteps approached me. For a moment I considered taking off and making sure he wouldn't catch me. Torn between not wanting to face Aidan after my shameful departure and hoping that maybe I hadn't managed to scare him off, I waited until he caught up with me. Even if he'd only chased me to tell me how big a wanker he thought I was, it wouldn't make the situation any worse. And although I knew the chances were slim, I couldn't help hoping he'd followed me because he did want to be friends, despite my foolishness.

"I'm sorry." Aidan was out of breath when he reached me and his words escaped his mouth on big gulps of air. "I should have known better. How angry are you?"

"I…" Lost for words, I stared at him. "I'm not angry. Don't say you're sorry. My childish reaction is not your fault. If anybody should apologize, it's me. And I do." I should have stopped there but the words just kept on coming. "Look, I know I'm a fool. Just walk away and forget you ever met me. I'm sorry I ruined your night."

Aidan tilted his head and examined me for a moment. "Dear Mother of God, they really did a number on you, didn't they? You didn't ruin anything and I don't want to forget I met you. I enjoyed our evening."

"So did I." I whispered the words, afraid I might spoil the moment if I talked out loud.

"You're on your way home now?" he asked.

"Yes. It's just a few streets away." I vaguely pointed in the direction I'd been walking before he caught up with me.

"Can I walk with you?" Hearing uncertainty in Aidan's voice took me by surprise. His quiet confidence had impressed me throughout the night and it bothered me my hasty reaction had stripped him of it.

"Yes. Of course. I'd like that."

We walked in almost complete silence, close together but not quite touching. Our lack of communication should have been uncomfortable but wasn't. I enjoyed his company and appreciated the opportunity to just walk together without having to search for words or worry about saying the wrong thing.

It only took ten minutes to get to my front door. Aidan let out a low whistle when he saw where I lived. "You're renting a room here, on Adelaide Road? Nice one, mate."

"No, not quite." My embarrassment was back with full force. "All of this is mine." I pointed at the three-story building in front of us in what was one of the most expensive areas in Dublin.

"You own that?" Aidan's voice held a mix of disbelief and awe.

"It's a long story but yes, I do. I inherited it off a grandfather I didn't even know I had until three months ago."

Aidan whistled again. "Man, you're set up for life."

I laughed. "I know, right? I still don't know how I got this lucky." I saw the look on Aidan's face and realized what that must have sounded like. "Listen, I'm sorry my grandfather is dead. I'm even more sorry I never got to meet him. But it's hard to mourn somebody I never knew and this house couldn't have come at a better time."

More books from
Totally Bound Publishing

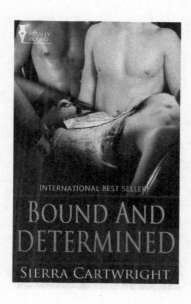

He will have her...

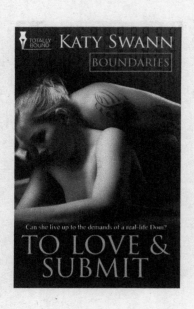

*Rachel Porter's dreams of being dominated are finally
about to come true.*

Bound For Justice

Against the Rules

She carried a gun and she knew how to use it.

Tori Carson

Is this fiery, redheaded submissive his lifeline or his downfall?

Who knows where pain ends and pleasure begins?

About the Author

Helena Stone

Helena Stone can't remember a life before words and reading. After growing up in a household where no holiday or festivity was complete without at least one new book, it's hardly surprising she now owns more books than shelf space while her Kindle is about to explode.

The urge to write came as a surprise. The realisation that people might enjoy her words was a shock to say the least. Now that the writing bug has well and truly taken hold, Helena can no longer imagine not sharing the characters in her head and heart with the rest of the world.

Having left the hustle and bustle of Amsterdam for the peace and quiet of the Irish Country side she divides her time between reading, writing, long and often wet walks with the dog, her part-time job in a library, a grown-up daughter and her ever loving and patient husband.

Helena Stone loves to hear from readers. You can find contact information, website details and an author profile page at https://www.totallybound.com/

Home of Erotic Romance